BEST
LESBIAN EROTICA
OF THE YEAR

VOLUME SIX

BEST
LESBIAN EROTICA
OF THE YEAR

VOLUME SIX

Edited by

SINCLAIR SEXSMITH

CLEiS
PRESS

Published in the United States by Cleis Press, an imprint of Start Midnight, LLC, 221 River Street, 9th Floor, Hoboken, NJ 07030.

Printed in the United States.
Cover design: Jennifer Do
Cover photograph: Pexels
Text design: Frank Wiedemann

First Edition.
10 9 8 7 6 5 4 3 2 1

Trade paper ISBN: 978-1-62778-313-2
E-book ISBN: 978-1-62778-526-6

for my boy

CONTENTS

INTRODUCTION

I'm thinking a lot about connection.

Even in the best of times, having a marginalized identity and being outside of the overculture can make us feel extremely alone. The more marginalized identities we have, the more it can seem like there are not any safe spaces for us.

Lately, we haven't been in the best of times.

In March, 2020, a deadly global pandemic quickly changed so many fundamental ways we operate. In some ways, it was fascinating to feel connected to people in Italy, Australia, and beyond, as we were all struggling together, fighting for information and safety.

Here in the United States, the effects of the pandemic have been so deeply felt in all aspects of our lives, from work to social to erotic and more. So many have been isolated and grieving, and the tragedies have been difficult to bear; at the same time, many have also used the time at home to reflect on their queerness, transness, nonbinary identities, kink interests, activism, and other community involvement. There have been opportunities to connect online in ways that are new and exciting—for some, the queer and kink events that moved online were the first access they had to those communities.

In these difficult times, I feel it's all the more important to celebrate pleasure, be in our bodies, connect with others, and feel like we are part of something bigger than ourselves. Connection helps the separation, and almost all of us have been more separated than we were before. Being isolated from our friends, our gathering spaces, and our community resources in person can start to feel as though a part of our identity is fading.

What I love about books like this one is that it can be a place to connect. We can lose ourselves in the feelings, communities, and identities described in these stories. We can see ourselves reflected, and feel less alone.

What I love about exploring sexuality through things like reading, writing, listening to podcasts, or watching films, is that there is a potential for healing inside of pleasure. I deeply believe that pleasure itself can be a healing act, and a radical act.

When we unapologetically claim what it is that fuels our desire as legitimate, valid, and real, we are healing a wound that tells us queer folks that what we love is wrong. When we write down what turns us on, it can be liberating. When we share it with others, we can find connection. We can feel less alone, less isolated, and less shame about our own desires.

Maybe it's impossible for everyone to see themselves reflected in just twenty-three stories—there are too many identities to capture the complicated aspects of every one. But I hope there are glimpses, at least. I am very proud of how much I've been able to bring in a wide range of gender and sexuality experiences in this series so far, including explorations of asexuality, kink, power dynamics, femininity, masculinity, androgyny, genderqueerness, transgender experiences, neurodiversity, physical ability, age, polyamory, and more. I am pleased that this year's volume features a wide expression of experiences and diversity.

With writers from Australia, the UK, the US, and Canada, with a wide range of genders, sexual orientations, roles, titles, and kinky activities, I am thrilled this collection explores connection and pleasure in difficult times. I hope you find some characters, feelings, or even phrases that you connect with and bring you pleasure.

I cannot wait to read from the book with the contributors at bookstores and in community centers, in person. I hope to see you there.

Sinclair Sexsmith
February, 2021

SOMETHING HAD SHIFTED

BD Swain

My fiftieth birthday was still a week away. I was looking forward to it but there was a nagging element of acceptance marking this birthday as different from previous ones. A little dread to dull the anticipation. Here it is, I thought, although what "it" was exactly, I couldn't name. Overall, though, I felt good and I knew being butch was making it go down easier than it otherwise would have.

My whole life, my identity and look have made me appear younger than my years to the mostly straight world I wander through. It's the same break men get. A masculine look doesn't age as fast as a feminine one does. The collective heteronormative culture prefers its women young. Men get to age and still feel sexy and viable. I was drafting behind a shitty male advantage. That cultural misogyny which uses up women fast reduced my overall drag. I was in my late thirties before I stopped shocking people when I got carded. Not because I truly looked so young but because people didn't bother to look past the masculine gender signifiers and my baby-smooth face. The combination dropped me into the "boy" category vs. "man."

Maybe that explains why fifty was the first time I felt the need to accept my age. It felt different and even though I felt content, my girlfriend Holly knew me well enough to see that flicker of . . . How do I name it? What was it? It wasn't sadness exactly. Not fear. It was . . . a settling. Settling in. Settling down a little bit. Settling for who I was about to be next. Holly who's six years younger than me isn't one to settle for anything. I don't imagine that will ever change.

She told me she had scheduled drinks with a friend for that evening. Well, drinks over Zoom. Video conferencing was the only way we could get together with anyone during the pandemic. We'd been sheltering in place for seven straight weeks and the virtual happy hours started early in week two. Everyone was connecting with old friends these days, so I didn't think anything about her setting up a get-together with a woman I'd never heard about before. I looked forward to socializing with a new face.

"It's almost cocktail hour," she said as she tugged me toward the closet, "let's get dressed up like we're going out." I looked down at the same sweatpants I'd been wearing for days and nodded. A change would be good. I picked out my best-fitting jeans and the sexy linen dress shirt she'd recently made me. I chose a brown blazer and a pair of dark caramel oxfords. She was still looking through her clothes when I headed to the shower. I couldn't just change out of sweats into nice clothes at the end of the day. I needed to feel clean.

The hot water rejuvenated me. Pretending we were about to go out felt like magic. As I rubbed soap in my hair, I pictured us walking out the door, turning the key to lock up, and walking down the sidewalk toward our favorite bar, her arm in mine. It felt new and long-lost at the same time. It felt needed. I scrubbed hard at my skin. Before I turned off the water, I put my palms against the still cool tile and leaned fully into the hot rush of water.

I was dressed and waiting for her on the couch. She walked in and stopped me. I hadn't thought about the fact that we were never getting dressed up anymore in this lockdown and how much I missed that moment of surprise when she walks in the living room, ready to head out. She wore a tight-fitting cream V-neck T-shirt paired with wide-legged pants of the same color and her signature green platform shoes. She looked so fucking hot. Her hair was pinned up in the back but fell loose around her face. I felt a jolt of excitement and she must have seen it because she seemed to roll her eyes and laugh.

"Your haircut needs a touch up," she said and went to grab the scissors. At week six, she'd agreed to attempt to cut my hair. We'd found trimmers at the drugstore by some miracle and she already owned her own haircutting scissors. She'd set me up on a stool with a sheet around my shoulders and made me look good again. I'd missed the feeling of stubble at the nape of my neck. I'd missed her fingers on a fresh haircut. When she came back with the scissors, she cleaned up the sides just over my ears. "There," she said and wrapped a hand behind my neck, "you look so handsome."

I set up the computer. We were all becoming good at finding the right angle for the computer and decent lighting to help these video chats feel as much like being in the same room as possible. With the card table in place and the laptop ready to go, I joined Holly in the kitchen to make cocktails. "Paper planes?" I asked. She nodded. I grabbed the lemons and a knife. We were also getting pretty good at mixing drinks. A necessity during this lockdown. She pressed herself against me as I poured from each bottle and it sent another jolt through me. "How long before this Zoom starts?" I asked, turning around to face her.

"Not long enough to fuck if that's what you're thinking," she laughed.

Drinks in hand, we sat in front of the computer and waited

for her friend to appear. Holly put her lips to my ear. "This is not an old friend of mine we're having drinks with tonight. This is a date." I shot her a look and nearly spilled my drink.

"What!?" She smiled at me and the image of a stranger popped up on the screen.

I was caught looking shocked and Holly laughed as she explained to our guest that I'd just learned what was happening. The stranger held a cocktail glass in the air, and swung it toward her computer camera, saying, "Cheers!" We introduced ourselves and I paused to take everything in while Holly and the stranger, now Alix to us, chatted.

We'd talked about threesomes before and when we could still go out in the world together, we'd gone out on a few dates but no one we met was the right fit for us. It wasn't just the shutdown that stopped our attempts at dating, I'd been hesitant to keep trying after only a handful of these awkward get-togethers. I didn't feel strongly that we needed something new but I knew it was a disappointment to Holly that we hadn't been able to make it work. I was surprised but not shocked. It was just like Holly to surprise me like this, especially when she could tell I was feeling a little low.

Holly had been secretly still looking for a date for us and had recently heard about the newish Lex dating app, which is where she stumbled across Alix's ad. The Lex was based on those old "back of the magazine" personals. The ads are all text, limited space to get your point across. It's a fabulous throwback and a nice change from the way hooking up works in our image-heavy world. As part of our introduction on Zoom, she showed me Alix's ad: "Older dyke. Chicago. Butch all my life but something has shifted. Not looking for love. Talk to me. Fuck me. Let's have a good time. Please be a reader. Tell me your favorite dirty book and I'll tell you mine."

I knew what had drawn my girlfriend to Alix. *Butch all my life but something has shifted.* The words excited me, too.

Alix had a beautiful, worn face. Her hair was mostly gray, straight, and grown out just long enough to wear it tucked behind her ears. The lines on her face suggested years of squinting into the sun and laughing. She had a warmth in her eyes and a ready but slightly sly smile. I couldn't see much of her body. She wore what looked like a thin, brick-red sweater. I could see the outline of a bra underneath.

We talked about cocktails—dirty martinis, basil gimlets, sidecars—and how and when to decide on a classic old-fashioned or something fancy. "Generally, I base my decision on the bar or bartender," I said, "and whether or not anything more than an old-fashioned is a pain in the ass." We all agreed this was wise. She was drinking an old-fashioned. "It definitely felt like a pain in my ass to make anything else tonight," she said with a laugh. Chatting felt easy.

We talked about books. I learned that Alix and Holly had already shared their favorite dirty books with each other. Jane De-Lynn's *Leash* was my girlfriend's choice (and possibly test). Alix knew the book and had been both fascinated and horrified by it. Alix's favorite was an erotica collection she'd recently enjoyed that focused on butch/femme scenarios from the point of view of a femme narrator. The fantasies in it had opened her up to exploring something beyond butch in real life. I didn't know the collection, but Holly had read it and I enjoyed hearing them talk over their favorite scenes.

It was easy to shift from erotica to ourselves, to this "date" and what we wanted. Alix wanted a butch to take control. Someone to explore her and take from her. I wasn't exactly sure how this would work over Zoom, but Holly looked at me and said, "Tell us what you want."

I thought about it. "I want to see you, Alix." I stood up to move our laptop further away and looked down to see that my belt was filling the video screen as I got closer. I stood there until Alix was back in view, being sure she saw me put my hand on my belt buckle. "You look sexy," I said to the screen and slowly backed up so she could see us again.

"Show me how you touch your mouth," I said as I sat back down on the couch and put my fingers to Holly's lips. I stared at Alix the whole time. I could see now that she was wearing slightly baggy jeans and her feet were bare. She looked tall with a sexy, big ass and thick thighs. "Do it like I do, Alix. Let *me* touch you." I pulled Holly's lower lip open with my thumb and ran it back and forth. Alix followed. The rush I felt was immediate. It hit all of us. Alix squeezed her legs together and lifted her knees. Holly grabbed my thigh.

I pulled Holly closer, her back against my chest, my arms wrapped around her. "Watch me Alix. Watch what I'm doing to you," I said and kissed her neck. Kissed Holly's neck. Alix's hand moved to her own neck. The connection felt so real. My words. My mouth, my hands on Holly and Alix's fingers followed everywhere mine landed. Everywhere I told her to go.

My fingers slid under Holly's shirt and my clit stiffened at seeing Alix shift a little deeper into the cushions of her couch as she slipped her hand under her sweater. "Let me feel your skin," I said and pulled the tank top over Holly's head. Alix pulled her own sweater off and modestly held her arms over her chest for a moment before placing her hands where mine were. I moaned seeing the rolls of her flesh and I imagined touching her skin. I rubbed her belly, squeezed my fingers into her flesh. My hands running up and down her arms and to her neck. "Where are we at, Alix? Am I making you feel good?" I asked and slid one hand between Holly's legs.

"Yessss," Alix hissed and sighed, "yessss." I rubbed a little harder between her thighs before moving on. I wanted to undress her. Them. The distance between us flickered on and off. I felt muddled.

"Take your bra off," I said and they were both quick to comply. "Your body feels so good," I moaned. I stared at the screen and at Alix's body. Her body was curvy and lush and a lot like Holly's. I imagined her struggling to hide it under more butch attire. It gave me a hard-on to think of her exploring her body in this entirely new way. She let me lead her hands over her own body and I felt honored. I rolled her nipple between my fingertips and we all moaned at the same time and then collectively erupted in laughter.

"Anyone need another cocktail?" I asked and Holly snorted back at me.

"Fuck us already," she said with a laugh.

"Stand up," I said quickly, tugging at her belt loops, "I want these off." They both stood and unbuckled, unzipped, easing out of their pants. "Leave your panties on," I directed.

I took a deep breath, settling us back down. "Alix," I exhaled, "watch me." We all stood, facing our computers. Alix's image filled the screen, but I could also see the small window of our video and realized Alix could see herself, too. I moved between them and turned to face Holly. Kissing her and pulling her arms around me. I felt Alix stare at us. I hoped she stared a little at herself too. I dropped to my knees and Holly ran her fingers through my hair as I pulled at her panties with my teeth. "I can smell you," I said. "Put a hand in your panties now." I tugged Holly's panties down and let them drop to the floor before moving back to the couch. "Sit on my lap," I whispered, "and open your legs for me."

I could see Alix again. Her thick, muscular thighs fell open. I felt sure the dark patch of hair between her legs was matted and wet. I licked the tip of my finger before softly brushing it against Holly's clit. "Can you feel me?" I asked. "I'm barely touching you." I felt my own clit swell hard with need. "Spit on my fingers," I said, raising my hand. Alix's fingers shined with slickness.

I circled her clit. "Pull my cock inside you," I said. "I want to feel you." I slid my fingers inside Holly and watched in awe as Alix grabbed her own fingers and pushed them inside her.

"Look up," I said. "Look here." It was impossible to lock eyes in this virtual setting, but I did my best to let Alix see me stare directly at her while we fucked. "Show me what you like," I said, and she rubbed a hand lightly on her inner thighs, first one and then the other, while she fucked herself with her fingers.

"I want my dick inside you until you can't take it anymore and need my fingers on your clit," I demanded.

Holly buried her head against me and whispered, out of hearing, "I love it when you use my body." I was so turned on I thought I might come with her. Them. My fingers were stiff inside her. Them. Alix begged me to touch her clit. Holly's pussy felt swollen, different. All of this felt so real. Holly came before Alix did. She grabbed my hand to keep it between her legs. Alix saw how she grabbed me and seemed to feel it. She came in waves, her belly rolling, her chest heaving, and threw her head back on the back of the couch.

I reached for my watered-down drink. "Will you make me another?" I asked and both of them stood up to go mix another cocktail. I leaned back with a hand on my belt and stared at Alix's darkened Zoom window. "Jerk me off," I said when they were back, taking a sip of my drink and spreading my legs. Holly tugged my jeans down to my knees and slid a hand under my briefs. Alix shoved her hand between her legs. I watched how her wrist moved. I tried to keep myself from coming too quickly but I was too jacked up.

Next time I'll be ready. Next time I'll know it's a date. When we can travel again, we'll book a flight to Chicago.

HOME

Ash Orlando

I had wept so much in those last weeks. I had said so many desperate things to Alice. I had offered a lot—let's have an open relationship, let's explore counseling, let's just live together as friends—all
the ridiculous things you say. But in the end, she still left.

It just killed me.

"I think that's it," I said, staring around. "That's the last box."

My friend Sasha and I were in the living room, packing up
everything I owned. I had rented a room across town and the new
keys were tucked in my jacket pocket. This was it.

The house belonged to Alice now.

My boxes sat like stones around me, witness to my life ending.
I was in limbo. I was between everything and belonging nowhere.
My thoughts ran in painful circles. The scent in Alice's hair, making me remember the thousand times I had bought the shampoo
she liked. The million times I had cooked her dinner. The four bil-
lion times we had laughingly said, let's get married in the spring.

The one time she had said—it's over.

"Sasha," I started, "I don't know how to do this."

"Baby, I'm so sorry," she said, stretching tape over the box and closing it shut. "There's no other way. You just gotta leave."

I clenched my fists, then let go. Nothing to hold on to. The feeling of falling through open air swept into my body, and I started to shake.

Alice was my first for so many things. It was the first time I had whispered to someone in the half-dark—*I think I'm non-binary.* The way she had put her hand on my chest then, and looked at me, really saw me and said, *Tell me how you want me to love you.* And kissed me, until I knew what my body wanted, and until I knew how to ask for it.

Alice was the first one to know my new name, after months of deliberation. That night in bed, in a holy storm of fucking, she called my name as she came. I was reborn.

And then, of course, the first time Alice had taken me to her mother's house. She said simply, "This is Jak. They're non-binary, so just use the pronoun 'they', okay?" I had stood there in shock, electric at being so visible. Her mother had said, "Yeah okay, that's cool. You're not vegetarian or anything are you? Because I've made lamb." I had laughed, and felt layers of shame lifting from me.

My beautiful friend Sasha saw my tears, and walked across the room to me. She rubbed my short-cropped hair gently.

"Hey," she said. I lifted my head to see her. "I'm so sorry it hurts."

I looked down again and checked my watch. Three hours till the moving truck came. Could I do this?

Sasha pulled me to the lounge and I lay on top of her, my breath coming in short bursts. She wrapped her legs around me and pulled me in. Gently she kissed the top of my head a few times. My head lay on her breasts and I felt mothered and warm and something in me softened for the first time in weeks.

"You're gonna be okay, baby," Sasha murmured. "You just wait."

The world tilted on its axis as I felt pain roll through me. I knew my whole new life was out there. But I didn't want it.

I shifted my body in her embrace and my packing cock pressed on her thigh. Something crackled between us, and a sudden need in me sparked.

"Sasha—" I started, but then she tilted her head down and kissed me.

I kissed her back hungrily. I pushed my tongue in hard, and she groaned in response. I bit her neck, firmly. I started to grind against her. Something in me woke up and wouldn't be quiet.

"My, aren't we a needy boy." She laughed, and paused. "Can I call you boy?"

Sasha's eyes met mine as she looked for my consent. I nodded, breathless.

She was nothing but lovely curves, all accentuated by tight jeans and a button-up shirt tied at the waist. She was stronger than me by far, and took pleasure in the way her body took up space. When she wanted to, she could conquer a man by undoing two top buttons and rubbing butter in her cleavage. I had seen it happen at more than one queer party. She was a goddess and she knew it.

Right then, she knelt before me.

"Open your legs my boy," she instructed. "Show Mama where it hurts."

"It hurts—it hurts everywhere," I stuttered, honestly.

"But where baby, where in your body? Show me."

So I got brave. I lifted my shirt off in a smooth motion and threw it behind me. My short white binder held my heart together but I pulled it off too, and sat there, my chest naked. With a swift movement Sasha straddled me, and took my breasts in her hands.

"Let me make you feel better, baby," she purred, and rubbing one breast in her hand she took the other in her mouth, making circles with her tongue. She bit gently.

I jumped, tensing.

"Honey, sometimes things have got to hurt a little before they feel good," she said, rubbing harder with her hand. "You gonna let me hurt you a little? You gonna take that for me?"

I nodded, breathless.

"Please, Sasha," I said, "all of this, please—"

"Hush, my boy. This is good for you. Now get on the floor."

I obeyed. The soft carpet on my back. The warmth of the late afternoon sun flooding the room, making me sweat a little.

"Arms up, above your head." She reached for a roll of strong tape that we had been using to seal up the boxes. She pulled out a length of tape and wrapped my wrists securely.

"If you move, I will stop. You get it?"

I nodded, shaking a little. She threw a big cushion behind my head so I could see what she would do. I was breathing so fast it was like mainlining energy.

"I'm gonna take care of you now. Now show me what you can take." She pinched both nipples hard again and laughed a little as I squirmed. Leaning over she took one breast in her mouth again, and bit down, sucking and moving her mouth firmly. I gasped but did my best to stay still.

"Good boy," she murmured into my ear. "Now don't think I didn't feel that little cock of yours before. Does it hurt there too?"

She unzipped my fly and slid her hand in.

"Oh, this is nice, my boy. What a beautiful little cock, look how it fits into my hands so perfectly." She tugged me gently, softly.

Her soft hand moved over my cock, warming it. It was held in place with a simple black fabric harness. I remembered suddenly the wild freedom it had given me, the first time I had slipped that harness on. I had tucked the cock into the fabric loop, and pulled on my boxers over the top. Something about the way it had sat perfectly made me feel like I was home. I don't understand why and I've stopped trying. But I know realness when I feel it.

All I know is that Sasha's tender touch was like gold to me right then, molten gold, like an alchemy of elements meeting.

She reached to her handbag near the doorframe and pulled out her purse. A square shiny package between her fingers. She tore it open, watching my eyes widen with desire. She knelt between my legs so I could see.

She kept eye contact the whole time while she pushed that condom onto my cock with her mouth. I closed my eyes and I felt the way it was real, the honesty of it, the push-pull of my dick between the warmth of her soft lips. It was gentle, it was kind, it was giving. Her strong hands were on my hips, urging me to tilt upwards onto her tongue.

I felt my tears start.

"Sasha, I—" My eyes opened to find her watching me still, but with a gleam in her eye.

"Yeah, that's it. We're gonna get all this hurt out of you. Let's go."

With expert grace she pulled off my old boots, my socks. My jeans she grabbed with both hands and pulled them free. I was naked before her, in the sunlight. My skin prickled with heat.

"Let's go, baby. Let's see you put on a nice show for me. Give your mama what she wants."

She thrust two fingers into my cunt, testing.

I bucked, hard. It felt good, in a way that shocked me. She grabbed a bottle of lube from her bag and covered her hand.

I pushed my heels into the carpet and my body lifted, beautifully. I was her handsome boy then, a boy that is a bit girlish, a girl that is a bit boy, but I was altogether hers and she knew it.

"More please," I mumbled. "Please more."

"I like a boy with manners," she said, grinning. "After I own you good and proper I'm going to put you between my legs and teach you how to lick some pussy. Would you like that, my boy?"

My whole body caught fire at the idea of it, but before I could register anything she started fucking me. Four fingers easily slipped in, right underneath my cock, the flooding wetness of me like a river. Then quickly, she expertly pushed five fingers into my cunt, right up to the bottom of her thumb.

"Yeah, I think you can take it. You gonna take it for me like a good boy? Are you ready?" And with that she slid her whole fist inside me. It filled me like fireworks and oh, god, I wanted it. It was good.

"Just for a little while, baby. Take it hard for a little while. Mama gonna make you feel all better."

With that she started fucking me. Slow, deep, powerful thrusts that echoed through me. I closed my eyes and I was nothing but my body, nothing but the lifting strong sensation of freedom. I heard my voice as I moaned but it felt like it was outside of me, that sound.

I started to rock my body into her rhythm and the tape around my hands cut into my skin. I felt a little bit of pain as I twisted my hands, helplessly.

"Hey," Sasha said, pausing instantly. "I already told you about this, baby. You move too much, and I stop. Did you get that from before? I know I warned you."

With her free hand she reached up and cuffed me on the cheek. A gentle slap, to put me in my place.

"I'm sorry, oh, god please. I'll do what you say."

"You promised that before." She eyed me, contemplating her hand still. "This is for your own good, you know that? I could be anywhere in town right now, fucking any boy I liked. But right now, I want you."

I started stammering appreciation, my gratitude, my thankfulness. I damn near begged.

"Please Sasha, please."

She looked at me, her wide brown eyes taking me all in. She was thinking. I started to speak again but was silenced by a single, powerful push of her fist inside me, all the way, hard, and fast. A delicious rush of agony. Oh. My. God.

"Yes, my boy, take that medicine." She laughed with pleasure. "Why don't I give you another chance and let's see what you can do."

The way she fucked me increased in pace and I let my heart open to it. I tried so hard to hold my body still. My hips bucked a little but I kept mumbling, "I can do whatever you tell me to. Whatever you say."

Sasha set one hand on my chest holding me down, so she could get the angle that she wanted. Sensing a shift in what I needed she tilted her fist up a little too, changing the angle so that it hit me inside just so. Perfect. I started to build and I knew I couldn't hold back much longer.

I started to follow that starry feeling that leads to release but then she paused again and met my eyes. "Can you take a little more?" She tilted her head. "Baby would you like a special treat?"

I had no idea what I could take but I said yes. She shifted back between my legs, and slipped some lube onto her other hand. She slid her free hand under my butt. With her thumb she circled my asshole, testing, nudging, all the while her fist rocking very gently within, keeping me ready. She took me slowly with her thumb, but with certainty, letting me push down, till I felt full and hot.

"Good?" she said, questioningly.

I nodded, yes, god, my whole body was saying yes, and then she started moving her fist some more. She built me up again, and it was tidal, like an ocean rolling. My whole body an ocean wave.

"You wanna come in my mouth, baby, like a good boy? I think you do," Sasha said, the sweat running deliciously down her breasts. She kept up the rhythm and put her mouth back on my cock, slipping her mouth around me, keeping up.

I felt the orgasm riding through me, pulling me—but Jesus Christ, I wasn't sure. I wasn't sure I could. I wanted to, god knows, but it was so much. I looked up at her, my eyes wide. I was nothing but sensation and need and willingness but could I?

"I'm not sure I—"

"Baby you can do this. You're gonna do this for me. You need this. It's good for you and you need it."

Her pounding was a heartbeat through me, she had me and I felt it. I felt home and I felt good and I said, "Yes, okay, yes, I will do it for you, yes," and I surrendered.

I felt open sky. I felt my body, and it was good and whole and perfect and goddamn it, it was mine.

My hands still bound I tucked them behind my head, opening up my body to it all. My body was joyous and wild and something dark broke in me. I would give this to her. I would give it. It belonged to me and I would give it.

Watching her mouth move up and down me made me primal and raw. The fisting was echoing through my body, calling me home. I wanted to go home. That's how it felt to me right then.

I am my own home, I suddenly thought, this body is my home and I own it and it is mine.

And with that I came, shouting, hard and beautiful, my strong cunt throbbing around her hand. It tipped me—I swam, headlong into it—I flew.

"That's it honey, my baby, my boy," Sasha murmured. "Let go, let go."

She gently pulled her hands free of my body and scooped me up in her arms, using the nearby blade to free my hands from the tape.

"I've got you baby, you're here with me. Jak, I've got you."

She sat and held me, whispering sweet things to me, pressing me to her breasts as all the pain I was holding filled the room in huge, rocketing waves.

It was a galaxy of grief and I felt it flow through me, and out, and away.

DOCUMENTING DESIRE

Luisa Margo Park

Your hands are sure. You know what you want and forget to ask sometimes.

You slipped your hand beneath my dress and roughly held my breast, pinching my nipple until you felt the shape and volume you wanted. It happened so fast I could not protest.

And I did not want to. I felt abandon, your lust mixed in with mine. There is no taking because it is already given.

You said you felt appreciated by my effort. My Sunday best hat and my dress. They express my invitation to come closer, my transparency in letting you know and letting you in.

Everything has been happening so quickly. I regret not remembering all the moments, the light caresses, meaningful looks, and alluring words spoken in between kisses. At home, feeling flustered and full, I jot down my little stories of the night. Perhaps I add some embellishments but I am certain I am also missing essential parts I wish I had retained.

* * *

On our first date, we lay under a tree with far reaching branches, shading us away from elements and other people. In the quiet I could hear the steady brushing of a snare drum. Some old-timey jazzy sounds played on. Real or imagined, I cannot recall.

Tired of sitting cross-legged, I finally laid down on my back, knees bent and feet on the ground. You stole glances that I caught each time. I pretended not to notice but smirked inwardly.

I looked up at the leaves and branches and patches of blue sky showing through the foreground. Your blanket of faded green and brown colors felt soft and soothing to my bare arms and shoulders. I took an intentional breath and felt that coveted feeling of peace and fullness in the present moment. However fleeting, I cherished this brief acknowledgment that there is nothing else to need or want, that I am part of a whole that does not need or want anything more than what it is now.

You looked at me with curiosity, guessing that I was having a philosophical moment. You admitted that you like this part of me, the one that thinks and wonders and questions the meaning of existence, dreams, dubious moral codes, and what we accept as everyday reality. I in turn find your nonconformity outrageously attractive, especially as it shows throughout all aspects of your being. Your distinctiveness does not read as forced or contrived in any way. Rather, I suspect that you are still peeling away conventions and cobwebs of cursory expectations. What then comes into view is a person of vast imagination, deep reverence for invention, and a whimsical passion for irregularities.

I don't think you veer off on purpose. I think you are already standing there wondering where everybody else has gone. Sometimes this makes you feel lonely, and I connect with you with my own deep loneliness.

I am grateful for this shared sense of solitude for accentuating the joy in meeting someone who makes sense to you. Perhaps we will feel more coherent in this world if we stay together.

At the beginning, you would paw at me and ask for permission later.

I laughed at you to tease you but also to let you know that you are within the bounds of my implicit permission.

Desire does not want to wait for words sometimes. We have done the work of extending invitations, recognizing and building chemistry, sharing increasingly fervent glances. We have delighted in the equilibrium of readiness and rapture.

Before you took me to bed, your hands already knew my contours and crevices. I knew what little sounds to make to keep your focus where I wanted it the most. You learned how to position me to play out your preferred parts. I held your gaze to summon your raw urges. You guided my fingers to your mouth and I made you promises with my swollen tongue.

I made it plainly clear that I wanted you. And at each point, you smiled in complicit agreement. Then you led me to bed.

You held my hand when I talked about my dying mother. She is six thousand miles away geographically, but even farther away after so many ruptures and heartbreaks. You listened as I told you about my family's struggles with communication, our different immigration trajectories resulting in linguistic differences and cultural misalignments. You did not criticize or demonize them, even though you felt the pull to protect me from the pain I carry for and from my family. You understood that I would resist and come to their defense, caught between loyalty and self-preservation. Yet neither did you let me justify the hurt by contextualizing everyone's actions and words. You understand rejection; the willful act of not accepting another human being for who they are. You understand the impact, the long shadows that fall upon our lives when our own people turn away from us. You held my hand and let me cry.

Your lips kept hovering just above mine, savoring the anticipation but not giving in, not just yet. Your touch is feather soft sometimes, just enough to make me shiver all over. I feel a searing warmth under my clavicles and above my full breasts. You find these pockets of skin through my layered clothing, not quite removing them but circumventing them. I wonder when you will undress me.

Will it be slow and deliberate? Or rushed and desperately demanding? Will you let me reach for your shirt buttons? Use one hand to undo each one, the other supporting me as I lean back on the bed, with your relentless arousal leading the way. Can I tug at your belt, slip my hands down your pants to caress the small of your back? A hollow holding an undulation of muscle and bone. Will you let me?

Once horizontal, will you grab my wrists and place them above my head, forecasting ties and restraints someday, maybe even today? Will you leave some piece of garment unattended because the urge to lay on top of me is too overwhelming? Would you like it if I squirmed and struggled slightly so you can press down against my hips and let me savor my deep desire for submission? Will you leave me to ponder while you take a moment to harness your strap-on and select the cock you have deliberated on and finally chosen weeks ago when we first met? Will you spread my legs and push hard into me, knowing I am so wet that I can take the sudden entry? Would I arch my back and moan as you forget to pace yourself and push your clit against me to the point of climax? Would I wait patiently until you notice me again, listen to my pleas for release, then decide you'll wait a little longer to build my desperate anticipation?

Will you gently place your hand on my open and vulnerable throat, signaling who is hunter and who is prey? Please let me be your prey.

Mmmmm. I have more ideas. Another round of me on top, conducting the score. Yet another with both of us in matching sailor suits. Where would you like to begin?

I had seen pictures of you before we met. You had read about me online. From these incomplete pieces we could have spun improbable stories and shameless projections. Instead I think we did quite well, letting each of our stories unfold rather than sketch them out of the thin air of speculation.

I do suspect that we spent some considerable time pre-worrying. What if this and what if that. What if they are stiff and don't know how to flirt? What if our stories are less enticing told rather than written? What if they don't recycle? What if I am vegan? What if they deny the reality and legacy of white supremacists? Absolutely not negotiable!

Then of course, some guesswork is involved in the gender identity fit. I don't always assume I know what any of the labels and pronouns mean because they are merely shortcuts to a much more complicated story. And while I accept and celebrate all genders, I know my particular spheres of attraction and magnetism. Thankfully my range has an impressive wingspan, but what I do worry about is the contrast we sometimes seek to our gender expression.

I've had trans male lovers heavily prefer my femme parts and inadvertently suppress my gender fluidity with well-meaning yet willful direction. I, in turn, am endlessly accommodating, something I am trying to shed from my upbringing. Thus I can't just blame them, I am part of the dance that skews us to the gender locations they want to inhabit.

In fact, there is no one or nothing to blame, since much of the time we are just being ourselves and hoping for the natural match. I know I too have tried to exert some direction when the fit felt a little off. My last nonbinary partner resisted my subtle yet strong insistence to extract out their masc sensibilities so I could move closer to my preferred expression. Neither of us enjoyed this. We soon let things dissolve.

I wonder, will I be femme enough to your masc leanings? Will this matter? Will you need to rely on me to locate you in the spectrum? Will I be able to experience the kind of gender fluidity I feel is most genuine within me? Will I recognize your spirit beyond these insufficient contours and casings? Will you recognize and support mine?

Thus far I am impressed with how easily we fit together without much effort, restraint, or shifting. You have a lovely mix of mismatched and playful gender parts, like the contents of a sock drawer that do not require perfect pairings. And I feel the freedom to roam aimlessly as I am bound to do.

When we hesitate to divulge hidden desires, we fall back on our legacy of voluminous writing to share our thoughts, stories, and of course, our confessions. As we grew closer and bolder, you asked me to describe my expression of submission. Like a map with dotted lines, I chose to share just enough to reveal the subtle exchanges of power I seek in kink play. This is what I wrote to you:

What makes me hot, you ask?

When you ignore my pleas.

Witnessing how my pain gives you pleasure.

Humiliating me slightly by making me aware of how wet I am while I beg you to stop.

Feeling precarious and exposed and in good hands when you are sneering, smirking, and looking down at me.

When you delight in my worried look when you pause to consider what you will do next.

When you push just enough that I cannot take it anymore but not enough for me to release my safeword.

That in-between space of self and other possession, my ownership of my own undoing.

When you hold me down with your weight and remind me that I'm not going anywhere. (I do not want to go anywhere, please keep me down here.)

I have been reading relationship self-help nonsense online. I'd like to think of myself as too cool and learned to seek wisdom in the press for the masses, but if you look past the hetero bullshit, sometimes you can find what you are looking for. I guess this is part of the problem, one always finds what one wants to see and hear. It is a massive infinite projection machine.

So I read that merely thinking and overthinking about romantic matters mostly leads to sheer confusion and potential misdirection. The author claimed that it is the noticing that can be most fruitful. I am to notice how my body is reacting to your presence and to your touch. Notice if my body and I feel at ease, or if tension and rigidity arises. Notice if our shared energy pulses in sweet, gentle motions like colorful parachuting jellyfish in an aquarium tank. Or does it dart in chaotic nervousness like pesky flies? Please don't let it be the flies.

I do not need to worry so. Our picnics have attracted nary a fly! Perhaps a mosquito or two due to my unusually tasty blood. And a couple of coyotes, not once but twice! And the rest has been jellyfish, the pink and floaty kind, both ephemeral and substantial, ensnaring us both in a rhythmic and trancelike dance.

I am noticing. That you make me happy. And at peace. And joyful.

* * *

Little by little, I plan to set up small boundaries so I can transgress them.

When your breath is on a steady crescendo, I will hold still with the slightest hint of unwillingness. An invitation with an innuendo of refusal. Riled up and ready, you will feel forced to dismiss the resistance. Your pent-up energy will turn to irritation and self-righteousness. I will be delighted. I will extract your desire to show me that you can and will take what is yours.

You will be rewarded with my increasing wildness and abandon. I will beg for more when you thrash harder into me, holding my body down firmly in my bent position and fucking me with your smooth, hard cock. My arms held back with your hands, my back artfully arched, and my toes tipping to reach the ground.

I will want to be punished from time to time. I prefer it swift and sparse. Sufficient to create another stretch of menacing anticipation. By then the promise of punishment will grow more exciting than the whippings.

My days have been filled with images and sounds from our latest trysts, and my phone is filled with snapshots of my favorite texts since our beginning. Like that Travis Tritt country song in the eighties, we are in T-R-O-U-B-L-E. I am sure of it.

Can one feel safely in trouble? I believe that is how I might feel. We are old enough in our forties and fifties to recognize the first signs of impending doom, the blurred boundaries that lead to regrets, and the tricks our chemically intoxicated brains can play on our already bruised souls.

I have been fretting that some recklessness is driving this bus, but I am also aware that overworry drives the meta of all buses. Like a clunky double-decker full of extra-opinionated passengers.

We have taken turns being brave. I have examined the sources of my doubts and mistrust, and they seem to reliably reside in old injuries and past betrayals. None of it can be traced back to you and me, at least thus far. At our age, our love histories need large maps depicting all kinds of roads, paths, and landscapes, as well as a detailed key of symbols to aid with legibility. I have drawn this map several times for myself and for others as a way to chart new territory ahead. I have decided that fear can come along with excitement and discovery.

I feel grounded. Grounded in preparation to take flight.

CODE

Meg Elison

Helen had the girl's wrists pinned up over her head. Violet was breathing heavier now, obviously turned on. It hadn't been this clear at the table, even with their ankles pressed against one another beneath. Helen was good at reading people, but she had accidentally ended up on dates with too many straight girls and had learned to doubt her instincts.

No doubts here, she thought as her knee came in contact with the moist heat in the crotch of Violet's tiny yellow shorts. Their lips met again in that hungry way, each signaling need beyond playfulness, beyond casual attraction. Helen leaned in, laying the length of her body against Violet's, feeling the curl of the other girl's body begin at once, as only an unconscious impulse can. Violet brought her body into maximum contact with Helen's, her hips pumping forward and slightly upward. Helen knew that not only was Violet into her, she was going to be a spectacular lay. It'd been a long time. She was aching for that kind of night.

They came off the wall, breathless. For a moment they were suspended in their own cloud of warm air and lust; a hot air balloon sailing through the night. Kissing the girl hard again, Helen began driving her firmly but carefully backward toward her bedroom. She silently thanked the gods that she had spent that all-important fifteen minutes cleaning up and shoving all the laundry into a hamper, at least. Violet's brown eyes were wild with risk and excitement as Helen's taller, more muscular frame led her in a savage dance toward the midnight-blue bedspread and tripped her backward onto it.

She covered the prone woman at once, hips aligned, belly to belly. Helen reached her clever hand beneath Violet's short top and brought a plundering hand to the woman's small, perfect breasts. She marveled at the sensation of satisfaction that came from the hard nipple in her palm, the heft and weight of it as she squeezed and stroked. How could a hand alone be so satisfied? How could one perfect breast live right beside another? How could she use both hands without losing her balance on top of this gorgeous girl?

She was clumsy in the way that lovers are always clumsy; teeth bashed together and forgotten. A hand placed for balance in a place that doesn't work and forgiven. All things forgiven, all things rendered endearing as Helen dragged her soft-parted lips over Violet's belly slowly. She kissed and fluttered a lick over Violet's skin, making a trail downward to where this could no longer be casual, where making out becomes something else. She went slowly, giving her heart time to slow, giving the other woman time to stop her. Violet moaned and arched and parted her thighs. This would not be stopped.

Helen read a clear *yes* in Violet's eyes and her tanned hands went to the little rivet-button barring her from paradise. Violet's freckled hands laid on top of her for an instant. Not a *stop*, exactly. More like a *wait*.

"When was your last debug?" Violet was biting her lower lip. She didn't want to be asking this, Helen could tell. But she needed to.

Helen sighed and let go of the smaller girl's button. She sat back on her heels, relaxing the predatory posture she knew had excited the other woman just a moment ago. "Kind of long," she admitted. "A year, probably."

Violet came up on her elbows, clearly considering. "Why so long?"

Helen shrugged. "I haven't had any new partners in a while. Hasn't been a priority. But I've had no unexpected shutdowns, no pop-ups . . . You know, I'm clean. As far as I know."

Violet was nodding, looking at the moody pink light on Helen's nightstand. Her long bangs fell into her face and she puffed them away with a jet of air guided with a side-cupping of her lower lip. "I have a firewall and all. It's just . . . I'm trying to be more responsible."

Which means you get around, Helen thought. She didn't mind knowing that, but she noted it just the same.

"I mean, everyone's caught a virus or two. It's bound to happen. Some of them are so common these days. Helen was trying to be reassuring, but she sounded nervous to herself.

Violet came up a little closer, looking to Helen like she was trying to reestablish contact. Her brown eyes were shining, mirthful. "Yeah, like a third of all adults have had iloveyou at some point or another."

Helen swallowed. "Yeah, my ex gave me that. I fell in code with her so fast, it didn't matter. And we went to the helpdesk together to get it fixed. But that fucker is persistent. Hides out in folders you didn't know you even had."

"I could help you find a pathway to some of those," Violet said, bolder now. She slid a hand up under Helen's crop top and brought her cool fingers to one brown nipple. It hardened at once, unused to any attention.

Violet grinned, then brought her cheek to the soft skin on the underside of Helen's breast. Looking up, she took a nipple into her mouth. She nibbled maddeningly at the very tip, making Helen feel like screaming, like stopping her. Just when she thought she couldn't stand it, Violet opened her lips and sucked the nipple inward. Her mouth was shockingly warm, rough teeth replaced by smooth lips, downy inner cheeks.

Helen moaned and Violet echoed back, carrying the vibration in a circuit between them. It had been so long for Helen that she was suddenly shy. Insecure in her own vast wanting.

"There's lots we can do without exposure," Helen said, her voice suddenly husky.

"Where's the fun in that?" asked Violet, coming off Helen's nipple decisively. Not shy. She was unbuttoning her shorts herself, this time. Helen followed instinct instead of worry. She reached out her strong right hand and felt at once for the port.

"Oh," she said.

"Oh?" Violet quirked up an eyebrow, laying back once again.

"You, uh . . ." Helen withdrew her hand. "You upgraded to UIV-D. I don't . . . I mean, I haven't . . ."

Violet sighed, falling back onto the pillows. "How old is it?"

Helen looked self-consciously down at her cutoff jeans. "I've had it since I was twenty-one."

Violet's eyes were now as narrow as those of the bouncer who had scrutinized them both at the club to see if their bios matched their scans. "You're like what? Twenty-seven now?"

"About that," Helen admitted.

"Okay," Violet said. "Switch." She was coming up, pushing Helen back toward the foot of the bed, stationing herself between Helen's knees.

"Wait a second," Helen said, surprised by this reversal. She tumbled back, laughing a little. "Just because I still have UIV-9—"

"It's a *nine*?" Violet's voice was that of an archaeologist finding a trilobite where she expected pottery shards. "Hang on, I think I have a carved ivory phallus in here somewhere."

"Okay, okay," Helen grumbled. "It's not *that* old." She settled back, still intent on connecting to this girl somehow, some way.

Violet stopped now, bottomless with her peaky nipples holding her T-shirt in a soft horizontal line between them. "My mom has a nine," she said, smirking and on the edge of a laugh.

"Great," Helen said, not thinking it was great at all. "Well, this was fun."

"Can I just take a tour?" Violet's eyes were merry and not malicious. "I'm still really into it, if you are. I just need to figure out what we can do."

Helen sighed, feeling the ghost of the loneliness that was always with her in this bed beside her, whisper in her ear that it couldn't wait to have her back to itself again.

"Yes, please," she whispered. She had meant to sound sexy and yielding. To herself, she just sounded lonesome and hollow.

Violet was the kind of girl who could bring her fingertip sensor to the port without even looking. She looked down into Helen's eyes. The two points of contact were unnerving, too intimate for a stranger who she had dragged home from a bar. But Helen could not look away.

The younger girl sighed. "Oh, you have so much memory."

"I've been using it for a long time," Helen said, smirking a little. Here was her power. Here was her whole self. Nothing to be ashamed of. Here was what she brought to bed with every woman she had ever loved. It was deep and rich and strange, and she was ready to share it again. She was. With Violet. This young, lovely purpling flower. "What are you, like twenty-one?"

"About that," Violet said, pink in her cheeks. She was breathing a little harder as she sunk into the link. She liked what she was finding, Helen knew. "Oh, god, I want to download all these files right now," Violet moaned.

Helen was spellbound, her pulse pounding. "Can you? Can you take all of me?"

"I don't know," Violet said, biting her lip again. Her rhythm was picking up. "I don't know if I have the space. We could just share access in the cloud," she said, looking down at Helen, panting but still holding back.

Helen turned her head on the pillow, so wet now that she couldn't regulate. Her background processes were slowed down. She was processing everything at once, rampant. "I guess," she said, knowing that that wouldn't satisfy her in the slightest.

Fingertip sensor and port went into overdrive together, and Helen arched her back, biting her lip. This was it. This was the deep dive. She was ready.

"I can do this," Violet said, her voice ragged. "There's a workaround. What's your public key?"

Helen turned back to face her, black hair clinging to the sweat on her face. "Don't you want the private one?"

Violent laughed, picking up Helen's leg with surprising strength and holding it against her chest, kissing the inside of her ankle and adjusting her fingertip sensor for depth. Helen moaned and bucked into it, split and splayed and dying to feel that final connection take hold.

"Yeah, why don't I take your last name while I'm at it?"

Helen transmitted, her hips moving in an unstoppable rhythm then waited. Everything got quiet. They were suspended again, not in their shared warm air, but in their own cold code.

Violet's fingers slowed, then stopped. Her eyes closed and for a minute, she didn't move. Her brow smoothed and her breathing slowed. She was somewhere else, waiting in some unknown vestibule.

Helen's arousal drained away all at once. Her breathing slowed and her skin cooled. Somewhere deep inside, she felt some vital process fail and enter shutdown. She wanted to hide. She wanted to turn back time and take back her invitation and make it so that she never opened herself up like this. She steeled herself for rejection, cruelty, whatever awful thing was about to come out of Violet's mouth.

But it wasn't that.

"You're password protected?"

"What?" Helen sat up a little, feeling her hamstring stretch against the shorter girl's body. What had been an exciting position a moment ago now only felt like vulnerability, like a bad idea. She clenched.

"There's a password to get in. Past your public key. It looks like a biometric?"

Helen though a moment, then flopped back down. "Oh, shit," she said. "It's a fingerprint."

Violet kissed Helen's ankle again, chastely this time, then gently laid her brown leg down on the bed. "I'm going to guess it belongs to whoever set all these subroutines you're still running. Honestly, name your files something better than 'how to get Anica off'."

Helen's face was burning. "Look, I swear I didn't know. I wouldn't have asked you to come home with me. I'm not a tease. I just—"

Violet disengaged her sensor. Helen felt bereft.

"Listen," Violet said, wiggling back into her yellow shorts. "I like you. I left you my contact info. Why don't you call me when you've . . . I don't know. Upgraded. At least allowed the auto-updates that are pending. Nothing has moved in there for like a year. Maybe more. You're too young to be locked down like this. To be obsolete."

Violet blew her a kiss from the bedroom door, so young. So far from her own zero day vulnerability.

Helen wondered whether Violet was going back to the bar to meet someone with newer hardware. With less complicated software. She wondered what it would be like to start over, to install a port where her wife had never touched her. What would it feel like to begin with a new system, no passwords, no subroutines, and just build together from the bottom up?

In the end, Helen put her own experienced but well-worn sensor to the port and dove back into her own deep memory, to the file pathway she knew the best. She went down to the place where her code was written when she was young, and she couldn't tell what was originally hers and what had come from someone else.

PRIVATE DANCER

Meka James

The lights were dimmed and the music lowered. From behind the black velvet curtain I could hear the murmured chants from the crowd. My heart rate spiked and butterflies warred in my stomach. No matter how many times I did this, I had nerves right up until I stepped onto the stage.

Plus I wondered if she would be here. My mysterious fan who'd been coming to The Candy Store for the last two months. I closed my eyes and shook my arms to get the jitters out and her face popped into my mind. Her smooth dark skin, and deep brown, seductive eyes.

"Now folks, get your dolla', dolla' bills ready. Coming to the stage is the one. The only. Caramel Delight!"

The sound of my stage name brought me to the present. I ran my hands down the feathers lining the white sheer robe I wore as part of the act. It was showtime.

Hoots and hollers mixed with thunderous applause, which died down as soon as my music started and I stepped out.

I began the seduction to a house remix of "Private Dancer"

while I searched the crowd. It didn't take long to find her. Front row, center stage, and eyes trained on my every move. She was here every night I headlined. In a sea of faces hers stood out to me from the beginning.

I twirled the pole waiting for just the right moment in the song, and then stopped. I ripped off the robe to reveal the outfit underneath. My body being exposed always drew bigger cheers and I loved it. Standing before the eager patrons in nothing more than a cream-colored G-string with a dainty bow situated at the back just above my ass crack and a matching cream pearl choker around my neck. The light colors stood out against my dark complexion, which is why I chose it.

Once I was on stage, being center of attention fueled me. And the act was all for her. Hell, even the song was a message I'd wanted to send after she'd been coming regularly. A strange sort of foreplay. As I moved, never was she out of my line of sight.

The crowd cheered and whistled as I danced. A little bit burlesque mixed with a little bit raunchy. Just what they wanted. Money rained down on the stage while I simulated dry humping the floor, ass cheeks clapping to the rhythm, as I visualized one person, and one person only to sell the fantasy.

She remained relaxed in her chair, ankle resting on her knee, and a slight smile on her lips. I held onto the pole to twerk, which drew more screams from the audience. They called out variations of "work that ass," a couple of marriage proposals, and the really lewd ones telling me how much they wanted to fuck me.

But she said nothing.

As I came to the end of my performance, she did the same thing as always. No applause, no calling for an encore like the rest of the patrons. No, my mystery lady stood and finished her drink while holding a crisp hundred between two fingers for my retrieval. And like always, I sauntered over, making a show of swinging my hips, then slowly bent over so my large tits dangled at her eye level to pluck it from her hands.

She winked and left. Same as always.

"Oh, girl, you killed it out there," Gina said as I entered the dressing room. "And I see your sexy stud was back, front and center."

I dabbed my face and chest with a towel. "Thank ya. And she's not mine. She never stays after, no requests for lap dances, nothing."

"Don't matter," Keeki cut in. "That woman comes to see you, and you damn near be dancing just for her. Be glad the rest of them fools out there be too drunk, and too horny to tell. Long as you flashing them tits and ass, they don't give a fuck who you lookin' at."

We all laughed and nodded in agreement. And she wasn't wrong, though I wouldn't admit that fact out loud.

"Yo, Delight. You have been requested in the VIP room," Darrell bellowed from the doorway.

We all thought it to be sweet that even though he saw us damn near naked every night, he never came into the dressing room.

"Who else is with me?"

"You rockin' solo."

We all exchanged glances around the room. Solo? In the VIP? Drunk businessmen or even drunker frat boys who'd pooled their money? Nah, Viv wouldn't set me up like that. She used to work the pole before retiring and opening The Candy Store, and safety for her dancers was her biggest concern.

"A'ight. Let me finish cleaning up."

After a refresh of my make-up, and a dash more glitter to my titties, I followed Darrell through the joint, ignoring the catcalls and men asking for a dance.

"How many?" I asked at the door.

"Just one. But if she gives you any trouble, you know what to do and I'll be in, in two seconds flat."

She? My heart rate spiked. Could it be? I nodded and he opened the black leather door.

There she sat. One arm stretched out along the back of the sofa and sipping on a drink. When she saw me, a full smile spread across her lips.

"It's taken me a while to work up the nerve to do this."

I slipped into my role. "Do what, baby?"

She rose from the couch and fuck if she wasn't tall. I had on six-inch heels and still had to look up to her. Damn, she was fine. Even in the terribly dim lights. Her dreads were neatly braided and pulled back. Her stark white shirt was stretched across her broad shoulders and was in direct contrast to her rich, dark brown skin. The top buttons being open allowed me a peek at three gold chains hanging around her neck at varying lengths. Slightly baggy jeans hung off her narrow hips, and tapered in at the leg.

"To . . . um talk to you."

"You rented out the VIP room to talk? Baby, a lap dance would have been cheaper."

"Maybe. But it would also be shorter." The same smirk she seemed to have whenever I danced appeared. "This way, for the rest of the night, you get to be my private dancer."

She winked and my mouth went dry. Maybe the message had been received.

"I'm Theo by the way," she said, extending a hand toward me. "Shall I call you Caramel, Delight, or both?"

"Delight will be fine."

She wrapped her long, delicate fingers around mine in a firm shake. I held on probably longer than I should have, imagining all the things those very fingers could do to me. Normally this was just a job, and the people that frequented The Candy Store all melded into one. But not her . . . Theo. From the first night she'd shown up I'd been intrigued. We'd been playing this sort of cat and mouse game ever since. But who was who?

In the main house, Theo appeared mysterious, but in here, there was a hint of something else, maybe a bit of shyness. I knew she appreciated my body, from my large breasts, thick thighs, and fat ass, but she didn't gawk.

I strolled over to the pole in the middle of the room and circled it. "You've bought me for the night, so, what's up first?"

"Don't say that."

"What?"

"That I bought you." She shook her head. "That's not . . . your time. I bought your time. Not you."

I smiled, her sentiment warmed more than just my heart. "Fair enough, Theo."

I made another strut around the pole. "Well, take a seat, baby, and I'll get your party started."

She didn't move. Like when she was in the house, she kept her focus on me as I began dancing. Her attention was almost voyeuristic even though I was performing for her. My nipples hardened and my pussy tingled.

I couldn't ever remember getting aroused while performing, but with Theo, the way she watched my every move, there was something about her that made it more than a job. More than a dance for a patron. Made it almost intimate.

She started to take a step forward, but stopped and shoved her hands into her back pockets. I smiled and sauntered toward her in rhythm with the music. Once in front of her, I bent forward, shaking my ass against her crotch. Part of me wished she'd give me a smack, but she kept her hands firmly to herself. Those were the rules, no matter how much she paid to be here.

"Lap dance."

The two words made me stand and face her. "Whatever you say, baby."

She sat her lanky form onto the sofa and took in a deep breath when I straddled her. Like when I'd danced in front of her, she kept her hands busy by gripping the cushions. I imagined her with a strap and me riding her hard. My pussy clenched at the thought. I'd fantasized many nights about her, getting off to the mystery and the what-ifs. Now she was beneath me, live and in person. Smelling delicious and looking like a full meal.

I held on to the back of the couch and gyrated my hips. "If you could touch me, what would you do?"

Theo licked her full lips and stared me right in the eye. "I'd palm your glorious tits. Then I'd pinch and tease your rock-hard nipples that are rubbing against me."

I tilted my hips forward, bringing my pussy closer to the small bump of fabric on the front of her jeans. My G-string was soaked and I probably should have cared I was breaking all protocol by dry-humping this woman, but fuck it. I needed to get off and she didn't seem to mind me using her to do so.

"What else?" My words were near breathless.

Theo stared into my eyes, the sly grin I'd seen so many times made its appearance as she began thrusting upwards. "I'd grab that thick ass of yours and help you find that nut you're chasing. And when you were done, I'd flip you on your back and eat that sweet, wet pussy until you came all over my face."

I dug my fingers into the leather. "Fuck, yes. Do it."

Theo grabbed my ass with her warm hands and squeezed. "That's it. Use me till you come. I need to see it."

Our movements became frantic and I was chasing no more as the drop hit.

"That's it. That's it," she grunted as she continued to pull me against her crotch while the tiny spasms overtook my body.

Theo lifted us and had me on my back before I could even catch my breath.

"Yes or no?" she asked, looking down at my soaked panties then back up at me.

I was falling into every stereotype and cliché of what went on in the VIP room, but I didn't give a shit. This woman showing up, and watching me dance only to leave again had been like foreplay and it was time to get my due.

I hooked a leg onto the back of the sofa and let the other rest on the floor. "Hell yes!"

Without another word, that fine-ass woman dropped to her knees, moved my G-string to the side, and got to work.

She spread me wide and licked the length of my flesh before thrusting her tongue forward.

"Fuck! Yes, like that."

I squeezed my tits and pinched my nipples. Theo shoved two fingers inside my wet pussy and began pumping them fast and furious while continuing to devour my clit, alternating between flicking and sucking it.

I pushed my hips up. "Shit . . . I'm about to come again," I groaned. My heart raced and my breath caught in my throat when the orgasm burst free.

She had my whole body shaking, but she didn't stop lapping at my pussy, drinking all I had to offer. Slowly, she withdrew her fingers and pressed her lips to my thigh. Then my stomach. Finally up to my chest. I watched as Theo swirled her tongue around one nipple, face glistening, and teased the other nipple with her hand.

If she kept that up, I was liable to go a third time. "You got me damn near speaking in tongues, and you're fully dressed."

She huffed a small laugh, then stood and retrieved two bottles of water from the side table. Theo handed one to me, then wet one of the pink napkins and quickly wiped her face then took a drink.

"You know when I booked this, I really only wanted your company. I wasn't expecting . . ."

I pushed into a seated position and drank half of my water in one gulp. "That makes two of us," I replied. "Fucking customers is not something I've done before, but I don't know, with you . . . Can I tell you a secret?"

"Yeah."

"I've masturbated thinking about you. A lot."

A lopsided grin pulled at her full lips. "Yeah, same here. And after tonight, I know I will be doing it a lot more."

This shit was probably reckless as fuck, but if ever there was a time to shoot my shot, it was now. I pushed off the couch and approached her. Theo didn't move when I raised my hands to cup her small tits in my palms. Or when I ran my thumbs across her hardened nipples.

"I like the idea of being your private dancer."

She reached around to grab my ass, squeezing my plump flesh, and licked her lips. "Oh, word? How much?"

I slid my hand down until I reached between her legs. "How much what?" I stroked her, putting pressure on with my palm, moving in small circles.

Theo widened her legs. "How much do you like being my private dancer?" she groaned.

I unzipped her pants, and managed to slip my entire hand in. Making contact with her damp panties brought a smile to my face. Leaning forward, I kissed her neck, moving up to her chin, the scent of me evident when I inhaled deeply. "Why? You trying to come back to VIP?"

Theo dug her fingers into my ass as I palmed her pussy, and rubbed up and down with the heel of my hand. I worked faster and really wished she was naked. But there was only so much that could be done in the confines of the club.

"You really don't have to . . ."

"It's not a matter of what I have to do, it's what I want. And right now I want you to come all over my hand."

She gripped me close and rested her head on my shoulder as shudders overtook her body and a stream of "fucks," "shits," and "damns," poured from her lips. I slowed down my actions, but kept stroking her, feeling the dampness of her panties grow. Once her breathing slowed, I reluctantly withdrew my hand and we stumbled back to the sofa.

Theo rested her head on the back of the leather furniture and turned to face me. "I want to hire you, for a private event outside the club. If you're game, that is."

"What we talking?" The sex high was fading. Being in the club offered a level of safety. I'd already been skeptical on doing the VIP solo, but to go outside these walls, especially if it was a party of some sort . . .

Theo sat up and wiped her hands down her thighs, keeping her gaze on her motions instead of me. The hint of her earlier uncertainty seemed to creep back into her demeanor. "Nothing crazy. Just . . . my birthday is next week, and I don't usually do anything, but I'm turning thirty and wanna treat myself so . . . if we can work something out."

My flight instinct to call this a one and done dissipated. I eased back onto her lap, rested my hands on her shoulders, and started moving my hips to the music. "Just for you, yeah, I can make that happen."

She stretched her long arms along the back of the sofa. "For real?"

I picked up the tempo, gyrating to the fast beat. I had no idea what the going rate was for a private event, but with her being my best tipper, I had no doubt I'd be paid well for my services. "Hell yeah. I'm into you, so I'm not about to pass up a chance for some alone time." I stopped moving and held my hand out toward her. "By the way, my name is Jada."

Theo's smile lit up her entire face as she wrapped her warm fingers around mine. She brought them to her lips and placed a small kiss to my palm. "I'm very pleased to meet you, Jada. And look forward to getting to know you better."

"Likewise, Theo." I let my gaze roam up and down her fully clothed form. "So, so much better."

OPERATION O

Therin Salem

Christy loved surprises. She loved it when Leila brought home flowers for no other reason than "just because." She was just as fine with being told to "Get in the car. We're going for a drive," without knowing where they were going, only to find out that Leila was taking her indoor skydiving.

Christy loved these surprises, but unfortunately that meant that she imposed them on Leila, who didn't share her enthusiasm for being on the receiving end of such things. If Christy jumped out from behind the living room couch and shouted, Leila's response was not laughter, but an earful about how Christy was going to send her to an early grave for scaring her.

"You should expect it by now," Christy would tease before apologizing. Leila was not a fan of surprises, but she had no hard feelings. Even if it wasn't her idea of fun to have no perception of what was coming next—something she credited to her precarious living situation as a child—she knew that Christy's surprises came from a love of life and her partner. It was Christy's zest that had drawn Leila to her, and despite their differences, she couldn't imagine living without her.

Leila hoped Christy's love of surprises would soften the blow when she had to put forward her proposition. She had put it off for weeks, but the more she lay in bed awake thinking about it, the more inevitable it seemed.

They had met at the closing night of the local lesbian bar before the owners' retirement—two old dykes who'd started the business in the 1980s and hadn't found anyone to buy the space from them. Amidst the live music and the throng of dancing women, Christy had spotted Leila sitting by the bar. Leila herself had only been there a few times, but when faced with the news of the bar's closure, she couldn't pass up one last chance to go.

Christy had seen Leila's face around before—one of a few Arab women whom she'd seen at the bar—but had never spoken to her, even if Christy had found her strikingly beautiful. When she spotted Leila on her own, she decided to finally make a move and talk to her.

Leila was unsure at first, as she always was when talking to someone new, but the two of them were soon deep into discussion about their interests: artistic, culinary, and everything else. Christy drew Leila out to the dance floor, her energy winning Leila over as they whirled around and around. But the conversation was just as exciting as Christy's wild moves. They kept talking long after they could no longer dance, staying until the bar closed for the night. While Christy usually felt she had to be suave, this time she didn't try to hide the fact that she was exhausted from staying up late. They exchanged numbers and agreed to go out again.

Leila had prepared for that first date with a mix of excitement and trepidation. She had told Christy with ease so many things about herself during that night at the bar and their subsequent texts—she'd never told anyone about how, over the course of three weeks during her undergrad, she had stolen over one hundred dollars' worth of snacks from the campus bookstore when she was between jobs—and yet there was one thing that she hadn't disclosed. She knew she would have to during this date, but also knew that it had the potential to end everything. She didn't want it to, but knew it was a real possibility.

They met at Leila's favorite Lebanese restaurant, where she ordered the best dishes for them to share.

"Oh, my god!" Christy had exclaimed with her mouth full. "This kafta is *amazing!* And the grape leaves, too!"

"Just wait until we get to dessert," Leila said. "These guys make the best nammoura in town."

"You mean this *isn't* dessert?"

"You won't want any more sweets for a week, but you'll love it."

Christy was doubtful about this, but when the nammoura came to the table and she tasted it, Leila was proven right.

"Wow," Christy gasped as she clutched her stomach. "That was very sweet. But amazing. This stuff was so good, I think it might be better than sex!"

Christy grinned mischievously, but the comment broke Leila from the pleasantness of the evening.

"I guess I'll find out later," Christy added, whispering into Leila's ear.

Petrified and unable to speak, Leila lowered her eyes.

"Aw, so bashful!" Christy said. "It's okay. We don't have to do anything you don't want to." This gave Leila some relief, but still she was unsure about how long things could last. Perhaps this whole evening, though fun, was a mistake.

When the bill was settled, they walked through the neon-lit streets until they got to Christy's apartment. Once inside, they curled up on the couch to watch an old movie. Leila's hand wandered down until her fingers laced with Christy's. She slowly shifted herself until she was resting her head on Christy's shoulder. Christy's head bent down and their lips touched, still tasting of nammoura. Leila clutched Christy's hand tighter, while her other hand cupped Christy's cheek with the ease of an old lover.

This bliss abruptly ended when she felt Christy's fingers de-lace from hers and creep between her thighs.

Leila jumped up from the couch before she realized what she was doing. Christy looked shocked, then hurt. Leila looked away.

"I'm sorry," she said. "I should have told you sooner. I'm . . . asexual."

"Oh," Christy said. Leila waited for her to get up and show her the door, as her previous girlfriend had done. But she didn't move. "You still like me, though, right?"

Leila looked up. Christy's eyes were curious, but no longer pained.

"Yeah," Leila replied. "A lot."

"Well, if that's all . . ." Christy said, her voice trailing off as she leaned in for another kiss. Leila wrapped her arms around Christy before tangling one hand in Christy's soft, short blonde hair.

When she pulled back for air, Leila said, "I love the way you kiss me."

Christy pulled her tighter. "Me, too."

They scarcely went long without speaking after that. The months passed. Christy's apartment became Christy *and* Leila's apartment, Christy's bed turned into Christy *and* Leila's bed.

They developed a system for what would occur in that bed. When they were holding each other and Christy got turned on, she would roll over and masturbate. While Leila had no interest in sexual contact, she didn't mind Christy doing this next to her. Eventually, Leila didn't even make her roll over, instead continuing to hold Christy in her arms, whispering things in her ear—sometimes in English, sometimes in French or Arabic—and caressing her partner's hair or back in rhythm with the pulsations of Christy's hand between her legs.

But while there was undisputed intimacy to this that Leila liked, she knew that Christy could only go on so long like that. Christy could only do so well with regularity. She had often moaned and reached climax when they first started doing this together, but one day she no longer did. And even if that climax was not the only pleasure to be had, Leila was sure that Christy was becoming bored and dissatisfied, even as Christy insisted that she wasn't.

And this was when Leila thought things had reached their logical conclusion.

"Do you want to break up with me?" Leila asked one evening over supper.

Christy looked up in shock from her spaghetti.

"Why would I want to do that?" she asked, concern in her eyes. "Are you unhappy?"

"No." Leila looked down as she thought about how to say things. Even after the weeks of worrying, the words didn't come easily. "It's just . . . I know you aren't asexual like me, and I can tell you want more. And . . . I don't think I can give it to you." She looked back up. "I love you, but I know you need—"

"Honey, no!" Christy exclaimed. She shot up from her seat at the table and swept Leila into a hug. "You will always be enough. I *love* you. You don't need to be something you're not just for me, okay?"

"But I want you to be happy," Leila said.

"I *am* happy," Christy said.

"Yeah, but you could be happier, right?"

Christy paused before saying, "Everyone could be happier. That's life."

While Leila found some relief in this, she was also saddened by what Christy was saying.

"I don't want 'That's life' to be how you feel about our relationship. Maybe there's something I can do to make you happier.

I can tell from the way you sigh when you're in bed that you miss orgasm. You think I don't notice it, but I do."

"Well," Christy said. "I guess I would be lying if I said I didn't miss coming a *little* . . . "

And so it began: Operation O.

With Christy's help, Leila set to work looking for ways she could please her girlfriend without having to make any concessions to her own comfort—Christy was adamant about that just as much as Leila had been at the beginning of their relationship.

They began with a relic from one of Christy's past relationships that she found in her drawer—a rainbow-colored strap-on. Christy presented it to Leila one evening by dropping it ceremoniously—and loudly—onto the coffee table. Leila, startled, dropped the book she had been reading and clutched her chest.

"Don't scare me like that!" she scolded, which Christy seemed to enjoy a little too much.

"I've come up with something to try," Christy replied simply.

"That thing is hideous," Leila said as she looked at the dick lying on the table.

"It can feel good inside me, though," Christy said. "Want to give it a shot? This one doesn't vibrate or anything, so you won't feel much of anything."

Leila shook her head and laughed. "All right." Leila bookmarked her page and then the two of them headed to the bedroom.

"How the hell am I supposed to put on this thing?" Leila exclaimed as she tried to untangle and orient the harness.

"Here, I'll help you," Christy said, taking it from Leila's hands. She stared at the intertwined straps, and started pulling one to untangle it, but only created a knot. "Er . . ." After some more fiddling, she finally got it. "They had simpler ones at the sex shop where we got this, but I insisted on this one because of the colors. What a fool!"

"Yes, but you're my fool." Leila laughed as she stepped into the harness and adjusted it on her hips.

They headed over to the bed. Christy lay down on her back and Leila climbed in after her. Leila tentatively began to straddle Christy.

"Wait," Christy said, gently putting up one hand and then starting to masturbate. "I need to get wet first." She rolled over and reached into her bedside drawer and tossed Leila a little bottle of lube. "Put some of this on the dick while I get ready." Happy to have a task, Leila set to work getting the strap-on nice and slippery, though she was unsure what she was supposed to do with her hands once they, too, were covered in the stuff. She didn't think getting it in Christy's hair would be very nice.

"Okay, I'm ready," Christy let out in a heavy breath. Leila positioned herself over Christy, but lost her balance and fell onto her lover's chest.

"Sorry," she mumbled, feeling the lube rubbing off on the sheet as she braced her hands against the mattress to hoist herself back up.

"It's okay," Christy said as she helped Leila up. Once reset, Leila tried again. She hovered over Christy's vagina before slowly guiding the dildo into her.

"Am I hurting you?" Leila asked worriedly. "How do I know I won't go too far?"

"Just keep going, you're barely in me."

"Oh."

She thrust her pelvis a bit more, watched more of the dildo disappear inside her partner.

"It's too big!"

"No, it's okay, Leila."

Leila thrust in and out.

"Slow down a bit," Christy said.

"Sorry." She moved a bit slower, then accidentally inserted farther than she meant to. "Sorry!"

"You can go faster now," Christy said, her breathing getting a bit heavier with each thrust. Leila could see the beads of sweat forming on her lover's brow, watched Christy's eyes close and her mouth begin to open. They were getting somewhere, but Leila couldn't hold herself up anymore. Afraid of what would happen if she fell, she hastily pulled out the strap-on from Christy's vagina before landing on the bed next to Christy.

"Please don't ever make me do that again," Leila sighed, covering her face with her hands in embarrassment.

"You were doing fine," Christy said.

"I know I shouldn't have stopped, but I couldn't . . ."

"Honestly, if you can't enjoy it then I can't enjoy it," Christy said, cutting Leila off. "What we did just now felt pretty good, but I couldn't completely relax knowing you were stressed out."

"Sorry . . ."

"No!" Christy exclaimed, before softening her voice to sound less angry. "Really. You have nothing to be sorry about. Come here." Christy got up and motioned for Leila to join her so that she could help her take off the strap-on. "Honestly, you're right about this old thing. It's kind of ugly." Leila laughed.

Operation O: Failed.

The next idea they tried went even worse than the strap-on episode.

"I've got an idea," Leila said one night after dinner. "You go in the bedroom and I'll stay here and call your phone. And I'll say dirty stuff to you."

"You mean, like, phone sex?" Christy asked.

"Yeah, I guess."

Christy looked skeptical but picked up her cell phone before slowly creeping into the bedroom and closing the door. Leila sat in the living room and stared at the floor.

"I thought you were going to call!" Christy shouted from behind the door.

"I am," Leila said. "I wanted to surprise you with my timing. Get ready!"

She waited another minute, then dialed Christy's number.

"Hi," Christy said.

"Hi," Leila said, trying to lower her voice seductively like she'd heard people do on TV.

"What's up?" Christy asked.

"Seriously?" Leila asked, not expecting that. She changed her tone to something more serious and, she thought, more authoritative. "You're asking *me* what's up? I should be asking you that. But I don't have to. Because I know . . . you've been *bad!*"

Leila heard Christy cackle from behind the door and through the cell phone speaker.

"I'm a bad girl, huh?" Christy asked.

"Very bad," Leila said. She tried to sound intimidating, but the words came out more like she was someone whose bladder was about to burst while waiting in line for the bathroom.

Leila listened to the sound of shuffling, what she assumed was Christy masturbating in bed, but was caught off guard when the bedroom door opened.

"I can't do this," Christy laughed. "You're adorable, but I can tell your heart's not in it."

"Does one's heart need to be in sex? I thought that was more the crotch's domain?"

"Are you saying you actually enjoyed that?"

"Well . . ." Leila thought perhaps the idea of "enjoying" that Christy was getting at was a bit misplaced, but she couldn't lie. "No. I don't get dirty talk."

"It's settled, then," Christy said, walking over to the couch to sit next to Leila. "Besides, I wanted to watch that new documentary tonight. The one about the lesbian baseball players."

Leila perked up. She had wanted to watch it, too. "Yes!"

They cuddled on the couch until it was time for bed and Leila was quite content. But she didn't sleep until she had thought a bit more about what to try next. Operation O needed to find success somehow.

One evening, she decided to venture into the sex shop a few blocks down from where she worked. Even though she'd seen Christy's sex toys around the apartment before, she was intimidated to go in the store. She was worried they would know that she didn't have much of a clue. She took a deep breath before walking in.

She avoided eye contact with the other people in the store and brushed off anyone's offer of help. She didn't want to have to explain things. She walked around to browse all the different toys the store had: strap-ons, harnesses, swings, huge dildos that she thought had no business fitting inside anyone's body, and some things the use for which she couldn't ascertain and was not sure she wanted to know.

She was thinking this trip would prove futile and was prepared to leave when something caught her eye. She quickly read the box and knew immediately that this toy would be perfect. She rushed to the register before hurrying home. While she waited for Christy to arrive at the apartment, she ordered takeout from the Lebanese restaurant where they went on their first date. When she heard the apartment door opening, she leaped out from the kitchen.

"Surprise!" Leila exclaimed.

"Wow!" Christy said sarcastically. "My girlfriend is here at the apartment where we both live. I can't believe it!"

"Come to the kitchen!" Leila said. She watched excitedly as

Christy opened the packages of kafta, grape leaves, and nammoura. Leila thought she could see her girlfriend beginning to salivate.

"Oh, my god! You really saved us tonight. I didn't know what we were going to cook for dinner." She kissed Leila in thanks before digging into the feast.

When she finished her portion, Christy let out a hearty belch, which Leila found adorable. Christy dutifully waited for Leila to finish so they could eat dessert together, but Leila could see the anticipation in her eyes was almost unbearable. She hoped it would not be for the last time that night.

"I think I might be too stuffed for dessert . . ." Leila teased, pretending to start putting away the leftovers. Christy's mouth went agape. "Just kidding!"

They divided up the nammoura, with the bigger portion going to Christy, and chowed down. Leila watched intently as Christy made the same orgasmic noises as the last time she had eaten the sweet treat.

"Is it as good as the first time?" Leila asked, though she already was pretty sure she knew the answer.

"It's better!" Christy exclaimed without taking the time to swallow the mouthful of cake she was chewing. Leila started to laugh. When Christy realized the view that she must have given of the masticated food, she lifted her hand to her mouth. "Excuse me." The look on her face made Leila laugh more.

When they finished dessert, Leila began thinking about how they would move on to the next step. Luckily, Christy helped without realizing it.

"So, what do you have in mind next?" she asked, waggling her eyebrows.

"I'm glad you asked!" Leila said. "Come on."

Leila took Christy's hand and led her from the dinner table to the doorway of the bedroom. Once there, she stopped and planted a firm kiss on Christy's lips.

"Do you promise to be patient?" she asked.

"That depends," Christy said mischievously. Leila raised her eyebrows mock disappointedly. "Okay, I promise."

"Good," Leila said before leading Christy into the bedroom and onto the bed. She gestured for Christy to wait, then knelt to get her surprise from where she had placed it in the bedside table drawer before her girlfriend came home. She passed the sleek pink toy to Christy and hid the other piece in her hand so that Christy couldn't see it.

"Is this a gift?" Christy asked. "Are you going to watch me masturbate with it?"

"No," Leila said, careful to keep hiding what she held in her hand as she walked around to the other side of the bed. "Well, not exclusively. Go on, lie down."

"Okay . . ." Christy said, curious about what Leila had in store as they got comfortable on the bed. Christy pulled down her pants and put the toy in position. She looked for buttons on the side to turn it on, but she couldn't find any. This was the moment Leila chose to begin. She pressed the button on the remote control and the toy began gently vibrating.

"Oh!" Christy exclaimed. "I see how it is!" She moved the vibrator back and forth along herself. She started to get aroused. "Mm . . . more!"

Leila waited, enjoying her control over Christy and her ability to surprise her, then jacked up the vibration another notch.

"Yes!" Christy moaned. Leila watched as Christy got wetter, excited that she could make this happen for her partner and that it was working. She jacked up the vibration another notch. Christy spasmed, Leila smiled.

"You still like surprises now?" Leila teased.

"Yes!" Christy yelped. "More!"

"More?" Leila asked. "More, you say?" She watched as Christy's eyes closed and her mouth began to hang open wider.

Leila turned the vibrator off.

"What?" Christy exclaimed, making Leila laugh almost maniacally. Christy, surprised by this side of Leila, joined her in laughter.

"Surprise!" Leila managed to say, clutching her side. When she was able to breathe more easily, but Christy still hadn't completely calmed down, she finally turned the vibrator on again, slowly working Christy back up to faster and faster vibrations. "I told you to be patient."

"Oh . . . yes! *More*, Leila!" At this request, Leila turned down the vibrator one notch.

"You're enjoying this, aren't you?" Christy teased. "Making me wait."

"Of course," Leila said. "I like to be in control. And I know you love it." She cranked up the vibrator to full speed.

Christy's head leaned back, sinking into her pillow as she let out a loud moan of pleasure. Leila could smell the sweetness of nammoura on her breath. Christy's toes curled, gripping the sheets tightly while her hands rhythmically rubbed the vibrator, now glistening, between her legs.

"Ohh! *YES!*" Leila was startled for a moment, never having heard Christy make such a loud noise. But then she knew that they'd done it. Christy had come. Leila slowly powered down the vibrator. She listened as Christy caught her breath, now the only sound in the room. Leila watched, strangely fascinated by the state Christy was in. She knew she would never experience what Christy was going through, but all the same Leila was pleased that she could finally give Christy what she craved.

Operation O: Success.

She thought they would just keep lying there until Christy's breathing got back to normal, but then Christy rolled over and pulled Leila close. She pressed sweet kisses on Leila's neck, chin, and nose, while rubbing her hands back and forth on Leila's back.

Warm in Christy's arms, Leila felt like she was melting. Each stroke of her girlfriend's hands released tension from her shoulders and back—tension she hadn't realized she'd even had. Suddenly things felt easy in a way they hadn't in a long time. Calmer.

"I thought you could use some loving, too," Christy whispered. "I really liked playing like we just did, but what we do in bed doesn't have to be all about me. We can take breaks. We can focus on you. You don't need to be responsible for everything all the time. I know you like it when we just cuddle."

Leila nestled her head in the crook of Christy's shoulder. Christy was right—this was her favorite thing. She didn't want to move from this position. Despite everything, she had underestimated Christy. Everything Christy had said was true from the beginning, yet Leila was still surprised by Christy saying it now. She knew that she would never underestimate Christy again.

It was nice not having to be in control of everything. A pleasant surprise.

BEING PRESENT

Tobi Hill-Meyer

I finish the knots on her wrists and pull upward so that her whole body is taut and she is forced to stand on her tip toes. With her body stretched out, she takes a sharp intake of breath. I run my other hand down her side and she shivers. My hand hovers over her naked pussy and I put my mouth next to her ear and say, "I want you to beg for it."

She pauses and doesn't say anything immediately. A flash of worry creeps into my mind. I'm trying to use this as a check-in, the last thing I want is for her to feel an obligation to beg for something she doesn't want. The breathing and shiver could be a sign of desire or a sign of panic. When she doesn't answer for a few more seconds, I decide to make it explicit. "If this is what you want," I add. "We could always do something else, or take a break."

"No . . ." As she says it, my worry spikes, but then she continues, "Keep going. I want . . . please . . ." She is talking very slowly and with great effort. Her body had been writhing, but she stops to try and gather her words. "I want you to . . . please touch . . . touch my cunt."

Suddenly I'm remembering a time years ago when I first hooked up with this guy I dated for six months. I thought he was so cool because his last girlfriend was trans and he had helped her through her transition. He knew all about hormones and could even give me advice on things now and then, like what doctor to go to. I looked up to him. His name was Dave.

Dave and I had been making out and he was groping me over my clothes. I reached over and ran my hand up his leg, then stopped. "Can I touch you?"

He gave me an odd look like I said something wrong and then laughed. "Uh, okay. Yeah."

The memories blur together between a handful of times we fucked. I always was very explicit about consent, but he thought I was being silly.

"You know, you don't have to check in all the time," he said. "It kinda ruins the moment. It's okay to just do something. You can trust me that if I don't like it, I'll let you know, and it won't be a big deal."

I had grown up with a lot of messages about consent. It was hard for me to do anything without explicitly knowing it was wanted. But he didn't want to do things that way. He was never upset or mad, but treated it like I was naive, still learning, and too anxious about getting things wrong to just let them go right. At the time, I trusted him more than I trusted my own instincts. I took his advice to heart, but it was still very hard for me to do.

"Please touch me more. I want to feel your hand on my clit."

I hadn't intended to hold out on her so long. The first couple of please's would have been fine, but I got caught up in my head. I've been doing that kind of thing as long as I can remember, but just in the past few years, I've finally realized it's a kind of dissociation. I pull myself back into the present and pull her to me.

I kiss the back of her neck at the same time I press the flat of my palm into her.

She lets out a gasp of pleasure, then sighs. "Sorry, sometimes when I get really into things I go a bit nonverbal, and it takes me a minute to pull myself out."

I start moving my hand slowly, warming her up. "Does that pull you out of the moment, too?"

"Well, it's almost like a trance. Like I'm deep in the sensations of my body. Refocusing my brain on language means less focus on those sensations, but it's necessary if I need to communicate." She looks me in the eye and smiles. And the relaxed pleasure in her eyes melts away my tension. That smile and the way she expresses pure joy is a big part of why I fell for her. I find myself hypnotized in her pleasure. I just want to give her more of it.

"I want you on hands and knees," I say as I shove her forward onto the bed. With her wrists bound, she catches herself with her elbows. Almost instantly her heavy breathing returns as she scrambles up into position. I'm leaning over her with my hand still reaching around to her front. I press my hips into her and growl into her ear as my fingers find and stroke her clit.

"You're so wet for me, aren't you?"

She nods her head up and down.

I'm starting to get hard, and I remember an earlier time when she said one of her favorite positions is getting fucked from behind. I savor the possibility. Maybe we can work our way toward that. I let go of her and sit back behind her. I press her knees apart, and as they spread, her labia opens up. My hand returns to her cunt, reaching through between her legs this time. My other hand strokes the back of her thigh, lingering on the crease just underneath her ass.

"Can you nod for me when you're nonverbal?"

She nods and moans out, "Mm-hmm."

"Nod for me if you'd like me to spank you."

She nods vigorously.

I can't believe I'm still thinking about Dave after all these years. He was so wrong, checking in can be really hot. You just need to be able to frame it as an expression of desire rather than an expression of anxiety. That's what I was trying to do when I asked her to beg me for it. I was giving her a chance to tell me how much she wanted it, what it was she wanted, how much she needed to be fucked. That kind of thing can be like rocket fuel for a scene. That's what is happening now as I watch her enthusiastically nod and press her ass back into my hand. She's begging me for it. Just like I asked her to.

I gave her a few light smacks, my left hand still wrapped around her clit. She gasps lightly at each impact. I pause a moment to stroke her tender skin, already starting to redden slightly.

Even when Dave had been telling me not to check in so much, ultimately the lesson he taught me was how important checking in can be. Toward the end of our relationship, he confided in me a secret desire he said he never told anyone else about before. He liked the idea of being a sissy. He even showed me some of the porn images and captions he got off to. They were all about being a come-hungry slut, just an open mouth and open ass for other people's pleasure. "I know it's not framed in trans positive terms," he warned me as I perused futa and trap hentai, "but it gets me really really hot."

"Do you think you might be a girl or something?"

"No, I'm definitely a guy. I just like the idea of being a sissy faggot hole to be used by whoever—men, women with strap-ons, trans women."

A week later, while we were driving around town, he told me he'd been playing with his ass when he masturbates. "Is that something you'd like to try together?"

He sheepishly said, "Maybe . . ." then looked away. A moment later he changed the subject.

We agreed to explore the sissy thing on our next date. He wore panties as we went out to dinner. At one point I called him a good boy and he flushed. I wanted so badly to give him this fantasy. When we got back to his place, there was a moment when I wanted to check in with him. In hindsight I wish I had. But I was trying to give him what he wanted. He had been hinting all week. This was what he told me he wanted. So I didn't "take him out of the moment." I grabbed his waist and I tried to growl it but it came out more like a whisper. "I'm gonna take your ass now."

He said okay and moved into position. I believed him. I often wonder if his answer would have been different if I asked a direct question. If he would have been upset with me. Or if he would have said the exact same thing. But the next day he told me things hadn't been okay. He froze up. He endured it because he thought he was supposed to. It wasn't good. And then . . . Then he dumped me.

Secret fantasies are like a spark of fire. Uncover them and give them enough fuel, and the heat can create mind-blowing sex. Expose them to the wrong element, though, and you're going to get burned.

Her ass is pink and I can feel her shiver when I let my fingers graze over her skin. I fall into a rhythm with several lighter impacts punctuated by a more significant one. Strong enough that she jumps forward slightly, causing her to rub herself up against my other hand. I'm trying to keep two parts pleasure for each part pain, and it helps that at this point she should be riding the endorphins well enough that this won't be nearly as intense.

I pause from the spanking to give her a break, and use the opportunity to place a finger over her opening. It lingers there for a while, just giving her time to think of the possibility. She starts nodding before I even ask her anything.

"Somebody is hungry for more." I press into her and give her a moment to adjust before resuming the spanking. I'm going lighter now, but still enough to cause her to jump forward, only this time there is no break in between. I increase my tempo and now she's fucking herself on my hand. She's moaning and yelling like some kind of wild creature, delight in her animal senses.

"Do you want me to fuck you?"

She nods.

I reach over for a condom and slide it on. "Show me," I say. "Show me how much you want it."

She reaches a hand back to grab my thigh, and pulls me closer. She presses herself into me and rolls her hips back so her cunt rubs against me. I can feel her heat and wetness through the condom. She turns her head back to make eye contact with me. "I want you to take me. You can use my ass if you want."

She puts her head down and raises her hips to me. A moment goes by. When I don't respond and don't start doing anything, she turns around again. I don't know what expression is on my face, but she notices something is wrong. I have to say something.

"But, uh, it's your body, what do you want me to do?"

"I want to be used by you. Fuck me however you want."

I sit back down. Now it is my turn to have difficulty with words. Is this her telling me that she wants anal? If I choose something else, will I be disappointing her? But we haven't done anal before. I don't know if I can do that without more negotiation, or at least more explicit desire coming from her.

I keep thinking of Dave and it takes all that I have not to shut down. I know he was the one who was hurt, but I was devastated to have hurt him. I'm pretty sensitive to the possibility of hurting someone or violating their consent. It's why I was checking in so much to begin with. But even beyond that, there is the stereotype of queer and trans people as predators. Transwomen in particular are constantly being accused of tricking straight men and lesbians into sex, and behavior that could potentially be called "male agression" calls into question your whole womanhood.

This stuff is still pretty fresh, too. It was just last week when we went to lesbian night at the gay bar and some TERF saw us together and pulled her aside to warn her that I'm trans. Even if I'm ninety-nine percent sure she wants this, my brain gets stuck on the one percent chance she doesn't. What if I do something that justifies that kind of a warning? What if she tells everyone I tied her up and fucked her ass when she didn't want to? Transwomen don't get excuses or second chances when something like that happens. It's as if it justifies all the bigotry slung my direction over the years, and proves right all the bigots who've said I'm not really a woman.

She's hugging me. Somehow she got out of the ropes. I don't think I undid them, but they were loose enough she could have gotten herself out. She's sitting next to me and wiping away the tears I didn't realize I had. She gingerly kisses my upper cheek. "Take your time," she says, "you can tell me when you're ready— or not if you'd prefer."

"Thanks. I got caught up in some bad thoughts." I reach for her hand and place it on my chest. "But your touch is helping me feel grounded."

She presses into my chest and moves me into a position lying back with my head in her lap. The weight of her hand is comforting. Her other hand is stroking my hair. I feel warm. Safe.

I've been doing activism in the community for well over a decade now. I've had my share of run-ins with TERFs and online trolls. I've protested. I've debated. I can hold my own. But still, running into one of them in person, at a place I went to so we could relax and have fun, I froze.

That bigot intentionally gave that "warning" in my earshot.

The goal was to antagonize and get a rise out of me. It's a standard tactic they have to antagonize, belittle, yell, and push all the dysphoria and trauma buttons they know transwomen tend to have. If they can get me to raise my voice or yell back, then they could say how all transwomen are aggressive and violent and claim to be the victim of my harassment. Maybe even appeal to the bouncer to have me kicked out. I didn't want to just sit there and take the verbal abuse, but I didn't have a good option. So I froze.

"It's a little stressful, sometimes," I say, "being in charge. Being responsible for things." She nods, listening intently and encouraging me to go on. "I know you were just saying you were up for anal, but was that your preference? Is that the main thing you wanted at that moment? Is that what you want right now?"

"I was—I am open to either option. I do really like anal. One of my favorite things is to have something in my ass and a vibe on my clit." She strokes my chin and pulls my eyes up to meet hers. "I guess I didn't ask how you felt about it. I mean, if it's bringing up issues for you, we don't have to do it."

"No, that's not it." I feel kinda bad. Things were going so well and were so hot and now I'm crying in her arms. This is not how I pictured our evening. "Sorry I'm not exactly dominant right now. I guess I just started worrying about doing something you didn't want. I knew you probably wanted it, but the consequences can be so high for doing something wrong. Sometimes I freeze up."

She smiles down at me and takes my hands. "I think I have an idea that might solve that." Then I feel the rope sliding around my wrists.

She's pretty incredible. I wish I didn't have to break down. I wish there weren't TERFs in our community, or that I could handle them myself. I wish she didn't have to come and save me again and again, but I'm grateful that she does.

As a cis woman in this lesbian bar, she would never be

accused of being a man for yelling, so she yelled on my behalf when I couldn't. She proclaimed that there's no room for transphobia there. I especially liked the moment when she said, "I'd only ever feel deceived into sex if it was with someone like you who hid how bigoted they were."

That's when that bigot accused her of not being a real lesbian if she was willing to date someone like me, and she responded, "Well fuck you, I'm not a lesbian, I'm pansexual."

I couldn't help but cringe. I know she's not a lesbian. I know that kind of erasure can suck. But I don't like the suggestion that someone would have to be pansexual to date someone like me. The truth is, I don't know many people our generation who call themselves lesbians. So many people who might otherwise have had non-binary partners, or are non-binary, or are fine acknowledging that rare guy they are kinda into, or maybe they are scared off of using that word because of all the people like this TERF who insist it's an inherently transphobic identity.

I'm not sure anyone I've ever dated or hooked up with has identified as a lesbian. At my most vulnerable, I sometimes worry there's an element of truth in what that woman was saying. Does someone have to be open to more than just women to be open to me? And what's that say about how they see me?

I'm lying on my back and my hands are bound tight to the bed's legs behind me. She actually seems more experienced at that than me. I'm not sure I could get out if I wanted to.

"Remember you can safeword anytime you need to stop or pause." I nod. "Where are you now? Red, yellow, or green?"

"Green."

"That's my good girl."

"And just to be clear, you're open to fucking my ass?"

"Oh yeah, if I know that's the thing you want, that sounds really hot to me."

"What about me playing with yours?"

I stop and think for a moment, doing a quick check in with my body. "That would be fun, especially with me all tied up like this."

She gets up from me for just a moment, rummaging through her purse. She comes back with a bottle of lube and a butt plug.

She warms the lube in her hands and then runs a slick finger around my asshole. The soft touch relaxing my muscles and giving me a chance to open up. Her mouth moves to my junk. I'm soft now, and she gently takes me into her mouth, running her tongue over the head. Everything is super sensitive and when she uses her hand to pull back my foreskin, it's almost overwhelming. She keeps a nice and slow pace until I start to get hard again, then begins to speed up.

I feel the firm pressure of the plug pushing up against me. I gasp as it goes inside.

"That's right, your ass is mine now."

It settles into a stable position. Pointing it upward, she presses on the base of the plug, working it to slightly rub back and forth over my prostate. Then her hips take over, thrusting into the plug in my ass and getting the same effect.

"Fuck, I love how you whimper so deliciously," she growls, and with each thrust I feel her getting deeper and deeper. I just want to surrender to her desires. Let her do whatever she wants with me because everything she's wanting is doing amazing things for me.

The first time I saw her, she was speaking at dyke march. There's always eight to ten speakers at the rally before the march itself. She was the one speaking right before me. She told a captivating personal story about her experience as an immigrant. Without familial support and not having access to legal work, she found opportunity in the underground economies of sex work, eventually being hired by a sex worker advocacy organization when legal work became an option.

She seamlessly weaved her personal experience in with calls for solidarity, with the need for policy change, and the need for community action. By the time she was reaching the end of her speech, each sentence she spoke ended with a strong punch that led the crowd into a cheer. She called out the tendency for people to help others only when it was more comfortable and implored everyone to take more risks when it means sparing others from risks they don't have a choice about. It hit home. Some people cheered louder, others were quieter. I began thinking about what I needed to be doing differently in my own work and I'm sure others were contemplating the same thing.

I usually spend the last five minutes before I speak meticulously going over my things and mumbling my speech over and over. This time, however, I was so engrossed in what she was saying, that never happened. Suddenly, the emcee was calling me to the stage, and I couldn't remember how I planned to start things.

I told the crowd to give her another round of applause and used the time to glance at my notes. Still, I kept having moments where I stumbled, had large gaps of silence, and I straight up read from my paper for the last several paragraphs. I thought I totally flubbed it, but when I came down from the stage she approached me and said that she really appreciated what I had to say.

I enthusiastically told her everything I appreciated about what she said. We marched together, holding hands for much of the way. Halfway through, she took off her top, then I did too. By the end, we were making out on the street.

It's hard to believe, sometimes, that things are going so well. It's like she's reaching into my brain, going right past all my hangups, and releasing pure and uncomplicated pleasure and lust. I am so ready for her when she straddles me.

"I can't wait any longer," she growls, "I want to feel you in me."

As she lowers herself onto me, she spreads her butt cheeks. I can feel her ass gripping me tightly. On most days, it might be difficult to get hard enough for penetration, especially for anal, but that is not a problem tonight. She's holding her breath until I'm all the way in, and then lets out a deep sigh.

"I want you to know, I'm glad you shared what was going on." She starts pulling back up slowly, then lowers herself again. "Because I really, really wanted this, and I'm glad we found a way to make it happen."

I've been holding back so I could let her set the pace and take things slow. But everything is so intense I can't hold back anymore. Instinctively I try to reach up and hold her but my arms are still tied. As I crash back into the bed I thrust up into her.

"Yes, that's right," she says, "keep fucking me like that. I want to feel how much you want this."

Each time I thrust upward I feel the plug inside me shift in a very delightful way. Almost as if she's fucking me right back. "Yes!" I moan out loudly. Then again quieter. Then again, until I'm keeping up a low mantra repeating the word.

She picks up a small vibrator she had on the bed next to her, and puts it on her clit. I can feel her clenching and spasming. It's getting me closer to coming. I want to be here for her as long as she needs me, but I don't know if I'm going to be able to hold off. Luckily, I can tell from her own pleasurable sounds that she's getting close too.

She starts to tense up and holds her breath as she reaches behind her and pushes a button on the bottom of the butt plug. Suddenly it's vibrating right into my prostate. I'm involuntarily moving now, faster, and she instantly starts screaming and coming.

I keep going at full speed. Desperate to come with her. It's not hard to. As my body tenses, the plug goes flying out of me. We fuck for a couple dozen more thrusts until we both collapse into a writhing, quivering, mess.

"Thanks so much for being so open with me tonight. A lot of people wouldn't have the self-awareness to be able to name it, and it means a lot to me that you trust me to share that." She snuggles up to my arm. "Sometimes I wonder what I did to have someone as wonderful as you in my life."

Tears well up in my eyes. It doesn't make sense. She is the one who is so incredible on every level. How can she think that of me? "But I'm such a mess!" I exclaim. "I don't even know if I deserve you."

She rolls on top of me and kisses me deeply. "You're a beautiful mess," she says, "and you know yourself well enough to pick up all the pieces. You're one of the most kind and caring people I know. Don't you ever forget how wonderful you are."

She unties my arms and pulls me into a spooning position. The cleanup can wait until the morning. For the first time in a long time, I don't have the slightest bit of anxiety that anything is going to fall apart as I drift off to sleep content, full of pleasure, and feeling loved.

NEW NORMAL

Sonni de Soto

With one hand on your toy bag and the other on Reena's back, you lead your partner into the room. Try not to scowl. This is supposed to be a fun night. Don't spoil this.

You should be happy. This is the first play event you've been able to attend in a long time. Even before quarantine, life had been too stressful, too emotionally charged, to play, much less play while surrounded by an entire party of people. It'd been so hard to get into the right headspace. Then quarantine happened and the world outside your apartment became too much of a risk. You've only started seeing Reena again in the weeks since the lockdown lifted.

Since the proven success of the vaccine, the world has begun to slowly creep back to normal. Or as normal as it can get. You're pretty sure that none of us will ever see *normal* again.

You look around the room. Yeah, *this* is not normal. Even though this is your community's first party since the lockdown lifted, there are so few people around. You know there was a limit placed on guests; first come, first served, to keep the party small.

Social distancing isn't being required anymore, but it's still recommended.

You look around the room and recognize some people, here and there. But it's not easy. Not with the night's dress code.

You had reservations when Reena told you the play party's theme. Mandatory masks.

Why would anyone choose *that* as the theme for a party? After having to wear masks everywhere you went for so long, you'd be happy to never see one ever again. Yet here you are, surrounded by people wearing little else. You adjust your own mask, just a plain cloth one left over from quarantine. Other people are wearing lace and leather parodies covered in straps and studs. Other people are wearing old-fashioned plague masks or new-fangled gas masks.

Don't think about it too much. Or celebrating—much less eroticizing—such an awful period will seem . . . distasteful. Disrespectful. People died from the virus. People were horrifically damaged by it. Our world was irreparably altered by all this. And seeing people—your people—playing pretend with it feels wrong.

Instead, stop and watch a couple on a nearby mat play. They're dressed up in cheap Halloween versions of a sexy nurse and doctor. You're slightly amused that the man is wearing the skimpy nurse skirt, hat, and mask, while the woman is wearing a loose pair of scrub pants, a surgical cap, a mask, and a stethoscope slung around her neck, brushing the tops of her bared breasts. She has him bent over a table, making him cough dramatically with each smack of her cane against his ass.

And, sure, it's a little funny and more than a little hot. Even the nearly naked couple is giggling through the whole scene, not to mention the other observers in the room. Conflicting feelings churn within you as you watch. You try hard to separate reality and play in your mind, but it's so hard.

Focus on the ferocious grace of the woman's body as she stalks around her partner. She's so much smaller than he is, but the way her muscles move and flex with each fluid step makes her powerful. She taps her cane against her palm, making him and the crowd flinch in anticipation with each thwack. Watch his naked body stiffen, his muscles tensing as he tries hard not to track her movements. His grip on the padded table is crushing, his knuckles white as they cling and dig into the cushion. Harsh red lines, left by the cane's stinging care, streak across his pale, cream-colored flesh, looking hot to the touch.

You stare into his wide, blue eyes, so filled with heat and awareness. You know that look. The overwhelming mix of emotions. The way you can both dread the next strike and long for it at the same time. And you know what it's like to inspire that feeling, to stir it in a partner's gaze. To make it flow through their veins. From either side of the scene, it's intoxicating.

But you can't look into his eyes without seeing that damned mask. Without seeing that reminder of all that's happened.

Look away.

"Are you okay?" Reena leans in close to touch your shoulder.

Nod. Smile. Do anything to reassure her. Just don't shake your head. Even if you think it'll clear your mind, it won't. "I think I just need some space." Don't run. Don't push people out of your way. Stay calm. Breathe. Just sidestep the people around you and head to the hallway.

You shouldn't have come. Shaking your head, you set down your bag that feels too heavy at the moment. You thought coming here would make you feel more connected, after feeling so alone in lockdown for so long. But it's just too much, seeing your friends and play partners look like strangers with most of their faces covered. Their bodies and desires are, like always, displayed and celebrated here, but from behind their masks, everything still feels hidden. You feel separate from it all, sequestered.

"Are you sure you're okay?" Reena looks at you worriedly over her mask and all you want is to rip it off her face. You didn't lock yourself in your apartment, seeing the fewest people you could get away with, to then keep doing this once the crisis passed.

You want to feel connected again. You want to feel normal again.

Reena frowns. "We can go, if you want."

No. She's been waiting for this party for days now. For longer than that. She's been anxiously waiting for their first play party since lockdown was officially ended. Actually, like with the rest of us, she's been patiently longing for the opportunity to gather with friends and partners since quarantine was announced. You can't take this from her.

But just look around. You shake your head again. This place— this community—is supposed to be your sanctuary. Your escape from the rest of the world. Where the ugliness and horror of the real world gets set aside for the space of a scene. And instead it just feels like a contaminated reminder of it all.

You need to get a grip. Breathe.

Your kink is not my kink but your kink is okay. Repeat it in your head like a mantra.

But a part of you is terrified—is devastated and heartbroken— that this side of yourself, the part of you that you've loved for so long—kink, play, the sexual escape of exhibitionism, and the comforting kinship of community—is just another thing lost to lockdown.

"It just feels different now, doesn't it?"

You open your eyes at Reena's hushed voice. You nod. Yeah. "Everything feels different now." As an Asian woman, you'd spent so long feeling people stare at you with suspicion. Like, because of your race, you were automatically carrying the disease or, worse, were part of some plot to spread it. For so long, you'd heard people describe this disease, which plagued everyone, in the most racist terms, even from the highest offices. As a result of all that, you'd heard news stories and watched viral videos of Asian people being harassed, targeted, and attacked. The saddest, most shameful truth you hate to admit, even to yourself, is that you stayed locked away indoors not just from the virus, but because you feared falling victim to that more insidious social illness.

You remind yourself that the virus seems to be under control now. You can stop feeling so scared. So stop. Just stop.

You feel Reena grab your hand. You turn and see her nod as she stares out into the play space. "The world is different now. We—not just you and me, but all of us that went through this—are different now." She shakes her head. "How could we not be?"

She turns to look at you and she is so beautiful. Her deep, dark eyes stare up at you with a mix of worry and understanding that staggers you, reminding you of how much she loves you and how much she means to you.

"All through quarantine, I've felt so afraid. So powerless. Helpless." She frowns. "There's nothing like a lockdown to make you feel like you have no control over anything in your life."

You frown too. You hate the idea of her dealing with all that alone. Once it'd become clear that the virus wasn't going away for a long time, you'd discussed having her come live with you for the duration. But, since she'd still been working her retail job, and therefore had been at a higher risk of contracting the disease, she'd refused to put you at risk too.

You wish you'd insisted.

She sighs and looks back at the party. "And, even though lockdown has ended and everything seems back to normal again, I still feel afraid." Her brow furrows. "I don't want to but, after so long, I don't know how not to."

You feel something tense inside you loosen as your thoughts flow out of her mouth. Hold her hand tighter.

"I think that's why I needed to come tonight." She squeezes your hand back. "Because, when I'm with you, when we're here together, it's okay to feel out of control." She turns to look at you. "With you, I can take all that fear and frustration that's been building up inside me from the beginning of all this and I can just give it up." She brings your entwined hands up to her lips. "I want to give it to you. Because I know, in your hands, it's okay to feel all those things. In your hands, I can be helpless, I can be powerless, yet still feel safe."

Look at her, as you feel her soft lips on your knuckles, and feel grounded for the first time in a very long time. You'd forgotten this feeling. The surge of protective strength you feel around her.

She is so beautiful. Even with the lower half of her face covered, her beauty is undeniable. Her brown hair, bound up tight tonight, looks pretty and prim and makes you want to let it all down, let it all free, so you can run your fingers through it or fist it tight in your hands. And her body . . . . Every curve and smooth sweep of her makes you want to touch her, taste her, take her.

But more than that, she is sweet and soulful and vulnerable in a way that humbles and awes you. There is a breathtaking honesty in her voice and words and touch that reaches deep inside you and wraps around your heart. And, faced with all that, you feel a part of you that you feared you'd lost flicker back.

Grin and lean in close. Let the material of your mask and the heat of your breath tickle her ear as you whisper, "Want to find a space of our own?"

Excitement sizzles inside you when she turns that scorching gaze on you and nods. "Always."

Pick up your bag. Scan the room as anticipation rises inside you. Instead of seeing and analyzing the scenes around you, you just see taken space. There are fewer designated places to play tonight, with all the mats and furniture spaced out more than usual. But, even with limited attendance, there are always people clamoring to play. All you care about is finding a patch of mat where you can take Reena and do all the things you've been dreaming of for so long.

You spot it. Across the room. The padded table where the doctor and her nurse had been. Shoulder your bag, grab her hand, and hurry, before someone else takes it.

Once safely snagged, you purposefully push and poise Reena over the table, your fingers lingering over her skin. It's hot to the touch and you can almost feel her body tremble with pent-up promise.

Strip her. Peel each piece of clothing from her body to reveal her soft, sweet flesh. You smile as a blush sweeps across her skin. Before quarantine, she'd just begun to feel more confident about being naked in front of others. But, after so long being alone, that delicious discomfort seems to be rushing back.

As you pull her panties down her legs, you can feel heat wafting from her. Push her legs apart more and revel in the slight tremor of her legs as they spread for you. Yes. You remember this. This is what you've been longing for. This is what you've wanted—needed—for so long.

Her too. As you stroke her thighs, brushing a little higher with each slide of your hand against her sensitive flesh, you hear her breath catch. Muffled by that damned mask, but hot nonetheless.

You stand up straight and walk around her. Pacing the table, you let her feel your presence. You trail a finger up her spine, enjoying it as she squirms. Standing on the other side of the table, you bend over her so your pelvis presses her head into the pleather cushion. Her body tenses as you drag your nails up her back, leaving red trails swirling along the whole length.

But, again, with her cheek pressed into the padding, there's that mask again, continually taking you—just a bit, just for a moment—out of the scene.

Why does it bother you so much? It's just a mask. Just a bit of cloth held on by a few scraps of elastic. Why can't you just let it go?

You want to. So much.

God, she looks so helpless, almost gagged, making her every noise sound breathless and stifled. As you bend down to dig inside your toy bag, you can't help but think it makes her look weak.

You know that masks were—are—actually a sign of strength. Throughout quarantine, they protected those around you. As you pick out some of your favorite toys from your bag, you know that.

But the rhetoric around masks got into your head, no matter how hard you tried to block it out. In your head, masks remind you of sickness and disease. Of decay and of death. You can't erase all the images of frail, infirm people ravaged by a virus that seemed as if it would never go away. You've associated that bit of cloth with feeling—being—powerless.

Except you know she's not.

Look at Reena. Really look. Her lined back rises and falls in a steady, strong rhythm, waiting for you. Touch her. Her skin is silken heat beneath your fingers as she arches into your stroke. Hear her. "More, please."

She's here. With you. Alive and well. She, you, the whole world, has gone through this horrible event. But you got through. That mask, that little scrap of fabric, saved your lives. So, after so long, you could be together again. And, sure, it's not the same. It may never be the same again. But you're here. With her. Finally. Don't spoil it.

No, more than that.

Enjoy it.

With that thought firmly in your head, you stand straighter, clutching your favorite toy in your hand. Gripping the braided leather handle of the dragontail whip in one hand, you let the length of the tail slide through the other. Plant your feet behind her and stare at the canvas of her back. Like an archer, pull the tail back and take aim.

A jolt of sheer joy shoots through you as the whip's length snaps against her left shoulder with a loud crack. Reena gasps, her breath so obvious as her mask sucks in deep before puffing out. Strangely, you notice yours does too, involuntarily matching hers, as if your bodies—the excitement and the heat flowing through the both of you—are shared. Connected. "Like that?"

She nods. "Yes, ma'am."

Grin. "Do you want more?"

Her head bobs clumsily, needily. "Yes, please."

Heart racing, you strike her right shoulder, marveling at it all as if for the first time. Hungry for her every reaction, you hit her again and again, in different places and degrees. You love how she moans, her back arching, as the full length of the whip licks her back. The way her body twitches and her voice yips, when the whip's wicked tip snaps her side, makes you grin. The way her back reddens—in long red streaks and small, star-shaped welts— brings you a twisted peace as you read her resilience across her skin. It feels like a secret language between the two of you that should look like weakness but, to those who know, reveals the astounding depth of her strength.

Your mask feels hot and damp with your breath against your face. You can feel your every inhalation—deep and needy—and every exhalation—heavy and heady with want—in every brush of cloth against your lips. You never really thought about your own breathing before but, with your mask on, you are so aware of it now. It sounds heavy and loud, like the hungry huff of a hunter or the eager pant of a predator.

God, you need the taste of her.

Grip her shoulder and turn her onto her back. Grin when you see her wince as her raw back presses into the edge of the padded table. Her hot hiss shivers down your spine, flowing through you like an electric sizzle.

Lean in. Loom over her. You bite back a guttural growl as you move low to press your face against her belly. You know her scent. You know it's hot and heady, strong and so very satisfying. But the mask feels like a muzzle, trapping you with your own desire when all you want is hers.

It should anger you. Should feel like another loved thing lost. But it fuels you instead, heatedly feeds your longing, making you ache for more. And, instead of hating that you can't satiate that hunger, you let it simmer inside you, filling you like steam as it burns within you. Your mouth waters as you press your cloth-covered lips just above her mound, temptingly close to her wet heat. The memory of her taste teases you. Lord, you want to lick her, bite and devour her whole. But you can't. And that drives you wild.

But, more than that, you can see it rage within Reena. She writhes under your simplest touch. Each covered kiss teases—taunts—her, giving her so little when she craves everything.

Damn. You smile. Gently, so gingerly, trail your fingers along her thighs. Let your lips flutter cotton kisses along the soft flesh of her belly, over those pretty breasts, before letting the folds of your mask catch on and tease her nipples to tight, needy points. An almost mean laugh slips from your throat as her hips lift, silently begging to be stroked where she needs it most. Her muffled whimpers hit your ear. They mix with slight, stifled chuckles from the room, reminding you of the crowd around you, filling you with the harmonious sound.

This is what you needed. *This*—this moment, this feeling—is why you came tonight, despite all your reservations. After being so scared, so cautious and careful, for so long, you needed to remember how to be bold again. You need to feel in control.

You send a silent, slightly surprised thanks to whoever came up with tonight's theme. Whoever made you look straight into the face of your fear and take your power back. Whoever let you find pleasure again, after so much pain.

Seizing that feeling, you rise to grip the ties binding Reena's hair back and pull, reveling in the cascade of her tumbling strands while trailing a finger over the soft skin of her vulva. You lean in and breathe into her ear, smelling the sweet scent of her hair as you let the cloth of your mask tickle the sensitive curve of her ear. "Tell me what you want."

Reena gulps, her neck taut, letting you see the desperate slide of her throat. "You to touch me." Her body wriggles with need. "Please."

Your teeth clench in a ferociously pleased smirk. You dip between her wet folds and stroke her clit. She moans gratefully, her whole body bowing into that touch. Yes. Her hot sex presses against your hand as her arousal flows from her like molten honey, the feel of it familiar as you draw out her pleasure at your whim. You nuzzle her neck and know she's close. Against her exposed throat, you groan. You run your other hand through her silken hair, gently, reverently, only to then grip it in your fist so you can turn her face to yours. Staring into the building heat in her eyes, you feel yourself burn. "What else do you want?"

Her body strains. "To come."

That phrase, so small yet said with so much need, arouses you. Nudging a knee between her legs, you spread them further, making space for yourself as you press close. You can feel all of her naked body, flush up against all of yours.

Her hand dips between your bodies, climbing up your skirt

to push past your panties, and begins to stroke you. She lets out a pleased sigh when she finds your sex wet—drenched—too. She rubs at your clit, her fingers knowing exactly how to make you moan and press deeper into her. You can feel your own climax coming, but you hold off. It's too good, the pleasure of it flush up against her struggle to hold her release back too.

Masks be damned, you crush your lips over hers as you slip two fingers inside her scorching sex and stroke fast. Deep. Just how she likes. Even through the fabric, you can feel her soft mouth give to yours, opening on a deep moan. Her hips thrust against yours and her fingers race to meet your heated pace. Your tongues meet against masks, the press and slide almost what you know while still being completely new. The mix of your mouths, like a potent perfume, overwhelms your senses. Feeling the slick slide of both of you against your face, you groan into her mouth and let your own orgasm crash over you. "Come for me."

Her body tenses on a heaving gasp before you feel her let go and climax against you. Pleasure rushes through you both as you writhe against each other. The warm, wet feel of her release on your hand and her thighs is messy, but you don't want to move. Not yet.

As Reena's tense body begins to relax against you, you lay your forehead against her heaving chest, feeling her heart's pounding rhythm match your own. You should get up. Clean up each other and the space and move on. There are others waiting for their turn.

But, instead you hold her—hold this moment, this feeling— close as her chest rises and falls with deep, even breaths. Her arm slips out from between your bodies to wetly curl around you and squeeze. "I'm glad we came."

You nod and sigh deeply, feeling—for the first time in a long time—like you can breathe again. "Me too."

A GOOD DAY

Lianyu Tan

Jillian kills my character with a well-aimed burst of gunfire. As I'm waiting to respawn, her team claims victory, ending the match.

Damn it. I move my hands away from the keyboard and roll my shoulders, shaking the stiffness from my fingers. "Gotta go," I say into my headset.

"Bye, Feiyan," my teammates chorus. "We'll get them next time."

I take off my headset and set it down. We almost never have enough friends online at the same time to play on opposing factions, but when it happens Jillian always slaughters me—without mercy, notwithstanding who will be cooking her dinner that night. It ought to annoy me and it does, but I also find it so amazingly hot.

In the bedroom, Jillian is still on voice. "Thanks, Elena. I think that worked. Definitely try it again if you get the chance—"

As I walk in she looks up and grins, the high of winning easing the lines that pain has etched on her face. She's in pajamas even though it's late morning, her brownish-blonde hair tied in a loose braid. Pillows surround her on every side, lending enough support so that she can sit up without too much discomfort and game using the laptop in front of her. Her glasses reflect the blue and orange hue of the screen.

I slip into bed next to her and lean over the mound of pillows, resting my head on her shoulder as I glance at her player stats. "Are you getting that new skin?" I ask. "I thought it looked bizarre."

"It's a reverse mermaid, of course I'm getting it."

I watch as she applies the cosmetic upgrade to one of her video game characters, turning her from a normal fantasy-esque fighter girl to a creature with the head and torso of a fish, and the legs of a human. Her character gulps air, glassy eyes staring, gills pulsing, as she shifts her weight from side to side on her high-heel-clad feet.

"The next time we're on the same side, I don't know how I'm going to tell you from the enemy," I say, half-seriously.

She logs out and puts her laptop to sleep. "Don't be silly. I'll be the one not trying to kill you." She leans back against her pillows and checks her phone. I feel the siren song of mine tugging at me.

I watch Jillian instead. She messes with her phone for a few minutes before putting it down. "I'm feeling pretty good today," she says, looking at me.

"That's great." It is great. How many days this month? Not many.

"Yeah."

"So, you want to go out today?" I ask. Saturday. No work for me, at least none I can't squeeze in during the downtime. "Or the forecast seemed good. We could try a walk."

Jillian runs her fingertips through the ends of her braid, the same braid she'd slept in. "Maybe we could spend time together."

The smile freezes on my face. "Sure," I say, forcing my tone to remain light. "Some time after lunch?"

"Yeah. And then give me an hour for these to kick in," she says, as she pops two prescription pills in her mouth, following them with a glug of water.

"Sounds good."

The afternoon passes slowly, with the clock ticking down the minutes. We eat lunch in bed while watching some sort of cooking show on TV. The host's face seems too plastic, her forehead unmoving, her smile too white. A doll pretending to be a woman.

After lunch, I take the plates to the kitchen and wash up. My favorite knickers are in the laundry. Are stockings too much? I'm watching my gloved hands, sudsy and slick with detergent, when Jillian comes up behind me and grabs my ass.

"Oh!" I jump, half-turning. Water drips down my gloves and onto the tiles. "You said an hour."

Jillian reaches around me and turns off the tap. Her clothed breasts graze my arm. She's changed into a satin wrap, the neck open to reveal a lacy bra. "It was an estimate." She slaps my ass with the flat of her palm. "Go get dressed."

I shuck the gloves and head back into my study, closing the door behind me. I rifle through the drawers to put an outfit together. Yes to the stockings, after all: white and lace-topped. Pink and white bra and panties, a pink harness, and a ruffly dressing gown over the top. I take my shoulder-length black hair out of its ponytail, then think better of it and tie it back up. I hate it when hair gets in my face at inopportune moments.

Jillian is lounging in bed when I come back. She's shut the curtains against nosy neighbors, leaving the room illuminated by a string of party lights I'd draped across the wall one Christmas that we'd never taken down. She smirks at me. "Looking good."

"Thanks," I say, self-consciously aware of how the bra wires pinch at the side of my ribs. "What toys would you like today?"

She tells me, and I get them. I can't hold back a shiver as I pull out a crop, laying it alongside a pair of clitoral vibes and a set of steel handcuffs, polished to a mirror sheen.

"How about Chip?" she asks.

My pulse quickens. "Okay." I flip up the valance and pull out a box from under the bed. It's heavy, and its plastic wheels struggle on the carpet.

What's inside is silver and black, industrial. There are two metal legs, a black plastic body with motor and pistons, and a remote. I plug in its cable and then assemble the legs, attaching the motor. The whole thing is about a foot wide and two feet long, but it doesn't take long to set up.

At first glance, its purpose is not entirely clear until I attach the dildo. I turn the dial on the remote to low, and switch it on to test the connection. The motor slowly turns a wheel, thrusting the dildo forward. A fucking machine.

I turn it off and pick up the whole unit, placing it at the foot of the bed, out of the way for now. It rests there, gleaming and patient. Like an expensive coffee machine, built only for one thing.

"All done?" Jillian asks.

When I nod, she beckons. I move some of the pillows and cuddle up to her, resting my head on her shoulder.

"Have you been good today?" she asks. Her hand traces down my back, lingering.

I hesitate. "Maybe?"

"That means no."

I make some small noise of protest. She tuts, gestures. I take off my dressing gown, throwing it to the floor, and crawl over her lap.

I'm glad I kept the ponytail. It's easier to breathe without hair falling over my face. My head hangs off the side of the bed. "Am I crushing you?" I ask, leaning my weight on my forearms.

"I'm good." She grips my hips, easing me down until I'm draped over her, resting my weight against her thighs. Her hand traces down my spine and over my ass, drawing circles on my skin.

I wriggle to get comfortable. An O-ring on the harness digs into my stomach, but it's a pleasant kind of ache. Jillian picks up her phone and turns on music, something synthy and instrumental.

Her hand travels back up my spine, grips my hair by the base of the ponytail, pulling my head back. "What's our safeword?"

"Pegasus," I say, cringing a little inside. Not the sexiest, but she'd insisted, which makes it sexy in a roundabout way.

She releases me and my head drops back down. I'm shivering a little in the air-conditioning. It's a pleasant spring day, but Jillian overheats easily and so the room is always a little uncomfortable for me. My nipples stiffen against the inside of the bra, begging to be touched.

"Tell me how you've sinned," she says.

I should've prepared something, but as always, I'm caught off guard. "I forgot to pick up your parcel from the depot yesterday," I hazard, after a moment.

"Mm-hmm." A brief *whoosh* of air, and something hits me. I flinch. Not the crop—it felt broad and flat. I glance over my shoulder to see Jillian wielding a hairbrush.

She catches me watching her and shrugs.

She must really be feeling good today to use something that needs more than a light swing to hurt. I open my mouth to caution her, then close it again. She knows her own limits better than I ever could; if she thinks this is worth the (not fun) pain she'll have to endure for a day or two afterward, it's not my place to protest.

"What do you say?" she asks, and hits me again, harder this time.

"Thank you," I say, the muscles in my abdomen clenching. She strokes my skin with the back of the hairbrush, its hard plastic surface smooth and cool.

"Another," she says.

"I took an extra pen from the stationery cupboard at work last week." *Thwack.* "Thank you."

We continue for a while. I feel myself falling into the present, a little more with every blow. I yelp when she retraces old marks, setting aside the hairbrush for the crop. Its narrow tip draws lines of fire across my ass and thighs, brushing me in red and pink.

"Another," she says.

"I let Elena get swarmed last week because I'm still pissed at her for New Year's. That time she conveniently forgot to invite us, and never apologized for."

"Still? Feiyan, you've got to let that one go."

The crop descends. I scream, then follow it up with a whispered: "Thank you."

Jillian fills in the next sin for me. "Holding a grudge," she says, and hits me.

I grit my teeth, force myself to thank her. My skin burns where the crop's landed. I think about asking her to go slower, but I'm desperate for a cry—I need the catharsis that only a good sobbing can grant.

She pauses, pulls down my panties, and runs her finger along my slit. I whimper, pushing against her hand as she takes it away. As always, I'm achingly wet, my heat eager for her touch.

The crop replaces her hand. "For being a slut," she teases.

I squeal. My ass burns. "I can't help it," I mumble.

"What was that?"

"I was made this way."

"All the same." The crop strikes me, over and over again. "Wet. Open. Whore."

Tears well up in the corners of my eyes. I arc my back, pushing my ass higher into the air, but Jillian has other ideas.

She grabs my hair again, pulling my head back. "Come sit here."

I leave her lap with reluctance, pushing myself up. She takes my wrists, placing a metal cuff on each of them, then attaches my left wrist to the waist-level O-ring on the back of my harness with a carabineer, leaving my right hand free.

Jillian rearranges the pillows so she's once again surrounded, sitting upright with her back against the padded bed head. She peels off her own briefs, then discards them, hiking up her robe as she splays her legs.

I scoot toward her and lower my face to her pussy. I'm on my knees between her legs, my right hand braced under her thigh. I inhale her, sea spray salt and damp earth. My tongue darts out as I taste her, and her fingers rake through my hair.

She's wet. Once upon a time the cocktail of drugs she'd been prescribed made that difficult. Heat curls inside me in response. My tongue traces patterns on her clit, plunges down into her pussy. She doesn't speak, but angles her hips up toward me.

The cold air against my throbbing ass distracts me. She notices. Her hand fists in my hair, forcing me against her. I redouble my efforts, my tongue dancing a staccato beat over her clit.

My jaw is going kind of numb when she sort of curls up, her grip punishing, her thighs clenching around my head. Her breathing quickens and she groans before her fingers relax.

I go still, and then pull away as her hand falls from my hair. "Are you okay?" I ask.

She nods. "Mm. Thanks."

I crawl up beside her, using just my right hand for balance, the left still tethered, and lay next to her with the pillows between us.

She sips from her water bottle, then rolls over and kisses me. "Gimme five?" she asks.

"Sure thing."

We both relax into the sheets, the synth instrumentals still playing. The hard bits in my bra dig into me but it looks nice and I can't get it off while I'm still cuffed, anyway.

I squirm, trying to get comfortable. My lacy briefs chafe against the slick heat of my pussy, and I rub my thighs together, my toes curling against the sheets.

She watches me from her throne of pillows, her eyes half-lidded. "Touch yourself," she says, her voice husky.

I crawl down to the bottom of the bed and move Chip the Sexbot to one side, before taking its place. I rest on my knees, directly opposite Jillian, so that she can watch everything without craning her neck.

Her teeth rake over her bottom lip as I slide my panties down over my thighs, first over one hip, then the other. I pull them down over my feet and toss them out of the way. It's a bit awkward just using one hand, but I get there eventually. My left wrist clinks against its constraints as I settle back into my kneeling position.

My fingers trace down over my cleft, over the stubble on my skin. I part my lips, dip a finger into my pussy, and shudder.

"Taste it," she says.

I curl my finger inside me, and then pull it out. A long thread of wetness follows, clinging. I blush and put my finger in my mouth, my lips closing around it as I make a show of sucking myself clean.

Jillian watches me, her hand drifting to her own pussy, an egg-shaped toy clasped in her fist. It's buzzing as she turns it on, which makes me jump.

"Keep going," she says.

I return my fingers to my pussy, continuing to touch myself—two fingers either side of my clit, gently stroking in long, patient motions. I close my eyes and rock my hips, leaning my shoulders back, my chest thrust forward. I'm too wet for this; the stimulation isn't quite enough. I rock and whine in frustration, my voice an empty sigh of longing.

Jillian takes pity on me. "Put Chip back, and come here."

I scramble to obey. I drag Chip into position, and then lie down in front of Jillian, so we're both facing the end of the bed, my head resting on a pillow over her thighs, my knees bent so that my feet don't fall off the edge. Her knees are spread wide so she can still reach herself with her toy.

"What do you want?" she asks.

"I'd like you to use Chip to fuck me," I say, blushing.

"Do you deserve a good fucking?"

"No . . . yes? Yes." I raise my head off the pillow to nod.

She hums between her teeth, and then grabs Chip's remote. "I'm not sure."

"I would like very much to be fucked."

"By?"

"By you. And Chip." And oh, I wish to the stars she hadn't named it Chip, because who can say that with a straight face? But then she nods and I grab Chip by its pink silicone dildo attachment and I no longer care about its stupid name.

I rearrange myself, angling my hips to line up. The head of the dildo probes at me, cold and smooth and hard.

Jillian flicks a button. "Is this thing on?"

Ever so slowly, Chip moves. I grit my teeth as it nudges inside me, too dry on the first pass, achingly slow and rigid. I lean forward to take more of it in, my eyes fluttering closed as its entire length fills me.

Jillian presses a button and it speeds up a little, going from glacially slow to just slow. I shuffle down to get closer to Chip. My left wrist is falling asleep against my back.

"Am I leaning too much on you?" I ask, even though I'm not even touching her directly, my head on a pillow across her legs, her thighs to either side of my head.

"I'm good," she says, sounding a little breathy. The buzzing of her toy cuts through the music. She squirms behind me, the insides of her legs pressing against my shoulders. Her hand reaches down and roughly grasps one of my breasts, pulling it out of the bra. She pinches my nipple, and I gasp.

I could live in this memory forever, playing it over and over again until it wears thin like an old T-shirt, the fabric so threadbare that light shines through the weft. Chip fills me, and Jillian hurts me, her attentions moving to my other breast. I reach behind myself, one-handed, and struggle with the clasp of the bra. It unhooks, and I drag it down lower off my shoulders to give Jillian better access.

She thumbs the dial on the remote. Chip makes a rhythmic whirring noise, something like a stand mixer. It's both too much and not enough, this implacable, unstoppable force, pushing its silicone dick into my welcoming heat. My pussy makes wet, open noises, and I know I'll have to change the sheets later; I'm dripping.

Jillian slaps my breasts. I jolt with the shock. My arm grips her knee; her body grounds me. She turns up the speed again. I can't keep up, but I don't have to. I whimper as Chip plunges into me, over and over and over, relentless and untiring.

Beneath me, Jillian comes again with her arm pressed against my throat. I lean into her; I can still breathe, but it's harder. I relish the struggle, each gasp of air sweeter than the last.

When she slaps my cheek, I come undone; tears spring to my face, and I cry out, wordless and primal. Each shudder ripples through me as a wave crashing to shore; I cling to her, harder than I'd intended, as a tear rolls down my cheek.

She winds back the dial, and Chip slowly withdraws, dripping with my slick along its shaft.

My knees tremble. I press my legs together, and then sit up, turning to face her.

She smiles, reaches out to brush her fingers along my reddened cheek. I turn my face and kiss her palm.

She unhooks my left wrist and I pick up the toys along with the dildo and pop them in the sink, for washing later. Chip goes on the floor, waiting to be dismantled. I climb back into bed and wend my way along her side, her arm draped over me. "You feeling okay?" I ask.

She brushes a stray lock of hair from her face. "Yeah. I think it helped the pain, a little."

"I'm glad." She'll pay for it later by having to rest for a few days, but she knows that, too. For her to think this is worth it—that I'm worth it? I don't take it lightly.

"Love you," I say.

"I love you too." She kisses my forehead, and I enjoy the press of her bare skin against mine. The air-con's not too cold, for the moment; in fact, everything feels just about right.

SOMETHING SLUTTY

Mx. Nillin Lore

Biere's cheeks turned a soft red and a subtle smirk crossed faer lips as the words poured out, "I'd love to photograph you for your sex blog some time."

It was a surprising offer considering that Rory had really only recently started getting to know Biere—who was actually the life-long friend of their anchor partner, Sam—more. While the two were certainly sociable with one another, Rory hadn't really spent any alone time with Biere at all.

"That's a great idea!" Sam interjected, his eyes lighting up with excitement. "Biere loves your blog, hun. Fae read it all the time!"

If Biere was an avid reader, that meant that Biere had seen an awful lot of both Rory and Sam. Rory never shied away from sharing many of the most explicit and intimate details of their relationships and love life, be that with Sam or any of their other play friends. So long as those involved had fully consented, of course.

And wow, did they eagerly consent! You'd be surprised at how excited most people get at the prospect of being featured on a sex blog. Be it a close friend-with-benefits or a one-night stand from the local polyamory community, anytime that Rory slept with somebody who knew about their blog there almost always came that inevitable question: "So, are you going to write about this on your blog?"

They did. Most times at least.

In fact, Rory prided themself on how explicit and unapologetic their blog's content was. They tended to write a lot about things other sex bloggers didn't. Things like tips for ways to eat your own come, where to find the best hardcore femboy furry porn, how to safely masturbate with various household objects, the most ethical places to fuck outside, and what they love about pet play with their queerplatonic partners. Much of the time their posts detailed really explicit sex acts they had experienced, such as what it was like attending their first orgy with friends or how much they loved getting road head from their bestie whenever they went out of town.

Sam's involvement in their site was on a whole other level than most others though. Unsurprising considering that he was Rory's anchor partner and spouse. Their sexual exploits together had been well documented over the past several years and Sam took great pride in this fact.

Be it a candid shot of him looking up, slutty eyed, with Rory's girl cock in his mouth, or the aftermath pictures of come dripping down his chin or splattered all over his breasts, Sam loved to fuck the camera as much as he loved to fuck Rory.

Knowing that Biere had undoubtedly seen all of those pictures—ranging from some flirty gender play shots in cute lingerie to full-blown images of them naked and masturbating, including close-ups for their erect and come-covered girl cock—was an exhilarating feeling for Rory. As much as they primarily wrote to inspire self-acceptance and unapologetic sexual liberation in others, Rory was absolutely also an exhibitionist relishing in having a consenting audience in friends and strangers alike.

And friends like Biere, evidently, would also express interest in sometimes engaging with the site in a more intimate capacity.

"You okay?" fae asked. It hadn't exactly dawned on Rory until then that they hadn't responded yet.

"Yeah, no, yeah. I'm good! I'm sorry! So, you want to take pictures of me?" Rory asked. "For the blog?"

"If that sounds good to you. I have a really nice camera I don't get to use very often," Biere said. "Figured we could take some really sexy and affirming shots for you to use. Some flirty lingerie pics. Maybe some nudes, if you're comfortable with that."

Rory could see Sam nodding enthusiastically from over Biere's shoulder, giving them the thumbs-up encouragement they had come to enjoy. Sam was always incredibly encouraging of Rory to partake in and enjoy experiences like this with others.

"Uh, awesome! That sounds great! Sure, let's do it!" Rory clumsily blurted out. "When would you, um, would you like to do that?"

"How about tomorrow?"

It was sooner than they expected, but then again, now that the idea was in their mind, they would've found waiting long to be excruciating. Again, over Biere's shoulder, they could see Sam smiling and mouthing an energetic "Say yes!"

"Cool, yeah, cool!" Rory awkwardly said while nodding way too much.

Rory was quickly realizing that they maybe weren't as smooth in person as they were online. It was a lot easier to play it chill and come off as confident through writing than through speech. Not that it seemed to matter to Biere, who was clearly looking forward to a sex blog photo shoot as much as they were.

"Perfect, will see you tomorrow then!" fae exclaimed, then whispered sweetly: "Wear something slutty."

And with that, the plan was set. In less than twenty-four hours Rory would be hanging out partially naked—maybe even fully naked—with their partner's best friend while fae took lewd photographs of them. It wasn't the life that Rory thought they'd be living, but they sure as hell weren't complaining.

Wearing "something slutty" turned out to be much more of a challenge for Rory than they had expected. While they had originally excitedly purchased a lot of new lingerie and underwear early on in their coming out, scooping up all variety of cute bras and trying every possible type of underwear, struggles with dysphoria and body positivity kept them from really ever finding what felt right. Fact was that as much as they really wanted to enjoy wearing panties, they had a girl cock, and panties weren't typically designed with girl cocks like theirs in mind. Nothing felt as affirming as it should for a femme-leaning nonbinary person who had a penis to account for in underwear shopping.

Bras too were a challenge, as so few comfortably fit them in a way that felt complimentary. The cup sizes were either too big or, if they did find a small push-up that might work, the band size was often too tight to accommodate their broader chest and shoulders.

Overall it was generally a lot easier for Rory to be naked than it was to be "sexy." Because sexy tended to take clothes, and make-up, and planning that they just didn't really have the spoons for when so few of those things existed in forms that worked for nonbinary folks.

Ultimately they packed themself a small backpack full of comfy sports bras, some nicely fitted boxer briefs that accentuated their package in a way that they liked, and some miscellaneous clothing items such as shawls, scarves, thigh-highs, and even a gaudy, dark gray and purple, floral print silk housecoat. It was an eclectic mix of things meant to cover their bases for whatever Biere might have in mind. They quickly tossed on a pair of dark blue jeggings and a cute little black dress, then headed out the door.

They couldn't help but feel a little nervous though. All of the images on their blog currently were taken and edited with their complete control. Rory got to decide what angles of themself they shared. Got to decide exactly how they were posed, what lighting there was, and generally how their body was being perceived by the lens. While certainly exciting, giving that control over to somebody else was also pretty scary.

Then again, the prospect of posing sensually for the camera while somebody else took pictures of them definitely played into those exhibitionist desires they so loved. And the thought of being so vulnerable, so bare, in front of Biere was incredibly appealing.

Once at Biere's place, and having gotten the quick tour of the surprisingly large two-bedroom condo fae lived in with faer partner, the pair sat to discuss boundaries and expectations.

Biere, dressed in a tight pair of galaxy-print leggings and a comfy fit top, glanced through the oval lenses of faer large-rimmed glasses. Fae almost seemed in a whimsical mood as fae hopped into a large armchair in faer living room and started to playfully kick faer feet.

"I only really have two rules for this: I'm not touching your girl cock and I don't want to be in any of the photos myself. Does that sound cool?"

"Yeah! Of course!" Rory had no assumptions that they were here for sex, or that Biere was going to be making porn with them.

"Cool! Other than that I'm totally cool with nudity and you doing sexual things with yourself. Feel free to be as lewd as you want, really. What are we hoping for today?"

Rory only really had a vague, mostly conceptual notion of

what it was they were looking for. "I don't really know to be honest. I think I just want some really queer- and trans-positive stock photos, you know? Just some cool gender fuckery things, things that make me feel good about being enby, and things that make me feel . . . you know . . ."

"Hot!" Bier exclaimed. "Sexy! Fantastic! Affirmed and unapologetic! All of the above! I get it. I've been thinking about this a lot actually. Can I see what you brought with you for negligee?"

"Well, I wouldn't go so far as to call any of it 'negligee,'" they said, handing their backpack over to Biere.

Biere dug around in the bag for a moment, a slight frown appearing on faer lips. After a moment, fae hung faer head and chuckled to faerself before holding up a lace bralette with faer finger poking through a small hole in it.

"How do you have a sex blog again?" Biere said with a playful sigh as fae side-eyed Rory with a smirk.

"I guess I don't really do a lot of glamour shots," Rory laughed.

"Alright, come with me. I think I have just the thing for you."

Rory had heard all about Biere's clothing collection from their partner Sam. Apparently, it was a collection of legends. All throughout their childhood growing up together, Biere was known for amassing large quantities of unique clothes, in all sizes and styles, to wear and repurpose into faer own unique look.

Rory sat on the edge of Biere's bed and watched as fae excitedly threw open the large doors of faer closet to reveal an assortment of vibrant dresses, cute frilly nighties, silk camisoles, colorful shawls, suit jackets, housecoats, jumpers, and more hung up in a colorful display. On some shelves built into the right-hand side of the closet sat all variety of bras, panties, garters, boxers, stockings, leggings, thigh-highs, and even some of faer sex toys, which fae seemed completely unembarrassed about Rory seeing.

* * *

Biere immediately got to work, quickly glancing back at Rory on the bed before launching into the sea of items before them, pulling out a few picks before spinning back around.

"Get undressed," Biere said, and Rory complied. They lifted their shirt over their head revealing a salmon-pink sports bra covering their hairy chest, their tiny perky tits giving a slight raise to the fabric.

Biere pursed faer lips a little in an unsuccessful attempt to mask a gleeful smile. "Bra too, if you please! I have a look in mind."

As they took off their bra fae handed them a silky, black camisole with a lace trim along the bottom and put a make-up bag on the bed next to them. Rory pulled that top down over their frame, surprised at how perfectly it clung to their body, complementing their curves and even the shape of their tummy, which normally made them feel dysphoric and insecure.

"Wow," they said, running their hands over the fabric and their body.

"Wow is right," Biere replied, faer voice soft and affirming. "Can you look at me for a sec please?"

They looked up into Biere's eyes then quivered with excitement as fae grabbed them by the chin, faer soft fingers gliding through their beard, and began to apply a vibrant, creamy red lipstick to their lips.

"Maybe I should have shaved," Rory lamented.

"Don't be ridiculous, you look adorable," fae replied, rummaging through the make-up bag for a second, then pulling out some eyeliner. "Look way up."

Rory felt themself melt a little. They didn't typically go for very femme looks but there was something about Biere's confidence in dressing them, in taking command of preparing them, that felt really good to Rory. It was quickly eroding any and all worry they previously had about the shoot. They would be clay, allowing themself to be molded however Biere envisioned.

"Perfect. Take off your bottoms too please, if that's alright."

It was alright. Rory stood up, maybe a little too enthusiastically, and slid their leggings off over their plump ass. Underneath they wore a nicely fitted pair of boxer briefs that softly clung to their full hips and quite clearly betrayed their arousal in highlighting their now partially erect girl cock.

For a moment, Rory caught Biere looking down at their visible bulge. Fae seemed a little dazed even. Taking cue, Rory slid their boxers off, their girl cock springing back slightly as the band of their underwear passed over it. They then crawled onto the bed and laid on their side, looking up at Biere with longing eyes.

"You know what? That's just what I had in mind." said Biere, stepping back to the closet where fae grabbed faer camera and immediately set about snapping shots.

Click.

"Now, lay on your stomach and lift your hips up a little."

Rory complied.

Click.

"A little more. Really make it pop."

Rory strained against the bed to raise their ass up to where they thought it needed to be.

Click.

"It's not quite right. Here."

They gasped as Biere's hands gripped them firmly by the hips and pulled their body to where fae wanted it to be.

"There it is. Mm! You look so very fuckable right now!"

Rory let out a soft, happy moan and chuckle. This was all starting to feel so very good to them.

With each clothing change, each series of affirming statements Biere made while directing them, Rory felt themself almost losing control of their body. They instinctively moved themself about hungrily, glaring at the camera with wanting eyes, constantly moving their body around to show how much they wanted to be fucked by whomever it was that would be looking at them later.

Each click of the camera sent another jolt of arousal through their body.

By now, neither Biere or Rory even needed to talk. Biere moved about the room, taking photos from all angles while Rory, now wearing only a black lace bralette and matching garter belt attached to thigh-high, black kitten socks, writhed about on the bed and ran their hands sensually all over themself.

Click.

They traced their fingertips along their lips, then down their chin and neck, breathing in deep and arching their back a little as they went.

Click.

They carried on further down their soft chest hair and over the bralette to just above their tummy.

Click.

Biere took a couple of steps closer to the bed this time, watching intently as Rory now traced the treasure trail of hair from their belly button down to their pubic mound.

Click.

They flattened their hand against their mound and moaned, letting their fingers spread apart so that their hard, pulsing girl cock slid between them. Biere stepped closer to focus even more on the action starting to unfold.

Click.

Rory took hold of their girl cock and moaned, slowly stroking it while they squeezed their breasts with their free hand. This time, Biere climbed onto the edge of the bed, positioning faerself on faer knees next to them. They could hear fae breathing heavily.

Click.

Always one to produce a lot of pre-come, Rory began to drip all over themself. They gathered as much of the fluid as they could with their fingers and palm, gasping as they used it as lubrication for themself. It was then that they noticed Biere, still holding the camera with one hand, had slid the other down under faer leggings.

Rory could hear how wet fae was. They sighed, their breath quivering as the rhythmic rubbing sounds coming from underneath the fabric of Biere's leggings filled their ears. Now all they could focus on, all they could see was the outlined shape of Biere's knuckles and outstretched fingers working between faer thighs.

Biere's chest started to heave forward and back, faer perky breasts and erect nipples straining against faer crop top as fae thrusted faer hips forward while continuing to pleasure faerself. Now also moaning quite heavily, Biere had stopped observing Rory through the viewfinder of faer camera, and instead looked directly into their eyes.

Click.

Both were now completely lost in their own pleasure, looking deep into one another's eyes and soaking in the view of them masturbating for each other. In all of the excitement, Rory forgot to pace themself. Pleasure erupted through them. They cried out, thrusting their hips into the air as stream after stream of thick come shot out all over their stomach, all the way up over their bralette and onto their right shoulder.

This seemed to be a stimulating enough visual for Biere, who also lost faerself in a satisfying orgasm. Faer whole body convulsed before Rory's eyes. Huge shudders of pleasure caused fae to lurch forward several times, faer face turning red as fae threw faer head back and screamed, then slumped down to sit on faer legs with a satisfied whimper. Rory rested their elbows against the bed, careful to keep their come-covered hands above themself in case they started to drip.

Once the initial calm had passed, the pair fell into a giggling fit over what had just transpired between them.

"I don't think all of those are going to turn out very clear," said Biere, still catching faer breath and stifling more laughter. Fae grunted a little, then pulled faer hand out from under faer leggings and began licking faer fingers clean of faer juices. "So, are you going to write about this on your blog?"

Rory, feeling happy and sexy in their mess, let their tired arms drop to rest on either side of them. The come previously strewn over their stomach and chest now trickled down their sides.

"Yes Biere, I think I definitely will."

THE OFFICE HALLOWEEN PARTY

Bear Nicks

"Hey! Look, Val's here!" Shelia, one of the nicer older white women, shouts into the crowd of some fifty coworkers. More than half are still wearing their business casual shirt and tie combo with a devil mask or some obscure creature. The crowd gives a drunk "Hey" before continuing their bad dancing. Small towns do have more fun, it seems; I could smell the booze on Shelia's breath as she leans closer in her inappropriate white bunny costume. Her thick, freckled breasts flicker with different hues from the roaming, colorful dance lights.

Forty years my senior and twice my size, I'm still confident I could give her a night she'd remember. With all the day-to-day shameless flirting, it could happen.

"I'm so happy you came, Val. When I first saw you, I knew you knew how to party," she nearly shouts my ear off. The music isn't so loud, all the people around us just don't use inside voices.

"Yeah, Halloween is my favorite holiday. I used to go all out with my friends until I moved here," I tell her. She eyes my firefighter costume, complete with a fake ax and a red helmet strapped to my head. To say I've been in the gym for the last six months to pull the costume off would be a lie; however, adding a few extra arm reps paid off. My kingly brown skin and toned arms are glistening with baby oil, and I admit I look more like a male stripper than a real firefighter. More like a Frankenstein firefighter since my shirt has a white male's bare chest.

Maybe I should have put some fake blood on it or something? Killer Fire Queer?

"There's food here?" I ask her as she eye-fucks me. Smirking, I look into her glossy eyes, sliding my hand on hers to sniff her drink. She blushes, parting her lips, and nods, pointing toward the cubicles, then has a crisis of conscience and removes her hand.

I leave her pondering the thought of whether going home to Larry after having fucked someone their grandchild's age at an office party is a good thing or a bad thing. I'm just a little too horny this holiday to care for any consequences. The food doesn't seem to help curb my lustful appetite: half-frozen cookies and candy that looks like the type old ladies hand out in church. Should have known it would be like this. I'm the youngest person at this company and I'm twenty-eight!

Manager Robert "Bobby" MacMurray had a twenty-year affair with Gina Drews in accounting—to this day, his wife doesn't know. Henry, William, Shelia, and Sherley are going through a midlife crisis, they've been smoking weed in the maintenance elevator for as long as I've been here, thirty days now. To be honest, this place is kind of cool; a place where people don't give a fuck but know they are helping people, so they give a little bit of a fuck.

But the one reason I chose to work here is Ms. Daniella Rodriguez. Associate manager, single, Mexican-American, forties-ish, warm brown eyes, thick in the body, great skin.

I've had my eyes set on her ever since I first watched her walk past the hiring station, gray skirt fitting tight to that supple ass. Sun-kissed orange blouse, ruffles hiding her bosom from my almost desperate view. Lush, thick brown hair. But what drove me to take the job that day was the clicking of her heels on the solid tile floor. Ever since high school that sound turns me on; her legs in those black stockings had me drooling over the paperwork. Didn't hurt that I got my own office in the deal: the view of her across the hall has been the best part.

She stretches every day at noon before her lunch break. I try not to stare, but I know she likes it when I do. I've caught her staring as I do push-ups, fanning herself and biting her pen. We've only talked on a few occasions—in the break room, passing in the hall, on the way to the car—more with double meanings than casual.

This morning, when she entered my office saying her phone was on the fritz, I was a little too eager to have a glimpse into her personal life.

There was an app I recognized right away, one that controls vibrators by Bluetooth. By its pulsating neon pink light, I assumed it was in use the very moment she walked in. Did she know I would know? Or was she oblivious—nah. Of all the women, femmes, lesbians I've encountered, not one has come on so strong. I told her it would be a minute for me to figure out the issue. She wore a black skirt and blazer over a light blue blouse. Her stockings were anything but casual. This long, thick black line ran from the heels of her feet up to her calves and thighs and rose into the sweet unknown.

Biting her lip, looking over me, she nods her head. I took the plunge and closed the distance. Ms. Rodriguez closed my office door behind her with little patience. She cleared her throat, staring me in the eyes as her orgasm approached. Pointing to the phone, she almost lost her cool demeanor, but she made it clear that she wanted me to focus on the task at hand.

Giving her space, I sat on my desk and opened the app. The

pleading look on her face when I turned it off so close to orgasm was priceless. Just in time, too—Mr. MacMurray knocked on my door, expecting to speak with me, but Ms. Rodriguez answered my door instead.

"How am I supposed to push control, alt, and delete on this skinny damn thing? They expect us to work on these glorified e-readers? Jimmy D. is losing his damned mind—"

"Mr. MacMurray," she said, keeping the door narrowly open. I raised the vibrator slowly, wiggling the pink line up and down. She huffed enough to play it off, I squeezed my packer harder to my clit, watching her. God.

"Oh, hell, am I at the wrong office?" Mr. MacMurray looks back at Ms. Rodriguez's door with her name, then back to mine. "Is Val in there, Dani? Only kids these days know how to use these damn paperweights. Sweet baby Jesus, what happened?" Mr. MacMurray said.

"We're in a meeting, I'll send him to you right after." She is firm but her back ripples; the view is intoxicating.

"Alright then. But first . . ." Mr. MacMurray says, then launches into a ten-minute conversation with Ms. Rodriguez, all the while the Bluetooth controls are in my hand.

At lunch, I barely made it to my car before I jerked off with my limp packer to her moans. I've never wanted someone so bad. She said she'd be here tonight, promised it would be a wild party watching people do the cha-cha slide and some weird honky-tonk shuffle. She wasn't lying on that part.

"Well, aren't you a sight," I hear her voice behind me as she taps on my shoulder. The first thing I notice is her lips, vampire red, with fake fangs. Her neck and shoulders are exposed, shimmering with golden glitter, and the red dress was meant to kill.

"Thank you, and you . . ." I take a deep breath; she smells like cinnamon and heat as I hug her close. "You look delicious," I let slip, unable to tear my eyes from her, uncharacteristically roaming over her body a second time as we separate.

"What?" she says loudly, stepping closer as if the music was suddenly booming.

I move close to her ear. "I said, you look fucking delicious tonight, Ms. Rodriguez." No need to cover my actions with fear of consequences. If the ship goes down, I'll go down with it.

Her eyes grew hungry in the silence. She licks her lips, standing up straighter but not moving away. "You shouldn't say such things at work," she advises me, with little authority in her voice. She's not the only one out to kill tonight.

Nodding my head, I step back, smirking. "Right you are, but tonight it seems I'm a Frankenstein Firefighter, and you are a member of the drop-dead gorgeous club." I put on my best charm and take her hand. She looks over her attire before smiling; such an appreciative smile. I spin her to marvel at her vampiric look. Well, at her ass and tight black fishnets mostly. She laughs, walking into my embrace.

"If I am being too forward, Ms. Rodriguez, please tell me," I whisper in her ear. She grips my tight-fitting shirt near my ribs and moans a sigh.

"No, no, you are perfect, Val," she whispers into my ear. My eyes flutter as she kisses my neck quickly, unable to stop herself. The music seems suddenly too loud and my clit won't stop throbbing against my dick.

"Call me Mr. Jacobs," I tell her, holding my hands firmly on her waist, not letting her run away as coworkers pass by us. Her hands glide from my broad shoulders, down my arms, moving closer to me. I nearly go weak in the knees as she presses her hourglass figure to my hips.

"Your hands, Mr. Jacobs, are going to get you in a hell of a lot of trouble." Ms. Rodriguez's lips part in a threat as my hand finds the side of her ass.

I remove my hand slowly, leaving her wanting more. "Dare I say, fuck trouble tonight," I rub my hand down my chest and grip my plastic, black firemen's belt.

"Oh, there you are! Hey everyone! Dani's here!" Henry from HR interrupts us, staggering to my side. The roar of the crowd is larger than when they greeted me. I look him up and down in his inflatable dinosaur costume as he steadies himself. "How's it going, Val?" he asks me, muffled underneath the floppy T-Rex head.

"Peachy, Henry, real peachy. Wanna drink?" I ask, pointing toward the spiked red punch on Tyrone's rainbow desk across from the water cooler.

He shakes his head. "No than-k-you buck-a-roo, Shelia put too much vodka in it this time," he says, creating an awkward silence between the three of us.

I look to Ms. Rodriguez. "I'll catch you later, yeah?" I tell her, stepping away. She reaches a hand for me and I wink at her, nudging my head to my office upstairs. "Ten minutes," I whisper smiling. She nods, grinning, biting her lip. I slip through the dance floor, doing a hip-bump with folks from receiving before leading the conga line in a large circle.

I enjoy myself and my weird coworkers, but break off. Laughing and dancing is nice, but I need to get laid. Ducking past the line to the restroom, I head upstairs and spy over the railing. The DJ hops wildly waving his arms around and the crowd eats it up—all except for the vampire eyeing me. Ms. Rodriguez rubs her red nails along her brown arms and over her stomach in that tight red dress, then down her hips.

"Tease," I whisper to myself, walking to my office door. God help me. I unlock the door, closing it quickly behind me, then hurry and shove everything off my desk into one of the drawers.

Her moan echoes again in my ear from this afternoon, where I controlled her vibrator for three hours, watching her talk to Mr. MacMurray while tugging her skirt lower. She came enough times for me to smell her hot cunt later, when she walked by my office. Her brown eyes were tired, with a fire still deep within, when I finally returned her phone, "bug-free." Whatever composure she once had, by my graceful thumb, it was gone.

Knock, knock.

I don't even need to check the time; I hurry to the door and open it for her. My eyes drink her up again from stocking to hips; peeking breast, neck, bloodstained lips, and wild eyes. She looks hungry. In no time, my cougar pounces; her arms wrap around my neck and the first time our lips meet, I'm in her possession. Slippery warmth coating my tongue and teeth, my hands roam her wide sides and hips as I press her back into the door, slamming it in the process. Ms. Rodriguez thrusts her hips to mine as I smother her with my body. She tastes mint chocolate. Biting her lip in the darkness, she is my treat. Her hot tongue pours warm into me, driving me mad for every inch she roams.

We moan as I spread her legs, showing off my strength, lifting her legs onto my waist. Dripping fire down my neck, her tongue finds my sweet spot and I melt into her. She is my hell, and I, her demon.

"Oh, *dios mio*," her Spanish tongue makes my clit twitch. God? God, I want to rip this dress. I bite her neck and her nails grip into my shirt, daring to rip me apart with it. Our lips find each other before I lower to my knee. I kiss her breasts, sucking marks on each of them as I set one of her feet to the ground. She pulls the top of her dress down, blinding me with warm dark flesh.

Ms. Rodriguez moans loudly as I suckle her like a baby calf. She pulls the back of my head into her, nearly suffocating me in her bosom. Eagerly, I lick them, such a death befitting Halloween night. I bury my head into her, closing my eyes, biting along her breast before taking her nipple into my mouth.

"*Ay! Papi,* slow down," she whimpers, tossing her head back, rubbing a hand over my jawline. I nod, twirling my tongue over her nipple, rubbing my hand up her thigh to her ass and squeezing all I can hold. She twists impatiently as I move from one titty to the next. I make her gasp when I lift her leg on my shoulder, kissing down her dress-covered stomach.

She whines a moan as I hike her dress up over her hips. Even in the darkness, I can see nothing but hairy wet pussy, and black stockings. Taking Ms. Rodriguez's juicy ass in my hands, I yank her hips from the door, stuffing my face full of her cunt. I let her fill all my senses, steaming hot taste of her pussy, melting under the texture of her hair and stockings, seeing and feeling her body desperately wanting to fuck my face.

Best of all, she whispers *Santa María, Madre de Dios,* between each moan and venture of my tongue.

Losing myself, I bite her thigh for a groan, making her grip into my hair.

"*Papi! Por favor,*" she pleads, and pulls down one side of her stockings from her hips for me. I smile against her skin and kiss the bite before hungrily indulging in her hair. I rub my chin and cheeks all around it, dipping my nose deep into her cunt, spreading it. I press my tongue between her labia, sucking each lip. Ms. Rodriguez spreads her legs wider as I put my back into eating her out, tonguing as deep inside as she could swallow me. Tilting my head, I wiggle my nose on her pulsing clit, drinking up her wetness.

She gives up on prayer.

My hand finds her breast and I squeeze, massaging while bringing the other into her pussy.

"Oh, god! Oh." she starts to tremble as I suck her clit, thrusting two fingers slippery deep inside of her. I stop before she can come and move back, to stand. Ms. Rodriguez wastes no time and undoes my belt. I move my red suspenders to the side and remove my shirt. She licks my collarbone, tasting all of my sweat. Taking her by the back of the neck, I pull her to my mouth, flavored in her pussy, and kiss all of her essences into her mouth while I move her back to the door. Her hands slide up my waist to my breast beneath my sports bra. Moaning, my eyes cross before they close.

Kissing her neck, I muffle my sounds as she toys with my nipples. I am beyond overstimulated, I just want to bury myself deep inside of her. She teases my ears with her tongue as I pull out my thick black silicone. Her whimpering, trembling pussy allows me to lube up as I slowly move it between her worthy, juicy thighs. I'm in love. Kissing her more deeply, I rip her stockings partly as I move them down to her knees. I take hold of her hip, stepping closer, guiding my hose into her goddess fur, circling my tip on her clit.

"Do you want me to fuck you, Ms. Rodriquez? Do you want me to defile you? Possess you with my youth?" I whisper in her ear, my sadist not letting me sleep a second when an opportunity presents itself. Ms. Rodriguez bites back a moan, eyes glossing with tears as the party lights lightly dance on the ceiling. Close to breaking, I lick her breast back into my mouth and moan, teasing her nipples.

She hurries a nod, capturing me, her thighs wrap around my waist and ass. I slip inside of her, losing my mind, feeling her inner lips spread for me, her hot center welcomes me, embraces me. Her pussy feels like magic to my strap and I don't want it to end.

"Mr. Jacobs, I'm ready for you," she whispers, and I begin to work my hips slow. Our sighs and gasps sing together as the rhythm takes over. It feels as if I'm slipping deeper into the tunnel to hell. Ms. Rodriguez's hungry cunt eats my strap, leaving me to feel like a newbie, but I will play my part even if it is my last. I quicken my thrusts, feeling as if her depths never end. My mind clouds a moment as she bites my neck, scratching along my back.

The door begins to rattle as the base of my strap hits her clit, my loins dripping wet, my clit so hard without any friction. I fuck her harder to feel her fuck against me.

Taking her back into my arms I carry her to my desk. Weight training could not have prepared me for fucking a worthy woman in the sky, so we crash onto the desk and I lean her to her back as her tongue and cunt suck me into no end. I take Ms. Rodriguez's thighs, jerking her ass to the edge of my desk, and pound, with all of my stamina, into this relentless queen. My fingers dig into her thighs as I daze in the view of my dick disappearing into what my mind painted hot red.

Spanish syllables and accented remarks toy with my ears, even as my eyes close. I feel our sounds, I see them in the dark. Her wet pussy sends my eyes to the back of my head. Ms. Rodriguez cups my breast beneath my sports bra, sweat dripping down my back and stomach. Lifting her leg, we grind harder together, we groan in unison. My orgasm finally nears, and I pull her by the back of the neck to sit up, her thighs high to my ribs. She locks eyes with me, moaning on my lips. I hit her G-spot, again and again, crying out together. She bites her lip, not letting go of my eyes, her nails digging in my hips.

My brows lose tension in her loving kiss. I don't even want my orgasm, I just want her, like this. My hips don't listen and I fuck her like a wild animal in heat. She bites my lip and cheek as I take her over the edge. She screams in my ear, tightening her pussy with trembling aftershocks, bringing me my blinding moment of solace. My legs lock in my stance as if possessed before I topple over her. She wraps her arms around my shoulders leaning back.

"Ms. Rodriguez," I pant, feeling my clit and dick throb along with my heartbeat, still home inside of her. She strokes my hair back, shushing me with her eyes closed. I nod, listening to her heart, kissing her breast slowly, panting, floating on this cloud.

Time didn't make much sense anymore, had it been an hour, thirty minutes? Four minutes? Fuck if I care. She tastes too sweet to let go.

Her eyes open to meet mine as I lean over her, stroking her hair back she marvels at my body. Tracing her fingers up and down, I gulp as she opens her mouth while I slowly grind into her before pulling out. "I want to ride your face, Mr. Jacobs," she confesses, as if it were her darkest secret.

"Ms. Rodriguez, I'd be honored." I open my heart, kissing her deeply, wanting everything she wishes to give me tonight.

She smiles on my lips as I help her stand. I lay the long way on my large desk and slide my hand beneath my strap, gathering my juices to stroke my thick black cock. Ms. Rodriguez smirks, climbing over me. She prowls, showing her teeth, and positions her sexy brown ass and cunt over my face. I could die here. Her thighs meet my shoulders near my neck, her wet goddess fur bathes me as I rub my face deep into her, lifting my head. She moans something in Spanish, I can't hear her over her pussy mixing with the tip of my tongue.

Ms. Rodriguez lowers the rest of the way to my mouth. My head is against the desk and my hands shoot up to her hips, gripping her ass enough to not fully be smothered. I make love to her sex with my tongue, nose, lips as passionately as I did with my cock. Her moans turn into hisses as she shows me what it's like to have a thick woman reverse-cowgirl ride my face. I've never been so elated in my life. I smack her ass for encouragement and she fucks my face faster. Slippery lips all over my nose and chin, I'm in heaven; her hips buck back as I suck her clit, making my nose tease her inner lips.

Who needs to breathe?

"*Papi,* fuck, don't stop," she tells me loudly. I nod, sucking her clit, spitting all over it. My hips twitch, feeling her lips tickle my pussy hair. Moving my strap to the side, her tongue sends life into me again. I moan against her hungry cunt riding my face. Rolling my eyes in lust, I use my tongue to enter her and fuck her, reveling in her texture.

Giving it all my effort, I sit up, holding most of her weight in my arms. She catches herself on the edge of the desk.

"Fuck me, Mr. Jacobs, please, I can't take much more," Ms. Rodriguez says shakily, as I move to my knees behind her.

I grip in her hair, lifting her head back. "Yes, you can," I whisper, pressing my wet cock inside of her again, slamming in and out, holding her hip, forcing her back to me. Nibbling along her neck, she thrusts back in time with me, yelling out Spanish profanities. Moving my hand from her hip to her clit I tease her, sucking her neck, and take her breast in one of my hands. "Ms. Rodriguez," I moan, wanting to devour every inch of her until this lust dies. But it won't, it can't. I won't let it. She beares down, tightening her hold on the desk as it begins to creak. Lifting her leg, I angle my dick for her favorite spot and give her the last of me.

Her head lowers to the desk as her hand covers on top of mine, circling and circling until she screams, squeezing my hand. Ms. Rodriguez's thighs clamp together as her upper body drops to the desk. I finish off after two thrusts tumbling to my end. We listen to our panting breath together, smiling. I kiss her, then move to my desk chair, falling straight into it with a sigh.

"Best Halloween of my life," I tell her as she turns to her side facing me, her breast moist with sweat.

Ms. Rodriguez smirks, lifting her leg, looking like a scene from a movie. "Over so soon?"

CONDUCTOR

Megan Stories

I met Hilary at a kink class. I don't even remember what the topic was; it never seemed to matter. The takeaway from a class on flogging, play piercing, caning, whatever, was if you were a top, you should go home and practice whatever you learned. But I didn't have anyone to practice with, and I was way too broke to shell out eighty bucks for kink equipment I didn't even know if I wanted and didn't have anyone to use on anyway.

I noticed her because of the patches on the back of her denim vest: a rainbow-colored cat rubbing lovingly against an ankle, a hand-lettered ACAB, and an ace flag, purple, white, black, and gray. I wanted to talk to her as soon as I saw the flag; I'd come out as ace a few months earlier, but when I mentioned it to an older dyke at a play party, she'd laughed in my face. *You know this is a kink party, right?* When I replayed the conversation in my head, I gave all kinds of clever replies, but in the moment I'd just shrunk into my chair. I wondered if I was wrong to think I could be kinky and ace at the same time.

My friend Charlie, who'd stopped going to kink stuff, thought maybe the older dyke had assumed I was a bottom and wanted to give me a hard time as a way of flirting. I said disparaging someone's identity was a shitty way of flirting, and Charlie said yeah, that was why they didn't go to kink stuff anymore. I kept going back though. It was the only way I could think of to meet people who might, against all odds, want to do kinky things with me.

The group who ran the classes always gathered people afterwards at the Skylite Diner down the street. As I moved with the loose crowd of queer kinksters headed toward the diner, a voice behind me said, "I like your boots."

I looked down. The boots were calf-high lace-ups, vinyl and shimmery. I'd bought them over a year ago, but this was only the third time I'd worn them. They seemed like something the person I wanted to be would wear, but I wasn't sure the person I was could pull them off. A couple weeks earlier, I'd let Charlie chop off most of my hair and dye the remainder purple, and I felt the same way looking in the mirror that I did looking down now, as if I was wearing a costume that everyone could see didn't fit.

"Thanks," I said anyway, and turned around to see Hilary. She was a head taller than me, with broad shoulders and a curvy waist, wearing lipstick in a bright glittery violet that made me smile. Her skin was pale and dotted with freckles, and her honey-brown hair hung over her neck and shoulders in delicate wisps. "I like your vest."

"I'm Hilary, by the way," she said, though I'd heard her introduce herself in class. "She/her."

"Rae. She/her too."

We sat together at the diner. I usually didn't know what to talk about on diner trips. People sometimes asked what you did for work, and I didn't like to say. I was a library assistant in a children's department, and I was scared of it getting back to parents that Rae who did storytimes for kids also liked to hurt people for fun. When I did tell people about my job, someone inevitably said something about sexy librarians, and I'd only recently found the words for how alien the idea of being sexy felt to me.

Hilary and I talked about webcomics, and her cat, who could open cabinet doors, and I asked if she wanted to split a basket of curly fries, which she did. It wasn't until our orders came that I got up the nerve to ask about her flag patch. I told her about the woman who'd laughed at me when I said I was ace. Hilary took a deep breath and gripped the edge of the table, her fingers curling in like claws. "That's some bullshit," she said, loud enough that a few people across the table turned their heads.

I laughed. "I thought so too, but then I thought maybe there was a reason I hadn't met other ace people here."

"Well, it's not because we don't exist." Hilary picked up a curly fry and blew on it; I didn't dare touch them yet. "The scene's got some warped priorities sometimes."

Hilary had been away from the scene for a few years. She'd been in a relationship with someone who didn't like public parties, then she'd been depressed after a breakup, and now she figured it was worth dipping a toe back in. I told her how I'd been coming to scene stuff for a couple years, how I wanted to top, but how people looked at a small, awkward femme-ish newcomer and thought *bottom*. How you weren't supposed to top if you weren't experienced, but how you needed experience to get experience, like the old entry-level job problem. How I'd ended up making out with people at parties even though I didn't give a shit about making out, because sexual stuff felt like the only thing I was allowed to do without practice.

"There's a lot you can do without practice," Hilary said.

"Like what?"

"Rough body stuff. Hitting, pinching, scratching, hair pulling."

"I guess." I'd done a spanking scene with someone at a party once. "Don't people think that stuff's boring though?"

Hilary frowned. "Do you think it's boring?"

I thought about the person I'd spanked, how their voice had broken with each hit. How I'd stroked their back the whole time and felt warm and connected, how the few times I'd dared hit harder, their body had seemed to crumple, thrillingly, onto our padded bench. I'd played that scene back to myself for days afterwards. "No," I said, feeling faintly shy. "I don't."

"I'm a masochist," Hilary said, biting slightly at her glittery lower lip. "And a service sub. I like pain, and I like doing things for tops."

I had to stop my head from tilting quizzically. I knew Hilary was kinky, or else why would she be here, but somehow some part of me still thought she couldn't be, let alone have desires that matched mine. Maybe it was an ace thing, but until I saw it, I found it hard to imagine people as erotic actors of any kind.

"I don't know if you're looking to play tonight," she continued. "But if you are, and you're looking to try some hitting or pinching or something . . ." She trailed off. My heart was racing.

"Yeah," I said. "That sounds really nice."

The playspace was a large, black-walled room in the basement of a theater. Hilary and I sat on a bench by the entrance, and I looked around at the now-familiar sights: a padded cross, a clean-up station, a bench with stirrups. A pair of regulars strolled by, the domme in leather pants, the sub wheeling their toy collection in a suitcase. Someone out of sight shrieked; somewhere closer came the metallic clink of restraints being fastened. Across the room, I spotted the dyke who'd laughed at my aceness caning a bottom who wore a tutu, and I wondered what she'd think if she saw me topping too. Maybe it didn't matter.

We talked more about our scene. Hilary said she liked boots, and being lower to the ground than her partner, and having her hair pulled. I said I liked touch, like how I'd rubbed my partner's back in that spanking scene, that I'd never hit anyone's upper body or pinched anyone, but that I'd like to try. We had all the conversations I knew from classes you were supposed to: safewords, limits, where she did and didn't want to be touched, how she usually felt glowy after a scene and wanted to cuddle, how the few times I'd played, I'd wanted that too. It still felt surreal, like I was playing a part that wasn't written for me, but at least I knew my lines.

And then Hilary pointed to a spot in the back corner of the playspace where it looked like there was room for the two of us and asked if I wanted to go there. I nodded and rose from the bench, and she followed.

There was no equipment in the spot we'd chosen, just a bit of bare wall and a stretch of floor. Hilary sat on the floor and looked up at me, her eyes darting shyly away when I looked back. I felt a little power flow from her and into me, like we were sharing a secret. She unbuttoned her vest and lifted her T-shirt, and I watched her bra appear underneath, gray cotton, sporty and cute. It felt good to look at another ace person undressing and not feel that pressure to feel . . . something. Her boobs were a nice shape but knowing I wasn't supposed to want to touch them, wasn't failing by eyeing instead her exposed skin and downcast gaze, made something in my chest untighten.

She folded her vest and shirt crisply and carefully, then turned around on her knees to lay them by the wall. When she turned back toward me, she looked up again and placed her arms behind her back, presenting herself to me. That gaze up again, that smile, and I felt the space between us start to close. I ran my tongue over my canine teeth. A new friend was offering herself to me and I was accepting and something in my consciousness was shifting, righting itself.

"Are you ready?" I heard myself ask. I stopped briefly to wonder if I was ready, but I didn't have to look far within myself to
feel, incredibly, that I was. Hilary lifted her chin and nodded up to
me. Her arms were still behind her and I wanted to move in closer,
was moving in closer, stepped in close enough that the toe of my
boot pressed against the knee of her jeans. I reached for the nape
of her neck and dug my fingers into her hair.

Hilary's hair was soft and fine and delicate. I took the wisps
between my fingers, holding tightly enough to control her movements but not hard enough, yet, to hurt. I pulled her in against the
front of my leg, gazing down as she gazed up. She was taller than
me, but not here, not on her knees, not looking up with wide eyes.
The room shimmered like a camera coming into focus. We were
doing this. I was doing this.

Around us, other partygoers walked by, a few pausing to glance
at our scene. I froze for a moment, imagining myself through outside eyes, but when I looked back down at Hilary on her knees,
her face pressed against me, my insecurity receded. I kept my left
hand in her hair and ran the other down her cheek, over her bare
shoulders, smooth, warm skin that was suddenly, improbably,
mine to touch, and breathed with her there until my chest swelled
again with the steely certainty of my own power.

I wanted to hurt her. Wanted to know how her body looked
taking pain, what sounds she'd make, how deep under her skin I
could get. I reached for her face again, took her chin in my hand.
It felt like taking a liberty, intimate and condescending. "Stand
up," I said, and her breath caught when I tugged at her soft hair.
"I'm going to hit you now."

I moved her toward the wall. Lifted her by her hair and she
stumbled upwards, guided her face-forward, stopping her with a
hand on her collarbone. She made a little sigh as she jolted toward
the wall, pleased and vulnerable, and I wanted to hear more. The

nape of her neck was warm under my hand and I tugged at the hair in my fingers to hear her voice catch.

Kink was a miracle. Stepping into the space of someone who wanted you there, hurting someone who wanted you to hurt them, breathing together in the delicious haze of intimacy and intensity. This was why I kept coming to these parties: the outside chance of feeling exactly as sharp and joyful and hungry and *right* as I felt right now.

Was Hilary feeling it too? I turned her head to the side to see her face. "How are you doing?" I asked, and her voice was breathy in answer.

"Good. You're good at this."

Was I good at this? Wasn't I too new, too ace, too hesitant, too inexperienced? But the soaring feeling in my chest told me everything I needed to know. I breathed in, pulled harder at Hilary's hair, and sighed at the sound of her gasp, and the worry was gone.

I was going to hit her. I loosed my grip on her hair and readied myself, my hands palm-open against the broad flats of her shoulders. Then I stepped back and pushed forward, a gentle slap to start. Hilary made a small sigh and stumbled forward against the wall. My palms tingled with the impact. I felt myself grin.

I hit her again, and again, letting more of my weight fall each time into her bare, available skin. Her sighs became grunts; her expression, when I leaned in close enough for eye contact, was dreamy and vague. I wanted to be closer in, more in her space, more under her skin. There were red marks on her shoulders. The right one looked like an imprint of my hand, fingers outlined in flushed skin. Her body, marked up with mine. I hit her again, harder. Her body sagged against the wall and I drank her unsteadiness in.

I was aware of my own body but focused on hers, the hug of the boot shafts on my calves, shoulders loose and back and relaxed, each hit fluid if not graceful. Something that felt like joy in my throat, cheeks alive with grinning. I wanted—I think we both wanted—our scene to last forever.

After more hits, Hilary murmured something, and I paused and leaned in. "Do you want to try pinching me?" she said, when I asked her to repeat herself.

I had almost forgotten we'd meant for me to pinch her too, and I felt a welling of gratitude to Hilary for reminding me, for wanting this, for wanting me. "Yes," I said. "Do you?" She nodded so vigorously I could feel the strands of hair in my hand tighten and go slack.

Nobody taught pinching in kink classes. It was too straightforward, too low-risk, too unskilled. If all you had to do to top was press a fold of skin between your fingers, then anyone could top. *I* could top. I tugged at Hilary's hair, gently this time, and told her to turn and face me. She followed my lead.

I ran my hand along her biceps, fleshy and warm and mine to touch. I gathered skin between my thumb and index finger, closed my fingers together until I felt resistance, until Hilary breathed in sharp through her nose, her jaw set, eyes wide and locked softly on mine. She whimpered a little and I let go, rubbing the spot I'd been holding. "You okay?" It was still hard to remember that she had chosen this, that she really did like pain, that some people loved to bottom, that the things I wanted to do were things a lot of people wanted done.

Hilary's face was flushed, her voice quiet and breathy. "I'm good. I like this a lot."

That feeling of gratitude welled in my chest again. "Me too."

I liked the intimacy of it. I liked controlling the intensity, moment to moment. I liked our eye contact, the way I could watch her watching me hurt her, a dizzying feedback loop. I pulled out another fold on her biceps and pinched again, longer this time, watching her fight the sensation and then surrender. I held her there, letting her gasp and whimper, feeling myself grow bigger and more alive. I let go and tried the other arm. Hilary swayed against the wall and I held out my free hand to steady her. I let go and pinched again. And again. Eyes and whimpers and breath and my cheeks split open grinning. My thumb was tired. I didn't care.

Eventually, Hilary reached her free arm back and tapped my hip. "I don't think I can stand up anymore."

I thought about having her kneel. About making her put her arms behind her back and pinching her again while she gazed up at me, while I held her body close. But the pause made me more aware of the ache in my fingers and a dryness in my throat. As much as I wanted to keep going, maybe it was time.

"Do you want to wrap up?"

Hilary nodded, tugging gently at the hair in my hand. "I don't want to," she whispered. "But yeah."

I helped her to the floor. She draped herself over my boots and wrapped her arms around my legs, and I stroked her hair as she leaned against me. My heart felt filled up, and my face hurt from grinning. Hilary smiled too, her body slumping against mine. After a while, I sat down next to her, and we held each other there for a still, seemingly infinite moment.

Hilary spoke first. "Definitely not boring," she murmured into my shoulder.

"What?" I said, and then laughed. I'd forgotten I'd even worried about topping with my bare hands not being enough. "Oh. No, not boring at all."

"You made this face when you were hurting me," she said, and I tried to brace myself to be embarrassed but found I could only muster calm curiosity. "Like you were, I don't know, an orchestra conductor."

I gave a small laugh. "Yeah?"

"Like you were in the center of the stage, and you ran the show, and you were channeling all your passion and focus and art into . . . I don't know. Into something that felt really good."

I tried to imagine what she'd seen, me with my purple hair and my shimmery boots, holding myself like some kind of kink maestro. I couldn't picture it, but somehow, I believed her.

We returned to our bench and chatted a while longer. When scenes started wrapping up around us, and Hilary gave a yawn and I yawned too, I said I thought it was time to go.

"There's another party next month," Hilary said, as we took the rickety elevator back to street level. "I was thinking you could come with me, if you want."

I thought about walking into another party with a friend and play partner. A friend who wore an ace flag with pride, a friend who saw me in my newness and believed I was enough. I thought about Hilary at my feet again, the heady feeling of power flowing between us. It wouldn't matter what anyone else thought; I'd know I belonged there. We both belonged there.

"I'd love that," I said, as the elevator doors creaked open. We walked through them together, both still glowing.

BRIDESMAIDS

Katrina Jackson

I came here for True Lucas.

I mean, sure, whatever. Technically, I came here to be my cousin Janea's bridesmaid alongside True, but in reality, I came here to get with my childhood crush.

Again.

I met True when I was twelve. She was fourteen and the finest girl I'd ever seen not in a music video. From that moment on, I compared every crush I ever had and every girl I ever dated with True Lucas, and they all came up wanting.

I thought I got over True in college when I met my ex. She and I dated on and off for six years, and the whole time, I forgot about True. Or I pretended to forget about True. It helped that I never saw True except on my cousin's social media, and I could pretend that the hitch I felt in my gut whenever I did come across a picture of her was just nostalgia.

But then I broke up with my ex for good three years ago. In my post-breakup ho phase, I decided to take a trip to Atlanta to visit Janea. Just 'cause. No ulterior motives. Janea invited me to come party with her, and I took her up on the offer. Innocent.

Janea's boyfriend Keith—now very soon-to-be husband—was a party promoter and always made sure to get her into the hottest spots in Buckhead. We'd been in the VIP section for barely an hour when True showed up, and before she even looked at me, I knew that I'd been lying to myself.

I'd never gotten over her.

True bounced up the steps to our area, and when I say bounced, I mean there wasn't a part of her that didn't jiggle, and I drank in the sight. She was wearing some short, tight, low-cut dress that drew my eye—and I assume everyone else's—to the fact that True and I were fully grown now. Seeing her for the first time in years felt like a punch in the gut, but in a good way. I'd never felt anything like it with my ex. Suddenly, all those years of longing hit me harder than the bourbon, and I knew it was finally time to make my move. Janea reintroduced us, and I decided not to miss this chance.

"Oh, my god, little Renee?" True said, pulling me into a hug.

"Little?" I asked while wrapping my arms around her body.

Most of my family called me "little Renee" no matter how tall I got or how much weight or muscle I gained, and Janea's friends followed suit whether they knew me well or not. I wouldn't normally have minded, but the last thing I wanted was for True to see me as the twelve-year-old girl who used to follow her and Janea around like a shadow. So, I moved my hands to her waist.

"Little?" I said again, though this time I whispered the word into her ear and squeezed her soft flesh.

I heard a soft intake of breath as we pulled apart, and I smiled in triumph. Whatever she'd thought before, she didn't see me as "little Renee" anymore.

I poured her a drink and picked up my own, watching her over the rim of my glass as I took a sip.

I was buzzed and enjoying the atmosphere before True showed

up, but watching her lips wrap around the rim of her glass and her tongue trace the spill of liquid from the corner of her mouth while she locked eyes with me made this a damn good night. It didn't take long for the night to go from better to best.

Maybe half an hour later, I ran into True in the hallway near the VIP bathrooms. She appeared out of nowhere. I was holding the bathroom door open with my foot while I leaned away to toss a paper towel into the trash can. When I turned back to the door, True was standing in front of me.

"Shit," I exclaimed. "Where'd you come from?"

She stared at me for a little too long—enough time for me to realize that she was probably as faded as I was. "My bad. I wasn't trying to scare you," she purred, a lopsided, too-big grin that I found charming as fuck on her face.

"If you weren't trying to scare me, then what were you trying to do?" I asked, feeling myself because that grin told me everything I needed to know. My question was a challenge, and True didn't disappoint.

Her lips crashed into mine, and I pulled her back into the bathroom with me, locking the door behind us. True slipped her tongue past my lips and snaked her fingers into the collar of my shirt. When I finally—after over a decade—moved my hand around True's body and palmed the globes of her ass and squeezed? That moment and the moan I tasted on True's tongue was like every dream I'd ever had come true.

True pressed her back against the door, pulling me possessively along.

"Damn, girl," I muttered.

True laughed and swiped her tongue across my bottom lip before kissing me again. She tasted like gin and cranberry and mint. She felt like heaven and gentle curves, and I made sure to massage her ass, the ass that had been the center of my fantasies for years. True groaned, and I licked that sound from the depths of her mouth.

"I've had dreams about this ass," I mumbled, sucking her bottom lip into my mouth. I moved a hand over her hips, appreciating every dip and curve and the way the clingy fabric of her dress gave way to warm, smooth skin under my fingertips.

She shivered and spread her legs for me. "What were you thinking about doing with this ass if you ever got your hands on it?" she asked with a smirk on her face. Her red lipstick was smeared across her mouth, and somehow, that made all this filthier.

That was the kind of question that didn't need a verbal answer, so I didn't waste any more time.

I moved my hand between her legs, brushing the back of my hand and fingers against her inner thighs, touching every inch of warm skin at every chance.

True sucked in a sharp breath and held it, watching me with hooded eyes and panting breaths as I cupped her pussy, telling her, even though I didn't have the right, that it was mine. She smiled and exhaled on a loud moan that I felt all over my skin. She started shivering again as I pulled the thin, wet fabric of her panties aside.

"How long you been this wet?" I asked.

"Gin makes me horny." Her voice was shaking almost as bad as her body.

I moved the pads of my fingers up and down her lips, watching her brace herself for my touch.

Her hands smoothed over my shoulders to slip under my jacket and cup my breasts. "No bra? Nothing?" she asked with a smile.

My eyes went to her chest, where her dress had slipped down, and her breasts were damn near spilling out. I licked my lips, tasting True's lipstick on my tongue. I pressed two fingers inside of her.

True's moan was so delicate that I was almost shocked when she pushed her dress down to uncover her breasts for me. Her thumbs brushed over her nipples, and I lowered my mouth to suck hungrily on her right nipple.

She lifted her left leg and wrapped it around my hip, grinding her pussy against the palm of my hand.

I moved my thumb to her clit.

She cried out on a laugh, and there was something about the way her groaning panting breaths were wrapped in smiles and laughter that crawled under my skin. I moved up to crash my mouth against hers again while I settled my hips between her legs and started fucking her with my fingers.

We settled into a rhythm quickly, as if we both knew there was no more time to waste. I pushed a third finger inside of her, and she sucked on my tongue as she moaned. Soon enough, True was riding my hand so hard we were slamming against the door behind us.

"Fuck, baby, I'm gonna come," she moaned into my mouth.

I tightened my grip on her ass and squeezed, moving her harder and faster against me. "Then come. Come all over my hand."

True didn't even try to be quiet, and I loved that shit. Her pussy clenched around my fingers, and she screamed just as I told her. She came all over my fingers, her release pooling in my palm and running down my wrist. She wrapped her arms around my shoulders and buried her face into my neck, shivering against me as her pussy pulsed around my fingers. Her dress was bunched around her waist, and I massaged her bare ass and clit while her breath returned to normal.

"Fuck, Renee," she breathed against my skin.

I thought about her smearing that red lipstick all over me, and I was just about to tell her that I wanted that for real when someone started banging on the bathroom door.

We jumped apart.

True started fixing her dress, and I moved to the sink to wash my hands. I dried my hands and swiped a paper towel across my face. When I looked up, I saw True unlocking the door and slipping out without even a goodbye.

By the time I made it back to VIP, Janea and Keith were fighting.

We had to pull my cousin out of the club. True and her friend Karma called a ride, while me and Janea's best friend Amaya steered her toward the closest Waffle House.

I was in Atlanta for two more days, but I never saw True again.

That was three years ago.

So, when Janea asked me to be one of her bridesmaids, I only needed to know two things: Could I wear a suit? And who else was in her bridal party?

True Lucas was the third name she listed. I said yes and started working on a plan.

I could've gotten dressed at the wedding venue, but I didn't want to get up at the crack of dawn to do all that goofy bridesmaids stuff my cousin scheduled after driving all night to get to Atlanta. I loved Janea—but not eight in the morning massage and facial love her. I was good with getting a few extra hours of sleep and showing up in my perfectly tailored suit because the other reason I didn't want to get ready at the venue was that I wanted to look my absolute best the first time I saw True Lucas after three years.

I'd missed the rehearsal, so when I got to the Botanical Gardens, I got lost trying to find the bridal party suite, and the staff person I asked for directions clearly looked at my suit and sent me to the groomsmen's dressing room, where the first person I saw was Keith, Janea's future husband, holding the biggest bottle of Hennessy I'd ever seen.

"Aye, what's up, cousin?" Keith called.

I smiled politely back and wondered if whatever drunken she-nanigans were about to go down over here were my penance for not waking up for that massage. "What's going on, Keith?"

"Ah, nothing," he said casually. "Just, you know, about to get married. Yo, your suit is fly."

I'm not terribly vain, but I'm also not one to turn down a compliment. I smoothed my hands over my lapels so Keith didn't miss the impeccable tailoring I'd paid a grip for. The specific shade of lavender Janea chose for her bridesmaids wasn't normally my color, but the right tailoring could make damn near anything work, I'd found.

Keith brushed his hand over my shoulder. "I should've sent my dudes to your tailor." He rolled his eyes toward his dressing room.

"I'll send you her card."

"Bet."

"Actually, I'm lost. Which way is Janea's dressing room? I need to get there before—"

"Where the fuck is Renee?"

Keith and I both cringed at the sound of Janea's voice, but while I was shocked into stillness, I watched with an open mouth as the groom ducked into his dressing room and closed the door without another word. I wanted to be mad at him but also wanted to follow him inside and hide. But since I couldn't, I took a deep breath and headed toward the sound of her voice. I tried to prepare for the worst while reminding myself that whatever monster in silk I encountered wasn't my cousin; she was just a perfectly made-up shade of the person I loved freaking out about this special day. Or whatever.

I rounded a corner into a long hallway. I saw Janea's dress first and took a deep breath before she saw me. I wasn't prepared to see my cousin's rage-filled face relax into a pretty, almost serene smile as soon as she saw me. "Oh, there you are. That color looks perfect on you! It's time for group pictures. Let's go."

I let out a relieved breath when she turned away, only to come face to face with True Lucas standing just behind Janea, looking fine as fuck and staring at me with soft eyes and that same filthy grin on her mouth. She looked thicker than the last time I'd seen her, and if I were the praying type, I would have sent up a silent thanks to God for that. Her floor-length dress, in the same color lavender as my suit, hugged every new rounder curve. The sweetheart neckline made those titties I hadn't gotten nearly enough time with three years ago look full and ripe, threatening the integrity of that dress in the best way.

I watched her scrape her teeth across her bottom lip as she watched me watching her. I opened my mouth to say I don't even know what, but Janea was having none of that.

"I said, let's go," she barked.

True and I both jumped. Her breasts jiggled gently, but Janea's warning tone didn't even give me the space to appreciate that.

I sighed and headed down the hallway behind True, my eyes on that ass until the last second.

We made it through the wedding with as little drama as possible. I mean, yeah, one of Keith's groomsmen tried to propose to his boyfriend right after the vows, but Janea told him to cough up three thousand dollars toward the bill for the venue or keep it cute and mute. He chose the latter, and the rest of the wedding ceremony went off without a hitch.

I started looking for True as soon as the reception started. I went around to all the tables, ostensibly to say hello to my parents and the rest of my family, but really, I had my eye out for True's bare brown shoulder or curly ponytail at every table I passed. I finally found her at the mouth of the hallway that led back to the bridal party dressing room.

She was on her phone, leaning against the wall.

I tried to play it cool. "Hey."

She didn't acknowledge me, so I cleared my throat and tried again. "Hey, True, what's up?" I swear to God, my voice squeaked.

Her fingers stopped swiping across her phone. She lifted her head slowly and smirked. "Hey? That's all you have to say after three years?"

I'm not easily shocked, but I was shocked.

True crossed her arms under her breasts, which only made the precarity of that neckline even more stressful and also made my concentration waver. I tried to moderate how long I spent looking at her cleavage and her face but failed miserably.

She chuckled low, the sound reverberating across the distance between us. I felt it all over my skin, even if it was the tiniest bit mocking. "Mmhmm. Imagine if you'd called me three years ago. You wouldn't be looking at my titties like a starving child right now."

"I doubt that, but you could've called me too, you know?"

"Didn't you just finally break up with your stalker last time I saw you?"

"She only stalked me that one time."

"Is there a one stalking free pass?"

"Besides, she pled out, paid her fine, and did her community service."

"Anyway, my point is that I assumed you needed some time to get over all that." She punctuated those last two words with rolled eyes and a dismissive hand wave. "That's why *I* didn't call *you*. What's your excuse?"

"Damn."

"Mmhmm."

"I didn't—"

"Clearly."

"My bad."

"It was."

"Are you gonna let me talk or just give me shit?"

"Depends. Are you going to say something worthwhile? Or can you think of a better way to make your mistake up to me?"

Those questions—that challenge—let loose that punch to my gut that I'd been waiting three years to feel again. I moved down the hall with slow, deliberate steps. I stopped in front of her, close enough that I could smell her perfume. Peaches.

Now that I was close, she wasn't nearly as mouthy. In fact, she didn't even speak. She licked her lips and swallowed thick and loud, which honestly was a great description of her.

"Let's go," I breathed.

She took another deep breath and turned to walk down the hallway toward the dressing room. Once again, I followed her with my gaze firmly planted on her ass.

The reception was in full swing, but once I closed and locked the door, it all faded away. All I could hear was True's soft gasp when I reached out, grabbed her waist, and spun her around to me.

"I've been waiting three years for this," she whispered against my tongue pressing into her mouth.

"I've been waiting since I was twelve for you," I admitted.

"I know," she said, walking backward toward a couch against the nearest wall.

I should be shocked to hear that she knew about my childhood crush, but I'd never been quiet about it. Besides, what was there to be ashamed about? Especially when True pushed me down onto the couch and shimmied her hips as she pulled her dress up to her waist.

"Fuck," I breathed, watching as she spread her thick thighs to straddle my hips and lower herself onto my lap.

I placed my hands on her thighs. Her skin was just as smooth as I remembered. Maybe even smoother.

She took in a shaky breath as my hands moved toward the crease of her thighs. And then her hands were on the button of my slacks, stilling, asking for silent consent to keep going.

I looked up at her, and it was my turn to take a shaky breath in. I nodded and she undid my pants.

"I used to have the dirtiest dreams about you," I whispered, spreading my legs for her and pushing my right hand fully between her thighs.

Her hand snaked into my underwear and brushed the curls of my sex. We both jumped when her fingers grazed my clit. She grinned at me and began to gently caress my lips, lowering her mouth close enough to mine that I could taste the mint on her breath. "What did you dream about doing to me, baby?"

I moved her panties to the side. Her pussy was hot and wet, and she shuddered as I pushed my fingers inside of her. She released a warm puff of air that ended with a soft, sexy squeak of a moan.

I lifted my head and covered her mouth with mine. Kissing True Lucas was everything I thought it would be, every time.

"Can I put my fingers in you?" she moaned against my lips.

I nodded because I didn't want to stop kissing her, and then I moaned as her thick fingers pressed inside of me. I gave her another finger in return.

"Fuck," we breathed together, and that was the last thing we said for a while.

Our hands worked on each other in the quiet room that wasn't quiet anymore. We ground our hips toward one another's hands, pressing our clits into each other's palms and begging for more and more. Soon enough, the room was filled with the sounds of my moans mixed with True's, and our clothes rustling as we tried to get as close as possible to one another, and the wet sounds of our kisses.

Somewhere in the back of my mind, I realized that I was

missing my favorite cousin's wedding, but I couldn't muster up enough of a care to stop. I assumed Janea would understand. And if she didn't, this was worth her annoyance.

I broke our kiss and pulled True's dress down again.

"Oh, fuck, yes," she groaned as I sucked one of her nipples into my mouth. And then I watched as she lifted the heavy weight of her breast and brought the other nipple to her own mouth. There were perfect women, and then there was True Lucas.

I came all over her fingers.

Naturally, she grinned triumphantly at me as she snaked her hand from my pants and licked me from her fingers, still grinding her pussy down onto my hand.

If I had to miss a wedding for anything, it was this.

"I want to taste you," I told her, although it would have been more accurate to say that I needed her pussy on my mouth.

I think she understood that, though, because she hopped up from my lap immediately.

She took my place on the couch and began to roll her nipples between her fingers, watching me like a hawk as I slowly lowered myself to the floor and peeled her panties down her legs.

"This isn't going to be enough," she groaned as I bent her right leg and lifted it to the couch. "Last time wasn't enough, and this won't be, either." Her breath hitched as I ran my hands up her thighs and then back, spreading her pussy for my own visual enjoyment.

"Who says it has to be enough?" I asked, bending down to swipe my tongue up her lips, tasting True Lucas's pussy for the very first time.

Her body shuddered, and she moaned again. "Don't tease me."

"Answer my question," I breathed over her clit, tasting her between words.

She was breathless and panting, licking at her left nipple while she watched me. "We see each other once every three years," she said, lifting her hips toward my mouth. "That's not enough."

I took my time dragging my tongue over every inch of her, swirling around her clit, swiping up and down her lips, dipping inside her, imprinting her taste on my tongue.

"Ooh, fuck, yes. Right there, baby."

I smiled against her pussy because I was pretty sure "right there" meant anywhere by the way she was trying to grind her pussy against my face. I could stay here forever, but I don't just yet.

True whimpered and whined.

I kissed her inner thighs and pushed her legs open just a little bit more, marveling at how beautiful her pussy was from every fucking angle.

"Janea didn't tell you?" I asked, teasing but impatient to taste her again.

"Tell me what?" she whined, circling her hips at me.

"That I just moved here."

She smiled, relieved and just as impatient.

"Fuck. Thank God," she whispered. "Oh, fuck, yes, right there."

I dove back between her legs now that that was settled.

If I missed the entire wedding, I'd have to live with that—because I came here for True fucking Lucas, and I got her.

A YEAR OF LOVE,
AN EVENING OF LUST

Quenby

Madam bared her teeth in a sadistic grin as Jamie squirmed next to her in the taxi. Ze'd looked so handsome when she saw hir earlier, bouncing out of the bathroom, preening in a navy blue shirt, paired with red chinos and a matching bow tie, suspenders, and boots. Ze'd been so pretty and composed ready for a dignified date with hir girlfriend . . . no fucking way. So she'd had no choice but to take her precious Jamie apart with tongue, and fingers, and a remote controlled plug still buried in hir ass. Now here ze was, blushing, disheveled, with lipstick smeared around hir mouth and an achingly hard cock barely concealed by hir fly—perfect for their filthy anniversary plans.

Jamie was in hir own world of exquisite torment. Ze was torn between the visceral knot of humiliation twisted in hir stomach and the burning arousal that accompanied it, dilating hir pupils and flushing hir face. Ze clenched around the plug that held the delicious potential to reduce hir to a trembling mess. Jamie knew that ze could end this torment any time ze wanted, but knew ze wanted this every bit as much as Madam. Ze looked over at her and bit hir lip, it was utterly unfair how good she looked! She looked so composed with that immaculate outfit and her hand casually resting on the cane between her knees. A blue dress clung to the gorgeous curves of her asymmetric tits and squishy belly, paired with knee-high leather boots and a bare cunt Jamie longed to worship. Ze knew she'd eschewed panties because it drove hir to frenzied distraction. Ze wasn't sure if ze loved or hated her for that. And on top of all this Jamie had big news impatiently waiting to leap from hir tongue. Later—ze'd tell her later, after they'd celebrated their year together.

The taxi dropped them off just around the corner from the restaurant, and they gently strolled down the street. As usual, Jamie allowed Madam to set the pace, not wanting to tire her out. She took it slow, appreciating the warm air caressing her skin, blissfully content with her walking stick in one hand and her boyfriend in the other. Just before they got to the door she pulled hir to one side, and they kissed against the wall.

"When we get in, I want you to go straight to the bathroom and stroke your cock. I want you to think about me as you stroke the head, grip the shaft, and tease the plug in your pretty little ass. And when you feel like you're about to orgasm, when you feel your cock desperate for release, then I want you to stop. Okay?" She watched the blush spread across hir face, a delicious cocktail of excitement and humiliated arousal as ze contemplated this.

Of course ze might say no: there was always that option, but she knew Jamie better than that. This was exactly the kind of degrading filth her boyfriend dreamed about. "Yes Madam." She smirked to herself as ze peeled off while she walked to the table, anticipating a fun evening. While Jamie touched hirself in the bathroom she ordered for both of them, then sent a couple of messages to check everything was lined up for later.

Jamie returned just in time for the starters, flushed and pouting. They shared melted goat's cheese, dragging bread through the cheese and chutney, and making appreciative noises. Once they'd finished the bread, Madam stuck her index finger into the cheese and scooped out the last morsels. Feeling Jamie's eyes fixated on her, she stuck out her tongue and used the tip to tease the goopy mess. She closed her eyes, sighing in satisfaction at the rich, pungent cheese dissolving on her tongue. She opened her eyes and saw hir eyes, eyes heavy with lust. Slowly she reached across the table and slipped her finger into hir mouth, watching Jamie's expression as she felt hir tongue swirl around her finger. "Good boy, I love you." Her heart swelled as ze buried a big goofy grin in hir hands and wriggled happily.

As she pulled back her hand, Madam's face twisted with an unexpected jolt of pain. "Are you okay?" Jamie's voice dropped its soft, subby cadences, ringing with tender care for hir girlfriend.

"Just a bit of pain, I've got my pills in my bag. Sorry." She smiled back at her dork of a boyfriend—touched by hir empathy, and slightly annoyed at her body.

"Nope. You know the rules, no apologizing for your disability." Jamie's teasing tone softened the words.

She rolled her eyes and stuck her tongue out at hir. "Fiiiine, I'll try and be more like a straight, white cis man and never apologize for anything."

"That's not what I—you're a dick sometimes, you know?!" Jamie huffed in mock exasperation. They sat giggling at their shared silliness while Madam swallowed her evening meds. "How are you doing? Do you want to carry on?" Jamie reached out and gently squeezed her hand as ze spoke.

Madam took a moment to consider this. "Well my fatigue isn't playing up at the moment and the meds should settle the pain . . . I think I'm happy to carry on if you are. Thank you for checking in."

"Love you Madam."

She squeezed hir hand once again. "Love you too, Jamie." She slipped her hand into the bag and pulled out her phone and remote control. She turned on the plug and grinned as Jamie fought the urge to squirm in hir seat. While ze was distracted she sent a message to set the next part of her plan in motion. She smiled as Brick and Carla approached from the bar, waving them over. Jamie twisted in hir seat and whimpered softly as the plug shifted in hir ass. Smirking, she thumbed the control and turned it off.

Brick was broad-shouldered, bald, and bearded, with hands like shovels and a deep, posh voice. Despite their imposing build, they were a teddy bear: gentle and caring to a fault. Carla was slender, with brown skin and shoulder-length curls. She spoke with a Mexican lilt and a sharp tongue that loved to tease friends, lovers, and herself. The couples chatted with each other, pretending it was a pleasant surprise for everyone involved. Again Jamie had to bite hir tongue, wanting to share hir news with their friends but afraid of hijacking the evening.

Madam smiled to herself, Jamie had shared hir fantasy of being used as a toy by these two and they'd added it to their long list of things to try. What ze didn't know was that she'd spoken to them and arranged a surprise. Brick and Carla made their excuses and kissed Madam's hand goodbye. "Oh, I think Jamie's feeling left out, would you like them to kiss you farewell too?" A sadistic grin twisted her face as ze blinked like a deer in headlights.

"Would you like that Jamie?" Carla asked, with a grin to match Madam.

Blushing furiously, ze just about managed to squeak out a "Yes." Brick cupped Jamie's cheek and gave hir a deep, passionate kiss on the lips. Carla laughed at the soft gasp Jamie let out as Brick pulled away, then leaned in. She gently bit Jamie's lip before slipping her tongue into hir agape mouth.

Madam waited until they were out of earshot before speaking again. "Did you enjoy that, Jamie?"

It took a moment for her flustered boyfriend to gather hir thoughts "Yes! But also . . . you embarrassed me!"

"Awwwww, poor you," she chuckled at hir answering pout. "Well I think you should go to the bathroom. I have a surprise waiting for you there."

Jamie's eyes widened and Madam felt a twinge of uncertainty. "Are you okay with this? I know we talked about it bu—" she stopped as ze nodded enthusiastically.

Ze stood up and leaned over to kiss her. "They know red is your safeword. Just remember Jamie, this evening your orgasms belong to me."

"Yes Madam," Jamie replied in a voice thick with lust.

Jamie walked through to the bathrooms and paused—they were single occupancy and ze wasn't sure which to pick. As ze hesitated hands grabbed hir from behind, pulling hir hair back to kiss hir neck, before pushing hir into the nearest bathroom. Brick was waiting, their cock already hard and wrapped in latex. They pinned Jamie's hands over hir head and began kissing hir on the lips and neck. Carla had locked the door behind herself, now she unzipped Jamie's chinos and took hir cock in her mouth. Brick grinned as they felt Jamie moan into the kiss. Carla was sucking hir enthusiastically, filling the small room with filthy, wet noises. As she began to fuck the plug into hir ass as well, Jamie pulled away from Carla's kiss.

"My uh—unghh—-Madam said—oh, fuck—Madam said I couldn't cuuuuh—come without her permission."

Brick and Carla shared a laugh. "Oh, we know that," replied Brick.

"But she never said we couldn't torture you." Sadistic glee resonated in Carla's voice. She grinned up at Jamie's face, drinking in the look of desperation that twisted it as she edged hir once again. She leaned in to lick a dribble of precome off hir cock, then leaned back as ze desperately bucked hir hips toward the sensation.

"I think it's time we showed the slut hir place," Brick chuckled. They pulled hir away from the wall, then pushed hir down onto all fours. Carla pulled out the plug and used their bright purple strap-on to rub more lube against hir asshole, Jamie pushed back hungrily, feeling desperately empty without the plug. Brick slipped a metal ring gag into hir mouth, forcing it wide open, helpless and ready for their cock. Ze felt Carla's hands on hir hips and let out a guttural moan as she buried herself in hir ass. The moan was cut short as Brick began to thrust into hir mouth. The two quickly settled into a rhythm. Jamie felt degraded and dehumanized, a fucktoy who only existed to be used. Ze reveled in hir nothingness.

All too soon, the rhythm broke down. First, Carla began to fuck into hir more urgently and erratically. Finally she pulled out, and slipped her fingers down to her needy clit, frantically touching herself as she watched the scene play out in front of her. Then Brick pulled out the ring gag.

"Kneel in front of me and stick your tongue out. I'm going to come on it and you're not going to swallow. I want you to give that to Madam when you kiss her at the table." Their gasped words hadn't been a question, but ze nodded anyway. Carla moaned in desperate need as Brick frantically stroked themself. Jamie got in position just in time, as soon as hir tongue was sticking out Brick's cock pulsed and spurted hot come into and around hir mouth. Ze obediently held it on hir tongue as Carla smeared her own fluids and Brick's excess, over Jamie's top lip, filling hir nose with the tantalizing scents.

The couple kissed hir once again, careful not to disturb the prized mouthful. "That was hot . . . but next time we're going to take it nice and slow and explore every inch of your gorgeous body." Jamie blushed and nodded at Carla's words, hir mind swimming with delicious potential.

Madam smiled as a disheveled Jamie walked back over to her, ze leaned in for a kiss and she reached up to meet hir. Her eyes widened in surprise as hir tongue shared its prize with her, then hers reached out and began to roll the mess of come between their mouths. Her cunt grew even hungrier, a drip of wetness rolled down her thigh and she wished that she d been the one in the bathroom instead. They pulled apart as their main courses arrived: steak with sautéed potatoes and peas for her, salmon with rice and char-grilled vegetables for hir. As they tucked into their food she slid her leather-clad foot up hir leg until her boot was pressed against hir sensitive cock. Ze jumped and looked up at her, but she remained pointedly focused on the meal in front of her. As they consumed their food she alternated between gently teasing hir cock and balls and grinding them beneath her feet like a cigarette butt. Jamie was desperately trying to keep hirself under control, fighting the urge to squeal and moan and beg. Somehow they made it to the end of the meal without hir publicly disgracing hirself. When the waiter came over asking about desserts, Madam briefly considered extending Jamie's torment. But she was way too horny for more games now: she wanted to get hir home (and herself off) as soon as possible.

Jamie squirmed in the back of the taxi. Madam had turned the plug on for the whole journey home and hir cock was achingly hard and agonizingly needy. Hir hunger was reflected in Madam's face, her mask of domly composure melting in the face of intense desire for her gorgeous boyfriend. She leaned over and whispered in hir ear, "I'm going to take longer to get into the flat. By the time I arrive I want a cup of tea and a vibrator on my table, and you kneeling in front of my armchair wearing nothing but your hood. Don't disappoint me."

As soon as the car stopped ze bolted through the door, fly-ing up the stairs driven by hir desire to please Madam. She took her time and made good use of her walking stick, not wanting to overexert herself and keen to give Jamie a chance to be ready in time. She left her cane by the door when she entered the flat, then followed the corridor down to the living room. Kneeling in front of her armchair, next to a cup of green tea gently steaming on the side table, was her beautiful boyfriend. A leather hood covering hir entire face, with only a mouth hole for hir to breathe through and service her. The butt plug was still buzzing away, and hir cock was gorgeously swollen and needy. It took all her self-control not to straddle hir then and there, but she knew ze wanted to wait. Ze wanted to feel like a degraded little fucktoy, a collection of wet holes waiting to be used whenever and however she wanted to. So instead she sank into the armchair. She took a moment to enjoy the weight lifting off her feet, and breathe in the aroma of fresh tea. Then, as she sipped her tea, Madam's boot slid between Jamie's knees, pressing against hir cock. Sub-consciously, ze began to rub against the soft leather in desperate search of friction.

"Such a filthy little slut, humping my boot like a mindless animal. My desperate little fucktoy to use however I want." As she spoke, Madam replaced the tea with a vibrator and began to finger herself while it rumbled against her clit. The first orgasm came easily, an amuse-bouche which only teased her ravenous cunt. The second, inspired by Jamie's helpless whimpers as ze ground against her boot, took a little longer but still she was hungry. Madam switched off hir plug and got up, pulling off her dress. She shoved her fingers into hir wet, pliant mouth until ze choked, the obedient throat convulsing around her hand. She pushed Jamie down onto hir back and lowered her cunt onto hir face. Ze moaned and dived in with a frantic hunger, hir talented tongue joined by eager fingers as ze worshipped her cunt. Jamie alternated between gentle strokes and vigorous thrusts, loving licks and mauling teeth. She threw her head back and moaned as orgasms came thick and fast, one rolling into the next. Then, as her legs began to tremble with overstimulation and exertion, she gasped out a command. "Make me squirt all over you, I wanna drench my slutty little fucktoy." Jamie whimpered in desperate arousal, then hir obedient fingers curled inside her, relentlessly massaging her G-spot. Ze sucked hard on her clit, hir teeth gently gripped the sensitive flesh. Her lip trembled at the intense sensation, straddling the boundary between pleasure and pain as ze rolled her clit between hir teeth. Finally, she felt a familiar roiling ball of pleasure building within her, and Madam threw back her head and let out a full-throated scream as she squirted, soaking Jamie in her fluids.

She raised herself up onto her knees and unzipped the hood. She cupped Jamie's flushed face in her hands, feeling the mix of sweat, saliva, and her own wetness clinging to her skin and soaking hir ruffled hair. "Fuck you're so good at that, I love you so much Jamie." The words came out in a breathless tumble and ze smiled in response, too deep in subspace to form a coherent sentence.

"You know what I want now? I want to hold you in my arms and kiss you as you come deep into my cunt." The broad grin and hungry gleam in hir eyes was all the confirmation she needed. Madam slid down Jamie's body till she reached the achingly hard cock she'd been teasing all evening. Slowly she lowered herself onto it, feeling inch after inch sink into her well-fucked cunt until ze was fully inside her. She leaned forward onto her arms and they shared a kiss filled with searing passion as Jamie began to thrust up into her. She met hir thrusts in an exquisite symphony of movement, letting out soft moans as their bodies moved in urgent unison. She felt hir cock throb inside her and softly moaned into hir ear, "Fill me with your come Jamie." A desperate, primal scream exploded from hir throat as the long-awaited orgasm was finally granted. Ze arched up into her, letting out a soft-choked sob at the overwhelming sensations. Then hir hips flopped down, tension draining from hir body.

Slowly, Madam lifted herself off of hir cock, reveling in the sensation of her boyfriend's come oozing from her satiated cunt and dripping onto the wood floor. They lay together for a few minutes as their bodies recovered from the frantic exertion. Then—slowly, gently—Madam raised Jamie to hir feet and led hir to the nest of pillows and blankets ze had prepared for them on the sofa before going out. She pressed a bottle of water and a bar of Dairy Milk into hir hand, then wrapped hir into a cocoon of cuddles and blankets.

"I love you so much Jamie. I'm so proud of you, you did so well this evening." Jamie's brilliant smile in response melted her heart.

Ze nuzzled into her chest and cuddled her even tighter before putting words together, soft syllables that barely reached her ears. "Thank you Madam. I love you too . . . there's something I need to tell you though."

Her heart jumped with anxiety at that. "What is it love?"

"You know how I've been trying to meet with the doctor for months? Well today I had my appointment and . . ." Ze reached into a bag and pulled out a prescription packet. "Today isn't just our anniversary, it's also my first day of HRT."

It was a moment that was years in the making and both were grateful to share this triumph together. Madam and Jamie held each other tight as tears of joy and relief mingled on their cheeks. They cried because not every day could be as perfect as this one. They cried because it was a day Jamie had doubted ze would ever see. And most of all they cried because in each other they had found someone with which to share resplendent joy, as well as the darkest pains. For that they would be forever grateful, however long it might last.

REMATCH

Tiara-Jordanae

The Glass Ring was a miraculous place, the sort of establishment one visited to have their dreams come true. Wishes were granted, desires indulged, the clientele rich, and the queer company exquisite. Yet, if a person left the main floor to wander the halls, they might stumble upon the well-guarded door that led to the Ring's more exclusive experience. A secretive world not exposed to the casual crowds above.

Rynn blamed that on the membership price.

The Glass Ring's underground was packed with spectators in various stages of undress and fancy, more than it had ever been before. The walls crawled with the buzz of whispered excitement, while the rumbling thump of bass-heavy music shook the floor. Rynn felt the bottoms of her feet tingle, bare as they were on the padded spot where she was centered.

"Are you ready?"

A feminine voice spoke out from an overhead speaker, easily heard over the sounds of clinking glassware and speculative gossip. Across from Rynn, her opponent nodded, serene in the face of

Rynn's own nerves. Rynn tried to emulate her opponent's action but was certain it came off more as a jerk of her chin. Her palms itched and her shoulders tightened. Were the lights in this room always so bright and invasively glaring?

Rynn didn't have time to ask, the speaker's announcer had already captured the crowd.

"Welcome to the Glass Ring's Vault, where we deliver the most unique experiences a lifestyle club can offer." The surrounding crowd tittered with murmured agreement. Typical, Rynn thought. "Here in the Vault, every Thursday night, we invite our members to enter the ring and compete in the league of submission and dominance."

The crowd gave a cheer as Rynn's face flushed, enhancing the warm undertones of her brown skin. The audience was playing their part perfectly, indulging in the spectacle of exaggerated sportsmanship. Every style of play was encouraged with the same vigor, and the Vault was host to many different engagements. It kept membership fresh and interesting.

Yet, the league was the main reason Rynn played.

"Are you ready for some wrestling?"

The roar the audience released was deafening, yet Rynn thought the rapid rattle of her own heart was louder. Warmth built within her chest, slow, *slick,* and melting as it swept lower. Across from her, her opponent mouthed, *'Getting hot already?'*

Rynn swallowed.

Beneath the hungry gaze of the spectators, Rynn felt practically *naked*. Suddenly, the clothing she wore felt far too tight. In a way it *was*. Her athletic bra and ass-hugging shorts were meant to be. The material accentuated every beautiful curve of her body while making her feel compact and powerful. It was a sensation she had lost after her last match, when the dud had resulted in a three-month stay in the cooldown room.

Rynn shivered and repressed a moan. Probably best not to think about the cooldown room right before a match.

As a serious contender in the Ring's league of sexual wrestling, there were contracts to sign and rules to be followed. Management made the experience feel *immersive* while keeping them safe. She enjoyed showing off for the community in the crowd but her mistress, acting as her sponsor, kept her serious by reminding her of her obligations, checking in and renegotiating the terms under which she performed.

That also meant she accepted the consequences of her loses too.

Rynn shook her head and focused on the announcer.

"In one corner we have Big Vik. Up-and-coming contender for a lifetime membership, number six on the leaderboard." The announcer paused, if only to let the crowd hoot and catcall, before they spoke again. "And in our other corner we have Swift Rynn. Freshly and newly returned from cooldown, here to reclaim her number from Big Vik, who has graciously offered to put it on the line for the match."

There was a scandalized gasp from the crowd as the announcer wove a tale of drama. "That's right! Three months ago, Swift Rynn failed to secure a *pin* against Big Vik and lost her placement matches. She has spent time in the cooldown room to . . . recover."

The crowd shared a chuckle and Rynn sucked in a shaky breath, *warmed* by the fact that more than just her sponsor now knew where she'd spent the last three months, bound and *controlled* by any woman her sponsor had deemed appropriate. Rynn had always considered herself a dominant person, a top who enjoyed the leisure of being with her sponsor and any other woman in Ring that expressed interest. Yet, some part of her—irritated by the stresses of life, disappointed by her loss—had *melted* in that room every night she'd come to Glass Ring. There was something addicting in being lost in the thoughtlessness of pleasure and service. A few weeks into her cooldown period, her sponsor had given her a reason for why the room existed for play wrestlers. It had something to do with her mental health and the tension she was holding onto in her muscles, but the exact words had been drowned out when Rynn's body had arched as something hot and wet sought out her clit—

"Contenders, please shake hands at the center of the ring."

The speaker's buzz disturbed Rynn's musings and across from her, Big Vik smiled.

Fanning her face, Rynn approached the padded ring's center. Vik, despite her contender title, was only a little taller than Rynn. A good five ten to Rynn's five seven, but where Rynn considered herself a lean and nimble individual, Vik was more athletic, all flexing biceps and muscular thighs, with the umber of her skin tinged pink due to the heat of the glaring lights. On more than one occasion Rynn had imagined this moment, that she'd step up to her opponent, look her dead in her eyes, and say something impactful.

Something about winning back her placement, something to intensify the rivalry, to get the blood humming.

Vik beat her to it. "You'll come before me, you know. You're already kind of revved up. Are you wet?"

Rynn sputtered, thrown off by Vik's statement and the rolling husk of its delivery. "That's a pretty vulgar question."

"Is it?" Vik smiled and Rynn was momentarily dazzled as memories of the last time she'd seen that smile flickered through her head. "I'll ask something different then. How was your cooldown period?"

"Fine," Rynn grunted, glad for the ambiance generated by the crowd. The last thing she wanted was to be reminded of her time in cooldown *now*. Rynn held out her hand, eager to return to her placement on the mat. Forget saying something profound.

Vik took Rynn's offered hand, the grip familiar, and brushed her calloused thumb over the back of Rynn's knuckles.

When Vik released her, Rynn's hand tingled with phantom touch. She ignored it as she took her place on the other side of the mat, though it took some effort.

Normally, these things—the crowd, Vik's presence, even the announcer's teasing—wouldn't have distracted her from the thrill of a match. Had her time in cooldown softened her? She was so aware of other, deeper, needs in her body now. Impatience squirmed through her.

Vik's nostrils flared and she bit her bottom lip as Rynn shivered.

"Girls! You know what to do." The speaker buzzed, before a loud ding filled the space and the crowd erupted in cheers.

Vik lunged, easily crossing the distance Rynn had put between them and Rynn countered, twisting her body out of the way. They danced around each other, reactive to the *oohs* and *aahs* of the crowd, seeking openings and places to grab that would result in a sought-after *pin*. With the match started properly Rynn's various worries melted away. Her body reacted thoughtlessly, relying upon the experiences of previous well-fought matches and the rush of being *watched* as her body was in motion. There was no way she'd lose this time; Vik's fluke string of wins three months ago had simply been due to Rynn's unrecognized stress. How could she give her all if half her mind was occupied by the inconveniences of the day? The cooldown room and its users had taught her that when they'd practically carved the taste of relaxation and *relief* into her body.

She shouldn't think so much about those hazy rose-tinted memories, but the freedom she'd felt through submission had been wonderful and *decadent*. It was distracting—

Uh-oh.

Vik grappled Rynn to the ground in one practiced motion, done with the sort of smooth grace that only the experienced could emulate. Vik took care to make sure Rynn wasn't crushed beneath her weight as she placed her on her stomach against the mat. Rynn wasn't sure she could have done the same so effortlessly. Not that she was impressed by the strength in Vik's grip or anything.

Well, that was a lie. She was terribly impressed and terribly embarrassed.

"*Shit!*"

The crowd stomped and whooped, enthusiastic and eager. The posturing, stalking, and waiting of their performance was little more than an appetizer for most. The true reason the Vault was full ever Thursday night was due to what happened *after* a contender was pinned. And Rynn? She was *pinned.*

This was not how she'd seen her night going.

Rynn bucked and wiggled beneath the weight of Vik's body, with a determination even the announcer complimented her on. Yet, Vik was unbothered. With a hissed laugh Vik placed a hand against the back of Rynn's head, and before long Rynn found her cheek against the mat and her hips immobile from the press of Vik's own.

Sweat-slick, panting, and tired Rynn ceased her struggle. It wasn't until Vik's dreadlocks, unleashed from their careful bun, tumbled into Rynn's vision that she remembered where she was and what was *next.*

Against her ear, despite the crowds swelling excitement, Vik whispered, "Color?"

As Rynn calmed she remembered the Ring's important system, universal in nearly all aspects of play, though structured simply for the purpose of the league. Beyond the rush of the match and the crowd, she carefully asked herself: Could she continue? Should they stop?

Rynn tapped the ground with two fingers. Green.

"Looks like Swift Rynn is in a pin!" The announcer inspired a fresh wave of cheers that stole Rynn's breath away. "Big Vik has thirty minutes to make something of it."

"I won't even need all of them, will I?" Vik husked against Rynn's ear.

"Fuck you," Rynn sneered, though she doubts it could be heard over the noise shaking the rafters.

"Are you afraid?"

Was she? This wasn't the first time she'd found herself on the mat, face down, ass being lifted up. Her body knew the position well. It was just . . . something about it felt differently. Anticipatory. The strange heat that had built in her chest had settled low and heavy in her belly. She wasn't sure when it had happened, nor *how*, but she was aroused, incredibly so.

The last time Vik had pinned her, Rynn had steeled her will with her pride and arrogance. Now, all she could think about was the gaze of the crowd and the heat that plucked along her skin, tightening her nipples and stealing her breath.

"Someone really enjoyed their time in the cooldown room."

Rynn groaned as Vik's lips brushed against the shell of her ear. She could feel the heat of Vik's powerful body through the thin breathable fabric they both wore. The sensation of her bare stomach across the small of her open back stirred memories only strengthened by Vik's words.

"You're already arching your back for me. Spread your legs a bit too."

Without any conscious input, Rynn's body obeyed. She spread her legs just enough to keep her body balanced and her back arched. With perfect control, Vik pressed further against her, holding onto Rynn's thighs to keep them spread and open. Belatedly, Rynn realized what she'd done, but no amount of flexing could get them closed again.

Am I really doing this?

Ryan's idle thought felt burdened, warmed by a building lassitude. It faded easily before the stronger sensation of touch as Vik drew nonsense patterns along her inner thighs.

"You're already so wet, I can feel it through your shorts," Vik cooed.

Despite the crowd (or maybe because of it) Vik was able to weave a sense of intimacy. The sounds of those beyond their circle did little to ease the growing pulse of desire seeking her surrender. Vik's husky whisper, the firm confidence of her hands, and the scent of their heavily breathing bodies cast a spell strong enough to put strain on Rynn's defiance.

How was she to survive the next act if she could barely contain herself now?

If only she hadn't been so distracted and so assured in her victory that her mind had slipped. The painful familiarity of her position conflicted strongly with her initial eagerness to changing her fate. Yet, as if her very thoughts had been trained, the longer she remained arched and vulnerable, the less sure she felt about regaining her place. The cooldown room wasn't that *bad*—she'd agreed with her sponsor that it had been needed. The experience had been enlightening in delicious ways, but nostalgia for the pleasures within had softened her before the bell had even rung.

Had she designed her own downfall, or had the trap been sprung the moment her cooldown time had completed?

"They're watching you, Rynn. The crowd is here for *you*," Vik said.

Rynn shivered, thrown by the idea that she'd brought them there. "No way," she hissed through clenched teeth, "this room is practically full to capacity."

Vik chuckled and the vibration rang along Rynn's spine.

"Three months ago our first match was intense. Did you not think the Glass Ring would heavily market the second one?"

"Th-they promote every match, not just mine." Rynn stuttered as one of Vik's hands began to explore her body. Rynn was about to snap more of her retort when Vik's long, sensuous fingers suddenly grabbed hold of one of her breasts. Rynn gasped in shock but resisted the urge to buck. She would give Vik time with her body, uninterrupted. Yet . . .

She could feel the warmth of Vik's hand through the material of her bra and her nipple began to pebble at just the promise of being touched.

Vik gave off a soft sound of interest, amused. "They like your attitude though, Rynn. How arrogant and overconfident you are."

Vik's hand began to move with purpose, massaging Rynn's breast over her thin athletic bra. The slow, methodical movement was done with a knowing firmness and Rynn had to clamp down on her body's urging for more. Rynn took a shaky breath and thought past the growing warmth that glowed pleasantly behind the tingling nipple Vik's massaging hand avoided.

"But three months ago, they found out how heavy your pride was and how sexy you looked when you lost. Now, they know how you really are."

Rynn gasped when Vik's deft hand grew bold in its exploration, joined now by its partner. The unyielding grip of her heavy breasts turned into a gentle caress. The sharp contrast in sensation was dizzying and Rynn knew her nipples were now easily visible, accentuated by their material prison.

"Soft. *Dripping.* Needy. The 'Rynn' they saw during our last match was only a taste of the humbled self you've become during cooldown. Gossip spreads fast in the Vault. They want to see that. Why don't we show it to them, Rynn? Your true self."

Rynn groaned as her endurance wavered. The pleasant warmth

in her chest had only sunk lower, stirring the heat that was already there. Her sex throbbed with anticipation as her belly flexed nervously. Was all of that true? Did the crowd really see her that way? Her heart thumped to the lustful beat of their sounds—they were encouraging Vik to conquer her.

Had her sponsor known this all along? Had Rynn become popular for her failure?

Her knees trembled as her strength waned, weakened by a growing pleasure.

"Let me help with that," Vik chirped, and all too soon Rynn found herself lifted and placed upon Vik's lap. Despite their actual difference in height, Rynn felt smaller held against Vik's chest. Or, maybe she knew she was helpless in Vik's grip as her fingertips began to coax electric sensation from her needy nipples.

Rynn attempted to search for the timer, knowing the announcer was keeping track, but found it difficult to focus beyond the pleasure that Vik had started to milk from her chest. Her hips twitched, reactive to sensation, and as Vik flicked and tugged playfully at her nipples Rynn's breath grew ragged.

"Does it feel good?" Vik asked.

Rynn's answer was a moan of irresistible pleasure. She hadn't realized just how much her body had yearned for this touch. *Still* yearned for pleasure as if she'd been made to submit.

"I'm glad you seem to like my touch," Vik smiled, "but if I want to win, I'll have to keep going."

Rynn's eyes fluttered as Vik's hands left her chest, only to rest on the tops of her thighs, waiting. Rynn took one breath, then another, and whispered, "Green."

Rynn watched, fascinated, as Vik's questing hands spread apart swollen lower lips, outlined and plump beneath the snug, form-fitting shorts. Her sex throbbed, *hungry* and craven as fresh wetness spilled from her depths. Something low in her belly clenched with heat and Rynn whimpered from the intensity. The arousal that Vik had built in her body was still growing, spiraling away from her, and all Vik had done was expose her pussy.

As if reading her thoughts, Vik chuckled. "I won't tell you how much time you have left. Try to endure it."

Vik started with a squeeze to her outer lips and Rynn's neck arched from the pulling-pushing sensation. Each touch of kneading and massage transferred the sensation indirectly to her clit, and it took everything Rynn had to keep her hips from rocking. Burning urgency whispered through her, to beg for more, to free herself once more from the obligations she'd shed during cooldown. And oh, *oh,* what she would give to *submit.*

But that was how the league operated. If she wanted her place back, if she wanted a chance to dominant Vik, she had to hold on, had to—

Something tight and *heavy* pulsed at her center, demanding her attention in exchange for pleasure. "Oh, Vik . . ." Rynn whispered, bucking as Vik drew tight circles around her clit. There was something decidedly *wicked* about being pleasured through her clothing, of having her body ache with the demand for more direct touch but knowing she wouldn't receive it—for the league was clear on their rules about nudity.

And yet, as Vik increased the cruelty of her teasing, the tight pressure dwelling Rynn's belly only increased. Lustful energy licked flames of fire up her spine, a warning and a seduction. If only Vik would soothe the angry throb of Rynn's clit or enter the dripping slit she rubbed so firmly. Everything was becoming so sensitive and slick. Desperation and insidious pleasure were blurring together, sharp in its taste.

"H-how much time is left?" Rynn panted.

"I won't tell you," Vik purred before she gave Rynn's earlobe a lick.

With each circle and stroke Vik dwelled dangerously close to Rynn's throbbing bud. Her clit had become a point of demanding focus, bending her will until Rynn felt on the verge of begging. When Vik finally nudged her clit with a finger, Rynn went so ridged she thought the anticipation alone would cause her to burst.

"You're so damn close already . . ." Vik seemed in awe. Rynn's embarrassment only enhanced her desire.

Still, Rynn growled with denial, "I'm not."

Vik's response was to firmly rub her clit in rhythmic circles.

Rynn moaned from the sudden stimulus, delighted and worried by the rush of ecstasy. Vik kept contact as she pushed and massaged her aching bud and her sex pulsed with a strange jealous emptiness. The ever-escalating waves of euphoria set her hips to gyrating as her breathing deepened. Before cooldown this would have been titillating, an alluring touch meant to tempt her. Yet, after greedily experiencing the joy of submission, her body quickly rushed toward what it believed to be one of many glorious climaxes.

"You're going to come for me *again,* aren't you Rynn? Right here, in front of all these people. You're going to show them what your body learned during cooldown and how *good* it feels."

Rynn bit her bottom lip to keep from crying out and trembled from the intimate intensity of her experience. The crowd's excited whooping had turned into focused murmuring. Even the announcer's speaker box had silenced. She now had their undivided attention. They were going to see her, *hear* her, come undone.

Rynn was floating. Unable to ride the sharpness of pleasure, it rode her. "Mistress—ma'am, I'm going to—!"

Vik hid her smile against Rynn's shoulder. "Oh, I know. It's alright if you do."

Vik's fingers quickened, expertly rubbing her clit in tight circular motions that left Rynn wheezing from the sticky heat of building pleasure. The pulsating pressure behind her clit began to throb in time to the rapid beat of her heart. There was nowhere for her to hide—not from the crowd, or the pleasure, or her mind begging *please, please, I need to come.* Her body wrestled for control, but Vik set the pace, holding Rynn steady with her legs held wide apart by the weight of Vik's own. The crowd could see her pussy spasm and drip, they would all know exactly when she'd come.

It was the intense thought of being watched that sent her tumbling over, moaning loudly in the suddenly silent room. Her body contracted as Vik milked her of pleasure, spreading waves of warmth that lapped at her senses and sent her soaring. Each pleasurable spasm was an undeniable signal of her loss, but there was relief in knowing what came next.

Cooldown.

As her body began to settle, wracked every so often with thrilling throbs and softening spasms of her satisfied clit, the announcer began to speak again, confirming Vik's win and encouraging the crowd to mingle before the next league round. The faces she saw beyond a veil of sweat-damp hair looked pleased and exhilarated. Rynn found that she didn't mind her loss as much as she thought.

"You did so well today, Rynn," Vik cooed, rubbing Rynn's arms with possessive affection.

"Thank you, sponsor."

Vik's laugh was warm and delighted. "I'm not your sponsor in the ring, you know that."

Rynn smirked, pleasure-drunk. "Sorry, Mistress."

Vik shook her head with a sigh. "I'm sending you back to the cooldown room. You can demand a rematch in another three months."

Rynn grinned and nodded. She truly did enjoy being a member of the Vault.

BE ROUGH

Kel Hardy

Boston is not a city for cruising. The mixture of Puritan values and old-school lesbian ethics deters casual lesbian anything. Between the third-wave feminist academics and the New England closet cases, I thought I was going to have to make it through my master's degree with the attention of my right hand alone. But as November whipped through the city cold and sharp, I started to get an itch.

Dating apps proved somewhat useless. The hyper-academic queers of Boston almost had a fetish for safety and status. I had prospective dates track down my social media, my job, and my writing all in the name of security. One even asked for references. The few dates I had been on, all firsts, had culminated in some kind of extensive examination of my life goals and non-existent five-year plan, which bored me to tears. I wasn't interested in being interviewed as a prospective wife. I was interested in being fucked like I wasn't respected, or being respected enough to be fucked any way that I asked for. I craved anonymous sex. If I was going to get my fix, I decided I would rather not know names, occupations, or who we both knew—and of course there would be someone we both knew, this was a small damn city.

Finally, I found a site in one of the less-reputable corners of the web. No photos allowed, just a headline and one hundred and fifty words, like old-school personal ads. *Have a friend write it for you!* the site advised. My friends would not approve of the risks I was taking.

Anon4Anon
WLW only. 7pm. Boylston Street. I have a hotel booked. Be rough.

As I walked to the meet-up point that evening, my internal women's studies graduate berated me. *"Always meet in public" is the number one rule of online dating. No one knows where you are. What if no one shows up? What if they're a murderer? What if more than one person shows up?* The last scenario didn't strike me as a problem.

At the station, I glanced around. A man with an ambling Dachshund eyed me as he walked by, from my side-shaved long blonde hair to my whore's red lips to the matching pumps. I pulled my trench coat tighter to my body.

"Anon?" a deep voice said behind me.

I spun around. A tall, lean butch stood six feet away, eyeing me cautiously. In a red shirt, black jeans, and swooped black hair, she reminded me of the boy bands I crushed on in high school. This could work.

"That's me," I said. She nodded, unsmiling. We eyed each other for a long moment.

"Will you do a turn for me?" I finally asked. I didn't particularly need to evaluate her, but I felt I should give the impression that I had some standards beyond any warm and willing Sapphic body.

She hesitated, then stepped awkwardly around in a circle, skinny arms held slightly out to the sides like a dykey music-box figurine. I normally had a penchant for buxom femmes, but if I was going to do something different tonight, it might as well be completely different.

She completed her turn and looked at me. I nodded and smiled.

"Open your jacket," she said. I noted with a small thrill that it was not a request.

I saw her eyes widen as she took in my low-cut shift, hardened nipples showing through.

"This could work," she said, almost smiling. "Do we need a safeword?"

"Yes, tulip. You?"

"No will suffice. Hard limits?"

"Piercing and blood play. You?"

"Bottoming," she said, her mouth giving a sarcastic twitch. I laughed. "Where are we going?"

"Follow me," I said.

A silent three blocks later, we checked in to a chain hotel. In the elevator, she positioned herself in front of me as I leaned as casually as possible against the back wall.

"Lift up your skirt," she said.

"What?" I stammered.

"You heard me," she said.

Breathing hard, I pulled my short hem up above my hip bones to reveal that I had nothing on underneath. She grinned for the first time. She reached down and grabbed my cunt firmly. I yelped.

"Do you normally go without panties on your dates?" she asked.

"I wouldn't exactly call this a date," I said breathlessly.

The elevator dinged our floor. She wrapped her hand around the back of my neck and steered me forward down the hall. She kept her grip even as I fumbled with the key card for the door. Once open, she shoved me inside.

"Coat off," she said, another delicious command. I stripped eagerly.

"On your knees," she commanded again.

"That's not a nice way to ask," I told her. She froze midway through pulling her arm out of her jacket sleeve. She gave me a look that made my knees press together. She dropped her jacket to the floor and crossed the space between us in three strides. She raised her right hand to grip my jaw so my cheeks squished and my lips puckered together. My heart was pounding; this was the rough handling I was after.

We stood in our tableau for a beat too long. She looked deep into my eyes. Underneath the sadistic gleam, I saw a question struggling.

"Can I slap you?" she asked in a barely audible whisper. We both broke for a momentary giggle, but lust had me back in line quickly.

"Oh, *please*," I practically moaned. "Please do."

She struck me quickly but not too hard. I turned my stinging face forward and I stared her down. She raised her eyebrows at my defiance.

"Knees, now," she commanded. I sank down slowly. On my knees, my eyes were just level with her silver-studded belt. Her long fingers unbuckled it hypnotically. I looked up as she undid her zipper, my lips parted and breathing heavily. I could see her staring down my dress.

A beautiful, black silicone cock emerged from her pants.

"You know what to do, don't you slut?"

I eagerly opened my mouth and wrapped both hands around her shaft to guide it down my throat. She twined her hand in my hair. I felt her other hand come under my chin gently and looked up at her. She smiled down at me.

"You look pretty like that," she told me. "A pretty little whore."

I felt my clit throb in response to the name-calling. I began to moan, just a little, opening my mouth wider around her smooth cock. She moaned back in response. She liked a show. After a few more minutes of deep throating, she tightened her hand around a fistful of my hair. I cried out.

"Up," she commanded with a corresponding tug.

I scrambled to my feet. She grabbed my shoulders, spun me around, and shoved me so I fell flat on the bed with a gasp. She kicked my heels to spread my legs apart. I began to pull up the hem of my dress again, this time to remove it, but I felt her knee between my shoulder blades crush me back into the mattress.

"No," she said sternly. "I like your slutty outfit. Keep it on."

I whimpered as I nodded. She stood and traced her fingers down my back and over my ass. I began to wiggle my hips back and forth in anticipation of receiving her cock in another hole. I was met with a firm spank.

"Stop that," she commanded. I froze momentarily, then wiggled again. She spanked me harder, and I yelped. Then I wiggled again. The next slap stung; I would have a bruise tomorrow. I wiggled again. Spank. Wiggle. Spank. Wiggle. Spank. I kept up my small defiance, gleefully crying out as she hit the exact same spots over and over. Finally, she grabbed me by my hair, yanked my head back, and pressed the head of her cock against my now dripping cunt.

"Someone needs to put you in your fucking place," she growled. She slid the full length of her cock inside of me as deep as she could. I screamed a little into the mattress. She growled in pleasure and her hips started moving in long, slow, deep thrusts. I felt so full, like she was pushing into my stomach. I whimpered a little with each stroke, enjoying the slight pain at the end. I began to gyrate with her hips, following her strokes, but her hands pushed me back into the mattress.

"Stop," she said, thrusting into me hard and deep, "fucking," another thrust, "wiggling."

And then she was pounding me. She had me pushed deep down into the mattress so I could do nothing but lie there and scream. I felt her nails dig into my shoulders, using her grip as leverage to fuck me harder and faster.

"Tell me you like it, whore," she grunted as she fucked me.

"Yes, yes, yes, *yes, yes, yes,*" I cried out in time to her thrusts. I could feel pressure building in my cunt and my legs twitching. My hips bucked even though she had me held down. I was insatiable. Even with her relentless fucking, my body still sought to be filled in the seconds she pulled back to thrust again. I could not be full enough. I pressed my face into the bed. I balled the starched hotel comforter in my fists. I screamed as I came, too loud for a hotel full of visiting parents and academics.

She thrust until I went limp, then slid out of me. The bed bounced as she collapsed beside me on her back. I peeked at her through sleepy post-orgasm eyes. Her black hair curled a bit on her sweat-slick forehead, and her narrow, wide-set eyes were closed. I wanted to reach out and stroke her broad, flat nose, but I stopped myself. Basking in the afterglow, I felt a rush of gratitude for her, that she was here, that she was willing, that she was so what I needed. She turned her face, eyes fluttering open to look at me. She flashed me a wicked grin and put her index finger over my lips.

"You have make-up everywhere, you dirty whore."

Heat rushed from her finger down my body. I loved sex-messed make-up, and clearly she did too. She pulled me in to her and kissed me deeply—our first kiss, I realized with a shock. When we parted, my lipstick was smeared across her full lips.

"And what can I do for you now?" I asked.

She bit her stained lip, and I saw a question swim behind her lust again. I waited patiently. This time, she appeared able to answer it herself.

"I want you to put on my strap," she told me. My eyes widened with shock. Her hand smoothed over my now tense back.

"I, uh . . ." I cleared my throat. "I've never actually . . ." Suddenly, I felt humiliated. I was a fraud. Who was I to initiate an anonymous lesbian hook-up in this god-forsaken, sex-adverse city when I had never even so much as tried on a strap-on?

She laughed deep in her chest.

"I do love being a first," she said with a look of unexpected glee. "Don't worry, I have something very specific in mind. You won't have to do a thing. Let me show you?"

My cheeks still burning with shame and my cunt now burning with curiosity, I nodded. She pushed me onto my back firmly. I became a ragdoll. She climbed off the bed, grabbed me by my underarms, and dragged me so I was splayed upside down and diagonally over the bed. She then took my wrists and brought them over my head, so they dangled over the bottom corner.

"Stay," she commanded. I heard her belt clink, and then felt the body-warmed leather wind around one wrist, then the other. I closed my eyes as she pulled my wrists down. When she released me, I was secured to the leg of the bed. Standing at my head, she ran her hands down my body, carelessly pressing her cock to my mouth as she did. I reached my tongue out to lick it. Her fingers caressed the hem of my dress and then pulled it up over my hips, my cunt, my belly, my ribs, my breasts, my collarbone, and finally my face. I felt the silky loose shift drop over my bound hands.

I opened my eyes as I felt her weight return to the bed. She had the harness in hand and a small silver packet in her teeth. She wore only her T-shirt. Gently, she threaded each of my stilettos through the harness.

"What a good little sex toy," she cooed through her clenched jaw as I lifted my ass to help her pull it all the way up. I shivered deliciously at the praise.

Once secured, she tore open the packet to pull out a clear condom, and slid it over her cock. The sight of her fist gliding down its length thrilled me, and I suddenly understood the phenomenon of strap blow jobs and hand jobs. I almost wanted to ask her to suck it, but I decided that particular act was not for the obedient sex doll I now wanted to be for her.

Once protected, she straddled my hips and positioned her glistening cunt above the cock. I took in the moles on her hips and sparse whorls of pubic hair, inhaling the smell of her even though she was nowhere near my face.

"Like what you see?" she asked, cocky.

I shrugged as best I could with my bound arms.

"Not bad," I said with a sly smile. She leaned forward and slapped me again.

"Be good," she said, and then sat back. She slid down onto the cock slowly, groaning as she did. She closed her eyes and held still. I held my breath. Her hips started to gyrate slowly. I dug my high heels into the mattress, wanting to thrust up into her, wanting to make her feel good, but she reached back to touch my leg gently.

"I got this," she said, eyes still closed. She rose up and lowered herself down slowly. Ropey muscle in her thighs bulged and relaxed as she set to a rhythm of fucking herself on me. Her mouth hung open in abandon as she began to breathe more heavily. I watched, mesmerized. I felt useless and used. My wrists pulled against her restraining belt, overcome by the urge to grasp at her flexing thighs or reach up under her shirt. She opened her eyes, sensing my distress, and grinned her wicked grin. One big hand grasped at my throat, making me gasp.

"Have you never been used like this, pretty whore?" she taunted through heavy breathing. "Isn't this what you advertised for?"

She was completely correct. She steadily increased her pace on the cock. Her breathing deepened to moans as she closed her eyes and bowed her head. I curled my toes, willing my whole body to be good and still for her. I surrendered to being hers to use.

She threw her head back, face scrunched as she cried out with each self-inflicted thrust. She placed her hands on my ribs and dug in her nails. I prayed for more bruises. Her pace became slower and harder, her moans growing to shouts.

"Fuck. Yes. Fuck. Yes. *Fuck. Yes. Fuck. Yes.*"

She fell suddenly silent. Her whole body shook, her knees clenched to my hips, her mouth drew wide open, and she bowed forward. Pressing her face to my tits, she unleashed a final scream. I released a breath I didn't know I was holding, feeling my own kind of release.

We lay immobile for an eternity, breathing hard. Finally, she pulled herself off the cock and lay flat on top of me, reaching over my head to untangle my arms from her belt and my dress. She went to push herself off, but I wrapped my newly freed arms around her.

"Stay here a second," I said, relishing her full weight crushing down on me. She obeyed, relaxing into me.

"Hey," she said after a long while, startling me out of a doze. "Thanks for this."

I laughed awkwardly. "You're welcome?"

"It's just hard to find a casual thing, you know," she said, her wrist limply gesturing between us. "I was starting to feel like a bad person for even wanting it."

"I know exactly what you mean," I said. We were quiet for a moment longer, then she propped herself up on her elbows and gave me a hard look.

"Let's not do the thing."

"What thing?"

"The thing where we trade numbers because it was so good that we think we maybe want to see each other again even though that's not what either of us came here for."

I laughed at her succinct analysis of the situation. "You're probably right. This was good because it wasn't meant to last."

"Exactly," she said. "Now, how long do you want to cuddle?"

"Ten minutes?"

"Deal."

TAKE ME TO CHURCH

"Excuse me, I'm looking for Church Street."

I approached the tall man on the corner. He turned to me and I saw that he was young. Maybe eighteen years old. Twenty-two at most. Dressed smartly in an argyle sweater and tie, I wondered where this kid was headed. A shock of curly hair stuck out from under the brim of his tweed flat cap. He looked like he'd just stepped off the set of a Depression-era film. He was certainly handsome enough to be an actor. He smiled, his baby-soft cheeks spreading up to wide cheekbones. His chin jutted forward.

"It's just a block this way. I'm headed there myself," he said and started walking.

I followed, surprised at his confidence as he swaggered along the sidewalk, escorting me, a woman at least twice his age. He looked at me again, a grin turning up the corners of his mouth, a gleam in his eye. Was this kid flirting with me? What was he thinking? Embarrassingly, I felt myself blush and smile in response.

"What's your name?" he asked, surprising me again with his forwardness.

"Sarah," I answered. "And yours?"

"Em," he responded.

"M? Just the letter? Cool!"

He giggled. "No. Em. E-M. It's short for my full name."

"Oh, yeah? What's your name?" I asked, wondering why he hadn't just told me outright.

"I don't always tell people, because my name doesn't always fit me right. But I guess I'm telling you. It's Emily."

Emily? I almost stumbled. This was not a boy. It was a girl. No. Not a girl. A woman. And now that I looked at her again, I wondered how I could ever have been mistaken. The softness in her face, the small crinkles at her eyes and around her mouth, her full lips. She was exquisite really. Exquisitely androgynous. And her voice, which had seemed slightly high for a guy, now sounded deep and rich.

No, wait! Maybe they were trans or . . . ack! What were all the terms I'd been reading online? All the gender stuff. Binary something?

They looked at me again and I realized I'd been staring, trying to piece together the puzzle, the intangible qualities of this person that had fooled me entirely. They had an amused look in their eye. They knew the assumption I had made and could sense the mental gymnastics I was now doing to adjust to this information. Recalibrating. Resetting.

"I use she/her pronouns," she smiled gently at me. "I'm cool with they/them but she/her still feels mostly right."

"She/her! Me too!" I proclaimed rather awkwardly, and she smiled. I was grateful for her deft maneuvering, and hoped I hadn't made her feel too uncomfortable.

"Where are you headed on Church Street?" she asked.

"The butcher shop," I answered. "I was told it was the best one in Toronto. I'm cooking dinner for my cousin tomorrow night when she gets back from her business trip. I've been cat-sitting for her. I'm actually from Kingston. Do you know it? The butcher shop I mean, not Kingston." I was babbling. Something about this woman, my misperception, the sudden revelation, had thrown me off my stride and I was flailing a little, trying to regain my balance.

"Yeah, I know it," she said. "It's right across from my favorite pub patio. That's where I'm going."

"Nice weather for a patio. Perfect afternoon. Are you meeting friends?" I asked. I wanted to keep the conversation going, still curious about the mysterious Em.

"No, actually. I just thought it seemed like a nice afternoon to sit under an umbrella, have a drink, and watch my people walk by."

My people? What a curious thing to say. I wondered what she meant by it but I didn't dare ask. Maybe it had something to do with her job. Her employees? That didn't seem right.

"What do you do, you know, for a living, like, what's your job?" I stumbled through the question, marveling at how tongue-tied I had become.

"I'm a pilot," she replied.

"Cool!" I answered, sounding like the kid I'd mistaken her for.

"I have one more day off and then I'm back on my route. Toronto Pearson to London Heathrow. Here's Church Street." She put her hand on my back and led me into the turn. Her hand was warm and strong. I felt the heat of it spreading through me. She dropped her hand as we made our way up the street, my back slowly cooling where she had touched me.

Church was a popular street. People moved in and out of shops and cafés. The patios were filled with diners eating and drinking, laughing together. I noticed rainbow banners hanging from the lampposts. The street signs had rainbow stripes painted on them. It was pretty.

"Welcome to the gayborhood," Em said.

Like I had just put on glasses, everything came quickly into focus. I looked at the people around me. Two men in tight T-shirts and jeans, shoulders touching as they talked together, walking down the street. A woman came toward me, walking with the same self-assurance I'd seen in Em. Grounded. Secure. I saw her clock us, me and Em. I saw her make an assumption and somewhere in my chest there was a tiny explosion of warmth. It caught me off guard.

I was still taking everything in when Em said, "Here we are." I looked up and saw the green awning of the butcher shop.

"Oh. Thank you. Thank you so much."

"No worries. Nice meeting you, Sarah."

"You too, Em. Have a great evening."

She left me then, crossing the street to the pub. I turned and entered the shop.

The door closed behind me and I felt the cool air of the place. It smelled spicy. Savory. And it was beautifully laid out. Bottles of organic olive oil and marinades lined the shelves on the wall. Baskets of artisanal bread were stacked in a corner beside the freezer. And the refrigerated cases displayed the most appetizing selections: steaks and chicken breasts marinating in various sauces, thick-cut bacon fanned out in one section, homemade sausages of lamb, apple, and rosemary, or turkey and asiago in another. I looked at everything and decided on the pork chops in maple balsamic marinade. I love food and I love shopping for food in specialty shops, but today I felt different. As soon as I had entered the shop and the door had closed behind me, I had felt the loss of Em like a hollowness in my core. I completed my purchases and walked back out into the warmth of the late afternoon sun.

My eyes scanned the patio across the street. At first I didn't see her and a little flicker of anxiety started in my chest. Then I caught sight of her at a table near the back. Next thing I knew, I was next to the railing separating the patio from the sidewalk, just standing there, frozen. What should I say? I didn't really understand what I was feeling. I wanted to put myself in front of this gorgeous, confident woman and . . . and . . . what? What was I hoping for?

I have been in a series of monogamous relationships with men since high school. The latest of which had ended rather messily about five months ago, hence the cat-sitting gig. Now, here I was, feeling excited and nervous about a complete stranger. A woman. And there she was in front of me and I didn't know what to do.

Suddenly, she looked up and saw me. Caught me staring at her. Again. She smiled and motioned me over.

"Hi, Sarah. Did you find what you wanted?"

"Yeah. I did. Thanks," I answered and wondered what exactly I meant.

"Want to join me?" she asked.

"Oh, sure, yeah. I'd love to."

I sat down across from her. Now what? I thought. I couldn't think of anything to say. Em looked at me, that playful glimmer in her eye, and asked if I'd like a drink.

"Yes, I would."

I almost said, "I'll have what you're having," feeling incapable of making a decision, but I saw that she was drinking beer, which I hate, so I looked around at the other patrons, hoping to find help quickly. Someone at a table behind her was drinking something red, leafy celery sticking out of the glass.

"Bloody Mary," I blurted.

"Great."

She called the server over, ordered for me, and then looked me in the eye.

"So, Sarah from Kingston," she said, "what made you come over here to share a drink with a stranger?"

Her straightforward manner had knocked all my defenses down. I answered her honestly. "Curiosity, I guess."

"And what are you curious about?"

There was going to be no small talk in this conversation.

"Well . . . you, I suppose."

" threw you for a loop back there, didn't I?" she said, smiling again.

"Yes. You really did. You enjoy doing that, don't you?" I asked.

"Sometimes," she said. "Depends on the person. You looked like you needed shaking up."

"Why? What do you mean?" I asked.

"You look like the kind of woman who always knows what to expect."

She was right. Not much surprised me. Which, I suppose, was how I liked it. I like to be in control. But today? Right now? I felt very far from in control. Normally I would do everything I could to regain my composure, my stability. But this was different. For some reason I had no fear of the confusion I was feeling. Instead I was intrigued and kind of excited.

We continued talking easily. We floated from subject to subject—childhood, relationships, favorite foods. We sailed through religion and politics with barely a ripple. The sun set pink around us.

Finally she said, "We've been here for a while and you need to get that meat refrigerated."

My heart sank. I don't know what I was expecting, but it certainly wasn't an end to this encounter. Not yet anyway.

"I live in that building right there," she said and she pointed to a condo tower over my shoulder. "Why don't we continue our conversation there and you can keep those pork chops safe for consumption."

My heart rose again on a warm wave. "Okay," I said. "Good idea."

I was going back to her place and my brain revved into gear. I didn't want to speculate about what the change of venue meant, but I knew that I wasn't afraid. In fact, I started to realize that I was hoping, really hoping that Em would make a move. At the very least, kiss me. And as that realization hit me, I was a little shocked. I had never kissed a woman before. I had never even thought about it, never pictured it, nothing. But now, faced with the prospect, or at least the possibility, of something happening with this striking woman, I was enthralled. Something about her androgyny, the mix of masculine confidence and feminine sensitivity, was thrilling to me.

We walked and talked our way to her place. It was a beautiful modern condo, sparingly decorated in neutral tones. Huge windows faced south toward the lake. Beautiful, huge Lake Ontario, stretching like an ocean to New York State.

She took my bag and put the meat in the fridge, then got us each a glass of wine. We sat down on the couch. There was a distinctive shift in mood, a sense of uncertainty and anticipation. It felt dangerous to sit so close to her on the couch, no table between us, nothing keeping us apart.

I was used to men making the first move and made an assumption that, because of the way she dressed and carried herself, Em would take the lead in what I thought was coming. But when she leaned back into the sofa cushions, took a sip of wine, and just smiled at me, I made a new choice. I took a drink, placed my glass on the coffee table, screwed up my courage, and took the plunge. I put my hand on her leg just above her knee. Her smile widened. I squeezed. She put down her wineglass, gently placed her hand on top of mine, then slowly ran her fingertips along the underside of my forearm. My breath caught.

"Are you sure?" she asked.

In response I leaned forward, put my other hand behind her

neck, and brought our mouths together. There was a moment of hesitation before our lips touched. A moment where we could feel each other's breath, warm and sweet with alcohol. And then we were kissing. The tenderest kiss. Our lips parted and the kiss deepened. I nibbled her soft bottom lip then she sucked on mine. Our tongues began to dip back and forth. Playing. Testing.

I became aware of her strong hands as they moved up my back, pulling me to her. I could feel the softness of her breasts as they pressed into mine. Unbidden, a tiny moan escaped my lips. The combination of strength and softness was dizzying. I felt a burst of heat in my chest and groin.

We kissed for a long time, hands caressing shoulders and backs. Her mouth left mine and travelled to my neck, her hand in my hair. I moaned again. I wanted more of this incredible woman. I wanted to undress her, to figure out the puzzle. What would she look like when stripped of her masculine clothing? Would I still feel drawn to her?

I grabbed her by the necktie and brought her mouth to mine again. I loosened the tie, pulled the short end through the knot, and stripped it from her neck. I gripped the sides of her sweater and started to pull it up over her head. She lifted both arms and I took it all the way off. I reached out and began unbuttoning her shirt. She did the same for me. With our shirts off, we sat in front of each other and paused.

Her skin was tanned, freckles sprinkled across her wide shoulders. I ran my finger along the top edge of her tight sports bra, barely grazing her skin, my finger dipping slightly into her cleavage when I reached the middle.

"Wanna help me with this? It's a bit of a struggle," she said.

I slipped my fingers under the band of the bra and pulled up firmly as she wriggled out of it. I dropped it on the floor next to me.

She was beautiful. And handsome. Womanly and strong.

Again I found the mixture of these two things intoxicating. She had small breasts, round and soft with nipples of the lightest pink. I extended my hand and cupped one, then bent my head and took her nipple into my mouth. Now it was her turn to moan. I sucked a little and her nipple responded, tightening under my tongue. I sucked harder and she gasped. Her hands came up behind my head and she held me there. With one hand, she snapped my bra open. I slid it off my arms and it fell onto hers on the floor.

She lay back on the couch, bringing me with her, my soft breasts falling onto her muscular stomach. Her fingers ran up and down my back and along my sides, her thumbs brushing my breasts. I was delirious with desire, could feel how wet I was getting. She pulled me up, kissed my mouth again, and then pushed me onto my back. She lowered her head to my nipple and my hips began to move. She teased me with her tongue and teeth, sucking sometimes hard and then very gently. With her fingers she played with my other nipple, tweaking and twisting it. I was practically panting.

She lifted her head. "Still okay?" she asked.

"God, yes," I said.

Em stood up and took me by the hand.

"Come with me," she said and led me to her bedroom.

With her shirt off I could see the line of muscles running down the sides of her stomach to her hips. I grabbed her around the waist, running my thumbs up and down the hard lines. Then I tucked my finger under the waistband of her pants, coming to rest in the hollow on the inside of her hip bone.

"Let's take these off, shall we?" I said.

"I will if you will," she teased.

We were both naked now. She lay me down on her bed and climbed on top of me. As she held herself up with her arms, the muscles in her shoulders popped and rippled. I ran my hands along them. She started kissing her way down my body, stopping in various places to suck or nibble or flick her tongue.

Finally, her mouth was hovering above my cunt. I could feel her warm breath. Then her mouth was on me and we both moaned. Her tongue began to slowly explore me. She sucked and teased and started making delicious circles. As my pleasure mounted, hers did too. Her whole body rocked in rhythm with mine.

I have had boyfriends go down on me many times, but I have always gotten the sense that they felt they should be praised for being such considerate lovers, giving off an "aren't I a great guy" vibe for taking a few precious minutes from the journey to their own orgasm to let me know that they cared about my pleasure too.

But this was different. For her this *was* the reward. I didn't feel like I had to concentrate hard and come quickly before she got too tired. I could relax into the glorious ripples of pleasure that were washing over me.

She very gently inserted a finger into me and, finding me so wet and open, she inserted another. And another. As she slowly began to move them inside me, I felt a giant wave start to gather momentum. A sense of urgency began to overwhelm me. It was hard to catch my breath.

"Oh, god . . ." I gasped.

Em moaned a reply.

I produced a series of unintelligible, guttural sounds as my body undulated with the swelling flood of sensations. The wave rolled closer. All thought ceased.

Suddenly everything focused as I started the final climb. Every tiny movement brought me closer and closer. Higher and higher. Almost there. And then, there I was, at the top, at the point of total surrender and I plunged over the edge. Free fall. Total abandon. Absolute bliss.

Never before had I given myself over so completely and I was amazed. My body shuddered and shook with the release. Em rode along with me.

Once the quaking had subsided, Em pulled herself up alongside me and held me softly.

"My god . . ." I repeated over and over, "my god . . . my god . . . I've never . . . my god . . ."

"Good," she said. I could hear the smile in her voice.

I wanted to say something to her to let her know just how incredible I felt, but I didn't have the words. I started to move my hands over her body, wanting to share some of what I was feeling. She grabbed one of my hands and brought it between her legs. She was dripping. Oh, wow! I thought. She got this wet for me?

"I would really like your fingers inside me, if you would like that too," she said.

"Yes. I would like that," I said, and then I froze for a moment and tried to remember just what she had done to me and how it had felt. I slowly inserted my index finger into her. It was the most incredible feeling. Smooth and wet and warm. And more open than I had expected. I quickly realized I should try more fingers. I added two more, enjoying the warm tightness around them. Em made an appreciative little moan.

"More," she said. "Another."

I inserted a fourth finger and we both grunted. My heart was pounding with wonder and excitement.

She brought her own hand down onto her clit and began to circle with her fingers. As she did so, the walls of her cunt contracted, gripping my fingers even more. I gasped in astonishment. I began to slowly move my fingers in and out of her.

"Yes. I want you to fuck me just like that," Em breathed and then moaned as I pushed a little deeper.

We kept up a steady rhythm. I watched her face, looking for

signs that I should go slower or faster or even stop completely. Mostly she had her eyes closed, focus turned inward, concentrating on the mounting pleasure. But sometimes she looked into my eyes with an intensity that made me stop breathing. I realized that I was throbbing just as hard now, if not harder, than when she had first entered me. I had never felt so aroused.

Suddenly her breathing changed and her rippling muscles went taut.

"Oh, yes. Oh, fuck. I am going to come for you, Sarah," she growled. Then she grabbed my wrist and pushed my hand even deeper inside her.

We began to moan. Then we got louder. And louder. An indistinguishable string of expletives escaped us both.

As she came, her body tensing and loosening and tensing again, her cunt rhythmically grabbed at my fingers, contracting and releasing as she quaked with pleasure.

As the aftershocks subsided and she opened her eyes and looked at me, she cracked a grin and giggled. "You liked that?" she asked.

"Did I like that?! It was amazing! Why? Do I look funny?" I covered my face with my hand.

"You look like a kid who just got a pony for their birthday." She laughed some more.

I realized she must be right. I could feel the mixture of astonishment and giddiness that must be showing on my face because it was exploding inside me. I started to giggle too. I collapsed next to her and she pulled me into her strong arms, my head resting on her shoulder. We lay there for a while, fingers tracing skin.

"Well," she said, "I guess you have to get home to that cat."

My mind cycled through reasons why it would be fine to stay longer. And it would. The cat didn't need me at all, really, not until morning. But I thought it wise not to ignore her hint that it was time for me to go. I gathered my trousers from the bedroom floor and the rest of my things from the living room. After I was dressed, Em came over and held me close, kissing me warmly. Then she walked me to her door.

"It was really nice meeting you," I said and we both laughed.

"Think you can find your way off Church Street?" she grinned.

"Yes," I said, "but I'm not sure I want to."

"When will you be back in town?" she asked. "Maybe we can get another drink?"

"Yes, please! I'm definitely coming back to Church!" I said.

Hearing the words as they left my mouth, I chuckled. "I've never said *that* before!"

I leaned in and kissed her one last time, turned, and with all the self-restraint I could muster, walked quickly away.

Then I remembered the pork chops.

I walked back and knocked on her door. She opened it, looking surprised at first, and then she smiled.

"Next prayer service isn't until tomorrow," she teased.

"The pork chops," I said.

"Right, the pork chops," she said. "I'll get them . . . in a bit." Then she pulled me inside, kissed me, and shut the door.

RELENTLESS

Sinclair Sexsmith

I'm on her before she closes the front door. One hand on the wall on either side of her head, forcing her backward. She gasps and cowers, bending herself under me.

"You know what to do," I say. "You have thirteen minutes."

It's not quite enough time. She prefers twenty, or even thirty. But I'm not waiting.

"Daddy," she says, softly. It's not a protest, not a whimper, but more of a release, a prayer. Her eyes sparkle as she looks up at me. She's technically taller than I am, especially in her almost appropriate work heels, the ones that show a little toe cleavage. But I put my boots on before she got home; the ones with the thick soles and the well-worn leather shined by the skilled boys at the Eagle.

I kiss her, softly, that full-lipped sweetness where we both melt. Fuck if I didn't miss her today.

I grin and lift my hands away from the wall.

"Thirteen?" she says.

"Twelve," I say, and she takes off her coat quickly, hangs it, and heads upstairs.

She likes her after work routine: empty her bag, empty her pockets, locate all the dry erase markers she might have accidentally swiped, change her clothes, put her lunch containers away, wash out her tea thermos, have a snack. Bedroom, kitchen. Then the bathroom: wash her face, take down her hair. She keeps it up at work. I love how she does that. Just a little buttoned up, just a little contained, just a little of her incredible sexiness held back just for me. Then she brushes it.

Or, sometimes, I do.

She likes to have time to thoroughly take her make-up off, to check her email, to check social media on her phone, to stretch on her yoga mat. Sometimes I watch her. Sometimes I'm still working. Sometimes I don't even notice when she comes back.

But I did today.

It's a fine line between taking care of her, my little girl, as her Daddy, and taking advantage of her. We've talked about this, of course. She likes to meander over that line in a wave as kinky as her hair. Back and forth. Pandering and possessing. Sometimes our friends don't understand what we do. We have tried to let them in on it, to explain or share how comfortable we are here, how we feel like ourselves. But the quizzical looks and the questions they ask show us they don't get it. Not really. We have mostly stopped trying, but we haven't stopped sharing it with each other. We haven't stopped showing each other that weird, sometimes shameful underbelly of us, the tender places that are so easily hurt or scared away. The part of me who wants to take and take and take, past the point of permission, even, because it's all about me and my needs are valid. The part of her who wants to be overpowered, overthrown, overwhelmed. The parts in us both who want to be wanted, to be needed.

For whatever reason, they are all twisted up with our desire, our sex, our play.

Sometimes, the line between taking care and taking advantage is clear, and I want to cross it. Or she wants me to. Today, she texted me at lunch with a proposal, and I promised her I'd deliver.

"One minute to spare," I say. I pat the wooden paddle into my left hand, gently, *pat, pat,* sliding my hand down the length of it. I still have my boots on. The boys at the Eagle would always leave the soles of them clean enough to lick, and if it's good enough for their mouths, it's good enough for my bedroom carpet.

She's kneeling next to the bed. Her hair is over her shoulders. Her silk turquoise robe with the white lace trim is tied around her waist, loose, and she's bare otherwise. Bare feet, bare pussy, bare legs.

She nods. She might be shivering. "Yes, Daddy."

"Up."

She rises, gracefully, intentionally, with a fluid movement that she practiced, that she still practices, and presents. Her robe is short and the bed is high, and it barely covers her ass as she bends over. She spreads her legs and brings her arms under her head until she's nestled comfortably, and she sighs.

I come in close, my body pressing against hers. "My favorite girl," I murmur, bending to be close to her ear. "You know why I have this paddle out, right?"

"Because . . . I deserve it?"

"That's right." And she does. She keeps me grounded, tells me I'm doing the right thing. She wakes me up with her mouth on me more days than not. She is excited for my experimental cooking. She knows where I hold all my demons, and she is slowly making friends with them. I wake her up stroking her thigh and wrapping my arms around her. I appreciate her for all the hard work she does to make sure our bills are paid. I make decisions when she wants to defer. I hold her while she cries at all the lesbian romance films. She deserves everything, everything.

I smooth my hand over her ass and thighs; she settles deeper into the bed. And I begin.

"One," she counts. My arm is fluid, liquid. The paddle is an extension of my hand, of my shoulder, of my heart. *Let it go.*

"Two. Three."

I drop into a dominant flow state. I was already flirting with it when she opened the door. I prepared myself before she even got home. I told myself all the things I tell myself when she wants me to perform for her, when she needs me to take the outside world away from her and let her be small, let her be mine and only mine, let her be released from the burdens of the work day and the ten texts her mother sent since noon and the sealed envelopes in her inbox tray on her desk and whatever public relations nightmare happens to be in her email since she logged off at work. I tell myself that she wants this, that it serves her deepest needs to give over, to surrender, to be taken care of and held safely. I tell myself that she loves it when I lose control, just a little bit. I tell myself that we have had dozens, maybe hundreds, of hours of negotiations, talking about what we like and don't like, debriefing after scenes and role-plays and fantasies and late nights of sex, sharing what we loved and what was hard. I tell myself that she knows me, she's seen into me in ways I don't know if anyone else ever has, and she trusts me. She knows what I'm capable of, and she stays, and she loves me. She knows how to take care of herself. She knows how to tell me to stop, if she needs me to.

"Six," she cries into the comforter. "Seven." Her body jerks as my paddle, hand, arm, shoulder, all connect with that sweet spot on her ass. She rocks against the bed, tucking and flexing her pelvis, showing me everything.

I stroke her hair. "Good girl," I murmur. "Good girl."

The tears start at number fifteen, and by twenty her mouth is open wide with guttural exhales that combine moans and gasps. She takes it. She thanks me.

"Please," she says, when we get to twenty-five. "Please, Daddy, please."

I slide two fingers into her slit and nestle next to her. "My sweet girl," I say. "You did so well."

She whines a little, still letting the cries come easy. Surrender doesn't come to me like that, it comes so much softer, so much more tenderly. I could never take as much as she does. I love how strong she is.

I feel her fingers start to rub her own clit and softly, slowly, I find the spots inside she likes and I press, I stroke. She blooms open, that cavern in her inside like a breath inflating.

"Daddy, Daddy," she chants as she comes. I feel the muscles of her pulse and squeeze from the inside. Her thighs quake. The tension in her slit pushes my fingers out and just my fingertips are left touching the soft folds of her.

She eases onto the bed. She won't be able to sit down for a bit. I nudge myself in next to her and she curls around my arm and thigh while I stroke her skin. Her robe is off her shoulders, pooled around her waist.

"Hi," she says, after a moment.

"Hi."

Her lips are red from scraping against the bedspread; her eyes are wet. She's glowing pink.

"Thanks for taking care of me, Daddy."

"The pleasure is all mine, sweet girl."

"You did a good job. I think my ass is going to be bruised!"

I rub my hand over it, gently, and she winces. I grin as a satisfying drip of sadism slinks down my spine. She'll think of me when she sits down. She'll think of me, and she'll remember my paddle, my hands on her, my fingers in her, and this release, this relentless absolution.

"What's for dinner?" she says.

I grin. "Anything you want," I say, though I know I'll be making the decision.

I JUST REALLY LOVE CATS

Cassandra Cavenaugh

"I love cats, I love every kind of cat. Sorry, I just, I really love cats."

The video played in the background, and I cackled at my desk. This playlist always cheered me up, and today I could use all the help I could get. There's nothing quite as demoralizing as being let go from a job you love, but these little morsels of fantasy held my morale together.

They'd walked me out first thing in the morning; I didn't even get to sip another cup of free coffee, or steal a bite of pastry before security called. I traced the embossed cubicle nameplate in my hand letter by letter. Years of work at the company, and this was what I had left. To say I was stressed was a bit of an understatement, but the job applications could wait until tomorrow.

I ran my thumb across the soft faux fur of the cat ear headband, and stroked my hand down the length of the tail. I'd had the set for a while, but the right moment just hadn't presented itself yet. Val and I had talked about pet play before, but short of some playful banter and well-intended rumination we hadn't actually done it. We both wanted it, but neither of us knew where to start without tipping the other off that they were clueless.

I, for one, was ready to fall to my knees mewling at Val's feet but the logistics always stopped us. You can't just throw on a pair of cat ears and a plug tail at the drop of a hat. Where's the romance in that? No, this would take time and that was something neither of us had in great abundance. Val worked nights at the restaurant, and I usually worked days at my fancy desk job. Of course, today's events had changed that.

Maybe it was time. I set out the kitten gear, a metal plug, and my play collar on the bed neatly as if it was some flat lay for Instagram or something. Val would be back from lunch soon, and she'd head for the bedroom to get some rest before her shift. A little lost sleep wouldn't hurt, just this once.

I was nervous as the key turned in the front door lock. Something about the anticipation, the worry, the anxiousness of *everything* just overwhelmed me. I was a frazzled mess, and the thought of letting go and having some playtime had entirely escaped me. I'd practically forgotten it all as Val dropped her keys on the table, and set her eyes on me.

"A-are you okay, Cat?" Val asked looking down at me as I gazed off into the distance pondering exactly how I wanted to answer that.

"I, well, where to start . . . They walked me out today. I lost my job. I'm a hot mess and I have no idea what I'm going to do next, but I do know that I need—I need to stop thinking and just be present for a while." My voice was rambling, trailing off after each phrase, waiting for her to pick up where I'd left off.

"I'm so sorry, honey. I know you love your work, and that just sounds awful. Why don't we get some rest, and I'll make you some tea before work?"

She headed toward the bedroom, and as her hand touched the doorknob I remembered the display I'd left on our bed. The lump in my throat was practically audible, but all that escaped my mouth was a long, drawn out "Uhhhh . . ." which, in retrospect, was not the most attractive thing I could have done.

I followed Val into the bedroom with my eyes cast down at the floor. The elephant in the room was actually a cat, and the cat was me. Or something. Look, I don't make a lot of sense when I'm stressed, okay? Anyways.

"Did you want to . . . I mean, we haven't, and I don't . . . but . . ." Val was reaching the same level of chaotic horny as I was, apparently. Neither of us knew what to do, but here we were standing at our bed with a shiny, metal butt plug between us. I don't know what got into me next, well, metaphorically at least—but I began to strip.

Val's eyes went wide, and she started to help me out of my pencil skirt and blouse. In mere seconds, I was bare. The lavender lace brassiere fell to the floor along with the matching panties, and with that I blushed deep crimson. Yes, she'd seen me like this many times—but never as her pet. Sure, we'd done some light bondage, a little play here and there, but this was different. This was a scene.

Val motioned me over to the bed and bent me over the side. My bare breasts rubbed across the rough comforter as she maneuvered her hand up between my legs, caressing my inner thigh with the cold metal plug. She'd already tied the tail to it with a lavender ribbon and applied a generous helping of lubricant. The pressure of the plug as it pressed into me was a sensation altogether foreign. Val pressed gently, slowly inserting the toy deep inside me.

"Tell me if I'm going too fast, love."

And with a final push, it was in. The soft fur brushed against my ass and down the back of my thigh. Val came from behind me, pressing herself against my body, and pushed the headband onto my head.

"Not yet, we're not done, pet."

Of course, the collar. Val wrapped the reinforced silk play collar around my neck; the bell jingled as I fidgeted under her weight. My mind had cleared, fully focused on the task at hand. It was hard to really worry about anything else when there's a fullness deep inside you that feels fleeting, comforting. I don't know how to explain it, but one thing was certain: I wasn't stressed.

"Get down on all fours. I can't have my pet walking around like she owns the place, can I?" Val said playfully. I, in fact, did own the place—thank you very much.

I slid off the bed, my hands and knees pressing into the thick carpet. Every movement brought with it new sensations. The sound of my collar bell jingling as I crawled across the floor, my tail swishing behind me teasing my thighs.

"I know this is new for both of us, but when you are being my good little kitten I expect you to act the part. You can meow and purr all you want, but words should not escape those pretty lips of yours." Val always had a way with words; it was disarming, undeniable. Even in this moment of awkwardness she knew what to say to give me permission to let go.

"Wait here, kitten. I have an idea that I think you will appreciate." Val dashed out of the room and headed for the craft closet. I could hear rummaging, a little cursing, but eventually the "aha" moment. Her heavy footsteps on the wooden floor gave me comfort that she hadn't left me alone, exposed. She returned with a small ball of lavender yarn and set it down in front of me.

"Why don't you play a bit while your owner watches? Go on."

I stared at the foreign object, took a breath, and batted it with my palm. The little ball of yarn skittered across the rug and bounced off the baseboard. My eyes widened and I chased it down, taking another swipe. Something about playing with a ball of yarn just made sense to me. My tail bounced as I chased it around the room, collar bell jingling with every pounce.

Val smiled down at me from her seat on the bed. I idly wondered what owner was thinking about, but quickly returned to my ball. I was getting rather good at moving across the floor on all fours, but Val had a better idea. She scooped up the ball and set out a bowl of water on the floor by the door.

"Drink."

I looked up at Val, and then down at the bowl of water. She didn't really think I would do that, did she? I mean, the water is going to go everywhere and most importantly all down my chin. I couldn't, but I *was* thirsty.

I crawled over the bowl and leaned in. My chin hit the cold water before my tongue could reach it. Lapping at the water like a cat was the only way I was *drinking* anything. It was embarrassing, demeaning, and practically dehumanizing but the blush of my face burned brightly inside me. Something about this whole scene was pushing my buttons.

When I looked up at owner I noticed her top was missing, her bra and blouse had hit the floor. I lapped away at the water some more; my thirst being quenched but also stoked by the sight ahead. Gazing back up at Val, her jeans hit the floor along with her panties. Stark naked, standing over me.

"Be a good kitten and lick me, pet."

She didn't have to ask me twice. I crawled over to her and nuzzled my head between her legs. Her scent was already hitting me, and I knew seeing me like this was turning her on. I spread her thighs ever so slightly and flicked my tongue against her clit. Val nearly jumped, but caught herself and stroked my head as I found her spot. My kitten ears brushing against her thighs, tickling them as my tongue went to work.

And then she came, and came again. Her juices flooding my mouth with her taste; her scent on me marking me as her own. I wanted more, I wanted to come too. I wanted that release, that euphoria. I pulled my body into a kneeling position and reached for my sex before Val grabbed my arms and pulled me back onto all fours.

I was on fire. The plug tail's weight, the sensation of the fur gliding across my bare skin, the embarrassment of not just being naked crawling on all fours but also having cute little kitten ears on with water and her juices dribbling down my chin was too much. I needed release, to get off and to bliss out—and Val wasn't having it.

"Kittens don't masturbate, sweetie. You'll get yours when I say you do."

I crawled over to the nightstand and batted Val's book onto the floor and smirked up at her. I've never been one to brat, but since I couldn't verbalize my distaste I could very well cause mischief to get my point across.

"You know, I shouldn't be surprised, but I think you've earned a punishment for that shenanigan."

Val stepped into the master bathroom and returned with something held deftly behind her back. We don't keep the paddle in there and I know she wouldn't hurt me. What could it be? My eyes were fixed on her movements as she crossed the space between us and raised her right hand. The cold water hit my face and it hit me, in more ways than one, that she'd retrieved the spray bottle I used to refresh my hair every other morning.

Sprayed. Like a kitten who can't keep her claws off the furniture. I looked up at Val with wide, pleading eyes, resting my ass against my heels to raise myself off the floor. She leaned in and tapped my nose.

"Be a good kitten and I'll give you what you want." She admonished me playfully, knowing full well I was being a brat, but still showing a hint of hope that I would come before the scene was over.

Val left me and found the low antique chair I used for my vanity and turned it to face me before sitting down with her legs pressed together.

"Come here, kitten." She beckoned me, her fingers curling to her palm to show me the way. Would this be it? Would I finally get release?

I crawled across the room toward her, my tail trailing behind me, the bell on my collar ringing with each step. She smiled down at me and patted her lap, and I put my two hands there looking up at her quizzically.

"Up, in my lap." Val patted her thigh again firmly, and I obliged by laying across her lap. Obviously, I was a bit larger than your average house cat. The underside of my breasts pressed against her outer thigh as I settled into place. In any other scene this would look like a punishment was coming.

"Good girl. Now, turn over. I want to see your face when you melt." I wriggled in her lap, eyes meeting hers as she smirked down at me. She slid open the drawer of my vanity and retrieved the Hitachi. Yes, yes this is it. I reached for the vibrator, but she batted my hand away. Come on, now, now, now. My disappointment must have shown on my face because Val booped my nose again.

"So eager, kitten. You don't decide when, I do."

She cradled me in her lap, pressed the vibrator against me, and turned it on the lowest setting. The hum of the Magic Wand shaking me to my core, I could feel the vibrations deep inside me. Something about being held like a cherished pet and pleasured at her will was intoxicating.

"Be a good girl and wait for me. You aren't to climax until I give you permission, pet."

I bit my lip not just because it was extremely *hot,* but because I didn't think I could wait that long. Even this little bit of motion was enough to set me on fire. Any more and I'd break. As if on cue, Val pressed a button and the intensity rose. I couldn't take it anymore, and I pawed at her chest demanding release.

"Let go, break for me darling."

I came so hard it felt like I was losing my mind, and Val maneuvered the toy so I wouldn't escape a second wave. The tail plug pressed into me as my body shuddered with pleasure. Each and every muscle tensing, pushing the plug closer to my core. I tried to protest, but I came again quickly as every last thought left my mind and all I could do was let out the softest mew.

Val set the toy down and stroked my hair gently, still cradling me with her safe, strong arms. She pressed her lips to my forehead gently, and smiled down at me.

"You did so well, honey. I'm so proud of you."

I nuzzled into her neck and closed my eyes as she held me close. My mind solely focused on her in this moment of quiet wherein I was her pet, and she was my owner.

LIKE A FUCKING MOTHER

Sarah B. Burghauser

It means "all people." All the bodies are infected. And the pandemic infects in myriad ways. There are the sick, of course. And there are the lonely and desperate. There are those of us who are going bonkers within our walls, and those who are infected with the illusion of invincibility. We each, in our own boxes, try in one way or another, to get out—we pray. We imagine, we yearn, we experiment, we decide not to give a fuck, we destroy ourselves and reinvent, too. But every body is affected.

I spent the day with my toddler, like I always do. We bake, we Skype and Zoom with family, we play in our gravel yard, and I let her run around naked. Sometimes I make her a bath in the middle of the day with lots of bubbles and food coloring and let her play with the bottle of shaving cream and we call it a "unicorn bath." At the end of the day it's dinner and washing up and stories before bed. Keeping her entertained and nourished while trying to take it easy on my eight-months-pregnant body is harder than I ever imagined. And made harder by quarantine. Every moment new worries emerge and swirl together with the normal ones that were already there. What would happen if I got sick? Would they take my baby away from me after he's born? Will I have to birth in isolation? What will I do on lockdown with a toddler and a newborn?

My wife leaves the house every day because she is an essential worker. The fear, the stress, encountering all the ways in which people are shitty to each other all come into play in her job. And she's always there—at work. Well, she says it's work. But I know that it's also *her*—the other woman—her co-worker. Sometimes my wife texts saying she's going to be late. Always late when she's working alongside her chickie. And that chickie? My wife's crush turned love affair? She's some average straight girl. Some blonde. And my wife thinks I don't know. Thinks I am so deep into my own body, my own anxieties and thoughts, that I don't notice anyone or anything else. But as it turns out, she doesn't know me at all, and I feel the way you might imagine one would whose partner is having an affair when she's heavily pregnant, chasing around a wily toddler all day, during a global pandemic, alone.

It's nighttime now and I've just put my swollen feet up for the first time today. I wrestle my way out of my sports bra—the only one that fits me now, and the maternity leggings that make me feel like a sausage in a mom-suit casing. My wife texts to say, "Leaving in five minutes." So you'd think, with an only five-minute commute, she'd be home in ten minutes. But I'm never sure anymore.

But I err on the side of caution and assume I have fifteen minutes, twenty tops, so long as my toddler, who is sleeping in the next room, who has been waking frequently in a stubborn, pandemic-stress-induced sleep regression, stays asleep.

During my first pregnancy, I never liked how orgasm felt. It was uncomfortable. Like wearing the coziest pair of pants, but they had an itchy tag sewn in the back. I wanted it. But also, I didn't. Orgasms gave me heartburn and panic. Orgasm made me feel frustrated, like a surfer enjoying the motion of the ocean, but unable to catch any waves. Orgasms during pregnancy induced the pain of worry and of a body negotiating what space it deserves.

But way before there was ever a baby in my body and before I met my wife, there was her. Imagine this and listen to yourself.

You are back at Folsom. Remember Folsom? Remember that fit butch nineteen years your senior with the small eyes and itchy smile? Remember when you knew what your body looked like and she knew, too, and so did all the queers in the women's play space? Remember when you marveled at the pictures of you she took while you were strung up in one of her rope traps? And the way you gazed at yourself in the mirror every day after that for as long as you could afford to, marveling, perplexed almost, at the way your skin looked when bruised and lashed, and how those marks changed each day as they faded from red and blue, to purple, to yellow? Remember your gorgeous butch—your top daddy power butch all the way—with her soft, cropped hair and mangled grin, who worshiped all the gentle curves of you and the severe ones, too? Remember all those times in the dungeon? And in her San Francisco fancy apartment with the anchor points on the ceiling and soft light coming in over the mantle? With oversized paintings of scenes abroad overlooking your degradation? Your utter pleasure?

Remember what we did together? She hardly ever fucked me. But it was everything else that goes into sex without the actual fucking. And even then, she once served me a beating so perfectly orchestrated that each lash brought me closer to coming—my body and my imagination, one.

I find my nipples. Both at the same time because nursing the first child has made my breasts stretch, and then balloon again with this second pregnancy. This is the part of me I always praised for its ability to take a beating despite its thin, delicate skin and gentle manner. This is the part that housed my heart, the warmest spot that pulsed with an even stronger story than my cunt. That managed to give me confidence in spite of their imperfect shape. My fingers wander all around and underneath and I try to notice the tender parts, the soft parts, the parts of me I can recognize. I notice the feeling of sinew just beneath the surface, and I swear I can feel the milk ducts revving up. There are stretch marks and discolored patches that shimmer with a purpose unknown to me. And now my nipples can kiss one another and connect. I skim right past the skin tags and rough spots, not wanting to dwell there, for they have their own stories to tell at another time. Yet each inch seems to threaten my attention, coax me away from what I want right now, which is to feel something else. To be me again.

She lit a candle scented "cedarwood cigar" and ordered me onto her bedroom floor. So I sat with my hands behind me, the way she liked. She might have used rope to keep me in place, but at that moment she did not need to do that. She was moving her body so languidly, like a wave. She knelt over me and told me to open my mouth and poured whiskey in, enough to coat my cheeks and tongue, and my lips went numb from alcohol and anticipation.

She said, "You're going to take me in. Listen to me, sweet girl." She handed me the glass. "Drink this," she said. "And stay here."

She got up and left the room. I sipped and savored, not caring that whiskey's not my drink. Loving it because she told me to drink it.

I find the top of my belly under my breasts where that deep crease is. There is no transition anymore between the parts of me—just abrupt changes from one place to another—breasts resting on the shelf of my belly, rolling off to the sides and back again when I move. Here is my fundus where the baby's bottom, his tailbone, shifts throughout the day from one side of my ribcage to the other. And just a little ways down is my belly button, wide and shallow from stretching. My belly button, the heart of the linea nigra. The line appears out of nowhere in pregnancy, winds itself in a small knot around my navel, and splits me lengthwise down the middle. What else has my body been hiding from me? Pregnancy reveals the body's potential, and also its dormancies.

I'd wanted to take mouthfuls of that whiskey, take it all in fast and swallow like the smoky throat-feel wasn't traveling up to my eyes and threatening to make me cough like an amateur pot-smoker. I could drink, make no mistake. I loved to drink. I could even make it look good. I could change my mind about the taste. I could drink, yes indeed. But this time I pretended to be an aficionado, making every swallow slow and count. I knew how to change my mind. Turn the turn-off into desire.

When she strode back in I'd only had a few sips. She might have accused me of being greedy had I finished it. I had to guess how much she wanted me to drink. Yes, and when my gorgeous butch came back in, I was lounging on her floor, propped up on one elbow. She stood over me in the same jeans and black T-shirt she had on earlier in the evening when she pick me up from the BART stop. Except now she was barefoot. God it drove me crazy when she went barefoot in her house while we played like she wanted to feel her feet on the ground. Like she didn't need the trappings of boots or leather to bring me in. To let me know what she could do. I trusted her completely. Especially when she was barefoot.

I find the bottom of my belly—all that space between—a long ways from the top. It takes time to stroke all that space where the baby lay, the very center—where the water lives—tensing up all the borders of me. I find the bottom of my belly over and over again, where I bottom out. Where my hair begins. Hair I haven't seen in months. Thighs I haven't seen in months. A vulva I never want to see again. My vulva. That birthed my first. That stretched, but not enough. A vulva that had to break itself open without any drugs, without any oil or coaxing. Without any fanfare or fore-play. Without any of the trappings of wet sex, hot mouth feel, or gentle love. My vulva tore. My perineum tore. My vaginal walls tore. My labia tore. And none of the stitches took. This is the very bottom of my belly, the very core of me. It is mangled.

So she's standing over me and she unzips her jeans—the top button was already undone when she walked in and I knew what that meant. She never fucked me because that's not what we did together. But this time, her bare feet and that opened top button was bespoke. She took my hand gently in hers. She was not bigger than me. Just older, and stronger because of it. So when she took my hand I knew I'd follow wherever she wanted to take me. I got to my knees and inhaled her denim. I rubbed my cheeks there first, and then my nose over her thighs and then stole a quick nibble from her fly and I knew then I was lost in her and I'd never be the same again. My head was infected. I was adrift. My whole body was open to her and I could feel myself stretching, wanting to open even further. She tangled her fingers in my hair—in the choppy queer tousle of the time—and groaned. She never made those kinds of sounds. Never emoted like that. What is going to happen, I wondered. It seemed obvious, but I never quite knew with her, how our time would unfold. Where we would end up. How dirty I'd get. How red or black or blue.

So now I am touching myself, traversing the bumpy terrain of both pregnant and postpartum. I touch the splits, the dips that are deeper than before birth. I touch the once smooth waterways that led effortlessly out to ocean, which now break apart the waves with their crags and peaks rendering the water white and choppy. I touch the skin tags. The three lips where there used to be only two. The scar tissue and mounds of raw, tender flesh. My fingers find new depths without ever going inside. And who knows what I'd find if I ever want that again. If I ever manage desire again— without pain or disgust—to slip into the surface of my very own, brand new earth.

I was lying on the floor again and she stood over me. She reached into her jeans and pulled out her cock, her fist around it, knowing how to control herself. Knowing what to do. She never showed herself to me and I felt so awed. So lucky. So fucking hot for her. And she lowered herself onto me, toward my face, and my mouth opened automatically, my chin extended, my jaw straining.

She's in my mouth now. I wanted to reach up for her ass to pull her in deeper, but she was pinning my wrists at my sides and leading her own way, knowing I'd take whatever she needed me to. My tongue slid over her, base to tip, and I noticed an opening at the top.

"What's this?" I asked.

"Sweetie, that's where my come comes out," she said matter-of-fact, and suddenly I felt silly like a naïve girl asking the most obvious of questions. And just then she slid down my body—tits and hip bones—to my open, dripping little cunt. She paused and I took a breath.

"I'm gonna get you pregnant," she said, and she pushed into me. All the way. Hard and steady and insistent, and my body called out its surprise and pleasure with a sound from my throat I hardly recognized. It was the sexiest thing anyone had ever said to me.

That was then. I don't want to remember, but I do. I have no choice. If I want to go on, if I ever want to be a real person again,

I have no choice. I feel the echo of who I used to be reverberating through me. The sex I had. The body I had. The dreams I had. The idea of myself that I had. I hate it all. I touch, I reach, I dig, I grip, I push. This is my body now. I feel the baby move and I come like a fucking mother.

I can't linger. Like a mother, my eyes open almost instantly to look for signs of a wakeful toddler. I take deep breaths, lie still, and let the contractions calm. I hear gravel crunching under tires as headlights flash through the window. *Go away*, I think. *Just another few minutes.* I hear the door open. My wife takes off her work shoes and I hear her walk to the bathroom straight away to wash up and change because the pandemic is on her clothes and breath and in her hair. The pandemic that takes many forms. The pandemic that has infected my home and my mind. The pandemic that is destroying my family. The pandemic of my life and of my body readying itself to be torn apart once more.

My jaw tenses and I think those last thoughts before I close my eyes and my pretend sleep turns into actual sleep. We are in a time when the skin is toxic, breath is toxic, saliva and tears are toxic. And our homes are both haven and prison. Like our bodies. Like memory.

THE MOON
AND YOUR EYES

August in Flux

Cold air pulls at my hair through the open car window. Summer in the Santa Cruz Mountains still has that hum of fog coming in off the sea, even after sunset. My lungs set still, I remind myself to breathe. I know what I need. Just one night to get this release. To feel my body breathe. I know what you need too. Just one night to be fully seen. To revel in my rebel and be able to scream.

I'm riding shotgun next to you. You've got me right here. Right now. Exactly how I want you. Taking me up to a place above the rest. Way above, up the crest of that mountain right there. Pull off here. We're gonna park it in the dark and under the light of the moon, I'm gonna love you right. Right up here above the treetops, the forest looking lit up from the top up, the light of the moon bright. White light pouring silver all over this here forest. Running up and over that plaid flannel I'm gonna rip right off you. That's it. Put it in park. Way up here in the dark. Here is where I'm gonna love you. I look you deep in the eyes and see the full moon magic sitting right there, staring right back at me. Drunk on lust and luck and ready for me to suck. Mm! Get out of the car, baby,

I wanna see you in that full moonlight. Up on the hood out in this wood, in this light you look fine.

The stars are trying to shine, but the moon's drowning them out, and you're drowning out the moon, so bright in your eyes, with that red plaid up your arms adding texture next to your smooth skin, glossed from brown to blue in the light of the moon. I'm not waiting anymore. My hands skim up your sleeves. Stop me baby, if you please, but I know you want this as much as me, and the way your breath catches when I stare you in the eye tells me that if don't get this shirt off you soon, it's gonna be my ass naked under the full moon.

Fingers slip buttons, fumble in the cold. You told me you'd never really been sold on this whole "indoor work" thing, back when your touch first gave me a sting. We were holed up inside with our hot coffee teas, watching the sea through the glass, the wood café table edged in brass. You told me all the names of all the trees. Every one in this forest you know it by name, but somehow, despite cruising by stars, sharing our scars, pointing out Mars, you say you never laid a dame outside? Hmm. Never done it outside before. Riiight. That grin right there told me you might be expanding the truth, the way your lip caught on the edge of your tooth. I m not foolproof, but I was ready to be fooled.

Well, now here we are. Far above the vast expanse of trees, looking out over the seas. I'm vast and I'm bold and I see how you're sold on exactly what my hands are doing, running up inside your shirt to flirt with your muscles under that cloth. I'm boss and you're free. Let's see under that plaid. One more layer underneath, white and ribbed, hugged next to your skin. I want to be in, but one eyebrow ticks up. I see you staring at me, the question in your eyes. A shirt is no disguise. Keep it on, babe, I've got no interest in scaring you, only caring for you. Let me make your skin sing.

My hands slide up and push that plaid off your shoulders,

holding you tight, pushing you back against the car and far up above the trees, letting your skin drink in the light of the moon, and my eyes drink you in. Thick and brown. My eyes move up to down. Black hair, long on top, short on the sides. Eyes like almonds, black in the night. Arms like heartwood, legs braced wide, Leatherman hanging out the side of your back pocket. Thick boots laced up, dusted with black dirt from the earth that we stomped back where we romped this afternoon, when I said I wanted to see you in the light of the moon.

I see the moon in your eyes. The way the light shines bright deep inside. Your lips are hot on mine. Breath hot, red hot, I'm hot and I've got you between my teeth. My teeth that bite and sink and scrape at the nape of your neck. The way you sway just so when my teeth sink in just right. My hands run up your arm, embossed with ink, embossed like rocks over sinking warm. Sink deep into me now, baby, and rock me till the dawn breaks hard and fast over that horizon.

You sing out, a sweet note breaking that black velvet night. Silent up here except for you, with your voice starting to break. I rake my nails down your back. You go slack. Breath starting to go ragged, my jagged breath matching yours, chest for chest. I'm pressed up against you, my leg between yours. My hand wraps round your hip, feeling my grip, pulling you to me. The edges of my eyes view the trees. I sink to my knees and find that button, shut in tight between rips in the denim. My hand in. Fingers splayed across the cotton covering your cunt. My manicured nails sail right over, fingertips bolder, gripping the sides of your jeans as this queen presses red lips to your covered sex. I can feel you getting wet. That lipstick'll stain, but I crane my head back up to look at you and with your eyes dark and your breath heavy, I know you don't care.

Your hands grip my biceps, dragging me up to stand on my

own two boots. The pink shoes I bought on sale at the mountain store that day when the floor was covered with boots. Shoes thrown every which way. I glanced up and saw you say hey. That smirk on your face as I tried to lace the too-big brown boots.

Get out of my face. I blew my hair out of the way.

Here, let me help. It fell back in my eyes, and to my surprise, you knelt before me, placed my boot on your knee, and laced it up, neat.

I remember I stood dumb. A stud on her knees. All that power bowed right down before me.

These don't fit, but I think those might.

You pointed to the pinks over to the right, looked up at me. I might as well have fallen right there and then. Your brown eyes knocking me over head over heels and I knew I wanted you. You saw my reaction and smothered a grin. But that hint of side smirk let me in, let me know that you see me how I see me too: a girl who loves loving girls like you.

You picked up the boots, brought them back over, standing too close. Much too close. Is it hot in here? Did the air leave the room? When you sank down, I caught a hint of your perfume, then tried in vain to reorient to the salesroom. You knelt down quick, slick, suave, flicked your eyes up to me. Took my hand and sat me down, directing me in a dance, breaking me from my trance. I watched you like a hawk, then, as you pulled the lace loose, slipped the tongue over the bridge of my foot, pressed up on my heel. I tried not to reel but I could feel you taking your time, more than you should, to spend bent over my boot, lacing it up slow and sure. Doing it right the first time. That's how you like it, huh, baby? Slow and steady and right the first time. I may be a little more reckless than you, but I'll do you right the first time.

I reached down to adjust my sock, locked my eyes on yours,

made sure your breath caught in your throat when you saw down my long pink shirt, too low on my chest, even the puffy white vest couldn't hide everything. I checked your hand: no ring. Not that that means anything. But still good to check. Especially if I'm planning already to wreck you.

The clasp on the necklace I put on this morning slithered down, thin metal slipping around my neck to dangle right in front of your face. You couldn't help but trek those delicious fingers up to check. A fine silver tree, the clasp disorderly. Your fingers wrapped delicately around the charm as you looked me dead in the eye, my hand suddenly on your arm, you gave the barest hint of a tug on the chain. Fire in my eyes, my breath caught in the rein. In that moment, I knew you were going to be my night tonight.

And here we are, just like I wanted, up high on the mountain, sea in the back, moon at the front, your body between me and the car and the earth. Your hands grip my arms, keeping me tall on my boots. Lick my lower lip. Nip. I can't help the grin that escapes, lighting my face like the moon up above. I shove you back onto the car again. My lips on yours, and I'm getting all of you tonight. Push all of me onto you, my skin screaming for every touch. Your hands slide down my arms around my waist and I feel your face sigh through my kiss, an ace pressed against my lips. Or maybe that sigh was mine. Hands reach round my backside, finding my ass and kneading and needing and rubbing and feeling, getting to know every inch of me just right. Even if it's just for tonight.

My hand's still down the front of your pants, cupping and rubbing over thin cotton. Your wet's leaking out and I'm ready to jet set through the sky with you. I feel my fingers slide against wet, sweat between my breasts drying cold in the chilled air, my hand warm with your heat. Your head rolls back, eyes closed, body arched against the hood of the car. The stars trying to twinkle overhead, but you won't let them. You're shining bright from the inside and you're the one I want to ride.

I take my hand back up. Your eyes open wide, panting, demanding, why? I look you dead in the eye and slip each finger between my lips, licking off your taste, salty as the sea and sweet as the trees. Hold you in that moment with me. I trace my fingertips across your lips, follow them with my tongue, my teeth, my need heavy as my tongue seeks you out. My hand on the back of your head, pulling you in, my mind spinning, racing as I'm chasing each sensation you're giving me so freely.

My hand trails down your throat, wanting to wrap my palm across that moat of power held inside. Take your voice from you. Take what you freely give. In this world where you are silenced without choice, giving you your voice by seeing you as you are. I see how you gleam in your dark blue jeans with the size too big seams. See how you stand with your lats flexed, reflexed at the defects of the pretense of the male sex. See how you need to scream, in pain and in ecstasy, to blow off that steam, put down your legacy. I see you standing next to me, ready to hand me your voice because tonight, it's your choice.

Witness you giving it to me, pressed against my car, far above the rest of the land. Hear you in my hand. My hand that trails down your chest to the old worries buried there. I can almost hear your thoughts scurrying around, hear the frowns from your mother, the gossip from your aunt, from too many unfriendly friends who just can't wrap their minds around why a pretty girl like you would want to dress like a boy. Too many lines from too many times, wrapped up and sealed in cloth. Silent. Bound landmines. I wish you were mine. I'd take those combustibles and bust them safely inside. Leave it so nothing could hurt you no more. Wrap my hand around your throat and hold you there, safe and warm and wanting and whole, mine forever; mine in a day; mine tonight; mine for play.

I trail my nails across your skin, keratin scraping the delicate skin covering your collarbone. Skin stretched tight over bone, over muscle over bone, in this body that makes your lived experience so much more than just this bone. Down I go. Down into you. Down into the abyss. Down where wet meets lips. Down where I can hold you down. Freeze you with just a breath. Arrest your chest. Your breath frozen in my teeth. The tip of my tongue languid on your peak.

My fingers slide deep inside and my mouth gets busy. You start bucking and sucking and fucking my hand deep into you, cursing me out with the breath finally unstuck from your chest. I'll stick to you like glue, baby, try to buck me off, it won't work. I'm with you till the end. Till you scream up to the sky and your fingers squeeze my arms and you think you're gonna die, but not on my watch, baby. On my watch, you get what you need. I feed your need with my wet lips, my tongue wrapped around your clit-dick, pulling and pushing deep inside, sucking you hard, giving exactly what you need. You're screaming and creaming and coming on me and it doesn't matter if your hand on the back of my head means I can't breathe, I'm gonna stay with you as you ride it out, as it runs out of you like waves skimming back from the sand. You're in my hand. And I'm with you. Echoing your yell into the well of the black night. Velvet in the sky, velvet on my lips. I kiss you, sip you, sway you down until you're done. Spent and vent.

I raise up as you come down, holding you steady, wait till you're ready. Set you upright, tug your jeans up tight. Let you brush my hair behind my ear just for tonight. Pull your plaid sleeves back up your arms, warm you up now that the heat has left and the cold come back. Open the door, gallant and femme, pulling you in to the dark inside. Curling up to your side, holding you tight, just for tonight.

The light shines in from the moon outside, dark and deep in your velvety eyes.

MAGIC IS COMING

Stephani Maari Booker

"Stop. Just stop," Maddi told Freya, who was holding a battery-operated vibrator against Maddi's clit. "Turn it off."

Freya shut off the vibrator and placed it on her nightstand as Maddi sat up in their bed and put her head in her hands.

"I'm so tired of this," Maddi said as she started weeping. "I don't even want to try to have sex anymore."

"Oh, sweetie," Freya said as she wrapped her pale, freckled arm around her distraught wife.

"It hasn't been the same," Maddi lamented. "It's been messed up ever since that damn Lupron shot. It was supposed to last only six months, but it's been eight and I still haven't gotten my period back. And now I can hardly have one orgasm even with a vibrator. I used to come ten times in row from a vibrator!"

Freya stroked Maddi's shoulder and let her talk without interrupting.

"The whole point of me getting fibroid removal surgery versus a hysterectomy was to make sure my sex life wouldn't suffer. But look at me now." Maddi lifted her head and flung her hands over her naked brown body. "The only reason why I let them give me that shot is because they said it would insure they wouldn't have to give me a hysterectomy. I knew that Lupron was fucked-up shit, but I let them give it to me because it was like a threat—take this or we might take your uterus!"

Freya continued to hold Maddi as she cried. After a while, Freya said, "We can find a way to fix this."

Maddi looked up at Freya with her teary brown eyes, sniffed, and then reached over to her own nightstand to grab a tissue from a box. "How?" she asked as she wiped her face and blew her nose.

"You can go to your OB/GYN," Freya suggested.

"Dr. Thao?" Maddi balled up the tissue and tossed it into the wastebasket on her side of the bed. "What she gon't do? It's not like she can prescribe me some female Viagra. There's no such thing as far as I know."

"We can do research." Freya rubbed Maddi's back. "We can try to find information and help online."

"Yeah, I guess." Maddi took another tissue from the box.

"Let's take those first steps," Freya said and then kissed Maddi's lips. "You go to Dr. Thao, and we go online. We'll figure out something."

"It's either that, or we'll be two victims of LBD," Maddi said.

"Lesbian bed death will not happen to us," Freya insisted as she wrapped her arms around her wife. "We'll find a way to help you."

A few days later, Maddi was sitting on her living room glider chair with her laptop resting on the blanket that covered her legs. As she stared at the screen, she shook her head and thought about shutting off the computer and tossing it on the floor. Ruminating over the online articles she read and scanned in her search for information about sexual response and arousal problems in women made her tired and irritated:

"Sexual Dysfunction Drugs for Men vs. Women: A Case of Inequality."

"The FDA, Sexual Dysfunction, and Gender Inequality."

"You okay, sweetie?" Freya came out of the kitchen and handed Maddi one of two saucers that held grilled cheese sandwiches.

"Oh." Maddi took the saucer, and Freya walked over to the couch to sit with her own sandwich. "I'm all right, baby. I'm just realizing that I'm being screwed over in getting any help for my sexual problems by sexism."

"Oh, honey, really?" Freya sat back on the couch and took a bite of her sandwich.

"Oh, yeah." Maddi put her sandwich on a side table between the glider and the couch, turned off her laptop, and then set it on the floor. "By all the articles I've read, because of sexism there's hardly any real medical or therapeutic help for women who have any kind of sexual function problems. There's like dozens of treatments out there for men who can't get it up or keep it up, including Viagra, but next to nothing for women who can't come or have a hard time coming or getting aroused."

"Wow." Freya shook her head.

"On top of that," Maddi continued, "the whole conversation and thinking about treatment for women's sexual problems is based on assuming all women want to have penis-vagina intercourse with men, and of course making women come while screwing men is the most important thing in the world." She rolled her eyes.

"Yuck!" Freya stuck out her tongue. "So it's sexism and lesbophobia getting in the way."

"Yep." Maddi picked up her sandwich and started eating it. "So it ain't looking too good for me."

"You have an appointment with Dr. Thao tomorrow, right?" Freya asked. "Maybe she'll have some recommendations."

"Maybe," Maddi said, "but after what I've read online I'm not optimistic."

"You're never optimistic."

"And you're never pessimistic," Maddi smiled at her wife. "You're always my Pollyanna baby."

"Yeah, and you wouldn't have me any other way." Freya blew a kiss at Maddi.

At her appointment with Dr. Thao, Maddi explained to the OB/GYN, who performed her fibroid removal surgery, about her sexual response problems and how she believed it was because of the synthetic hormone Lupron that she was injected with before the operation.

"Sexual dysfunction is a possible side effect of Lupron," Dr. Thao said. "I'm sorry that has happened to you."

"Well, that's great," Maddi said sarcastically. "I'd welcome the hot flashes I had the first few months after I got that shot if I could trade them for getting my sex life back to where it was before."

"I understand. Unfortunately, I have to be honest with you: There really isn't much medical treatment available for women with sexual difficulties."

"Yeah, I read up on it online, so I knew that," Maddi said.

"There are two drugs that have been approved by the FDA in the last few years," Dr. Thao continued, "but they're only recommended for pre-menopausal women who have low libido or sexual desire with no known medical cause."

"Well, I definitely still have sexual desire," Maddi said, "and we know the very medical cause for my problem, the Lupron."

"Oh, yes." Dr. Thao nodded her head. "Now, what I do tell women who have these problems is that they go get testosterone cream . . ."

"Testosterone cream? Like the male hormone?" Maddi asked.

"Males do have more testosterone than women, but in men and women testosterone levels are related to sexual arousal and response," Dr. Thao answered. "I recommend getting an over-the-counter testosterone cream and then applying it to the clitoris."

"Oh, okay." Maddi gave a noncommittal response, but she didn't want to take the doctor's advice.

"Testosterone cream? That's what she told you to use?" Freya said as she and Maddi were in the living room having a noodles and vegetables dinner that evening.

"Yeah," Maddi replied. "I know that testosterone is a hormone everybody has in them, but the idea of using it really freaks me out."

"If using an over-the-counter hormone cream might help you, maybe you should try using natural progesterone cream."

"You mean that stuff you put on every night?"

"Yes, and you could use it too, since like me, you're in the perimenopausal stage of life."

"I don't know what you're talking about. I'm still in my thirties." Maddi bobbed her head at Freya. "I'll be thirty-fifteen this year." The women both laughed.

"Anyway, you use that cream," Maddi said after she stopped laughing, "and you're not having any problems getting off; that's for sure." Freya bowed her head while looking up and fluttering her eyes. "But you haven't had your body hormones messed up by Lupron like me. Still, I might as well try that cream. If it helps, you can take credit for another one of your all-natural remedies working."

"You know that would make me happy, in more ways than one." Freya had a big grin on her face. "Also, I think maybe you should try a G-spot sex toy," she added. "Since you can reach my spot with your fingers but I can't reach yours with mine, a toy would make things more equal between us. Plus, you might experience some new sexual pleasure."

"You know, I always wanted to try one of those hard metal or plastic sex toys with the curves in them," Maddi said. "I'll have to check the Smitten Kitten's website and see if they have any of those. I hope they don't cost a lot." The Smitten Kitten was a local feminist sex toy store.

"Even if what they have is high-priced, it would be worth it if it helps you," Freya said.

"Yeah, I know after all these years not to cheap out on our sex life." Maddi chuckled.

The next Saturday night, Maddi and Freya were in the bed with a red tote bag that contained their erotic accessories. After applying the progesterone cream to her naked abdomen, as she had every night before going to bed since Freya recommended it earlier that week, Maddi stretched out on her side of the bed, bent and spread her legs, and then grabbed a couple of pillows to tuck one under each knee.

As Maddi made herself comfortable, Freya sat between her wife's thighs and piled up pillows behind her to support her back. She then reached into the tote bag and took out a black mesh drawstring sack. Pulling off the sack and putting it back into the bag, she revealed their newly acquired toy, the Crystal Wand. Shaped like an elongated "S," the translucent, purple acrylic toy was rounded on one end and pointed on the other.

"So," Freya said while twirling the Crystal Wand in her fingers, "which end do you want?"

"Hmm." Maddi raised her arms and put her hands under her head. "I'll try the blunt end first. If that doesn't do it for me, then I'll go for the pointy end."

"All right." Freya reached back into the bag and took out a small bottle of lubricant. After pressing the top to open it, she turned over the bottle and held it above the Crystal Wand to let the lubricant drip onto the toy. She closed the bottle, put it back in the bag, and then smoothed the lubricant along the toy's length. Reaching between Maddi's legs, Freya parted her wife's coily-haired nether lips with one hand, revealing deep pink, moist flesh. Tilting the toy almost vertically, Freya carefully slipped the curved wand into Maddi's poonani. As she pushed the wand deeper, Freya angled it down until the end of the curve was nestled behind Maddi's pubic bone, moving the toy down until it was nearly parallel to her lover's prone body.

With one half of the S-shaped wand curving up inside Maddi, the other half sticking out of her was curved downward, making a perfect handle for Freya to grab and gently pull.

Maddi hissed at the new sensation. The wand arched around the upper part of her vagina like a smooth, thick hook, and as Freya tugged the exposed end the resistance Maddi felt inside made the tip of her clit burn even though it wasn't being touched.

"Ooh, damn," Maddi groaned. "It's like it's stroking the other side of my clit. Ain't that weird?"

"It may well be doing that," Freya said. "The clitoris is bigger, longer, and deeper than the little bud you can see from the outside."

"That's true." Maddi had seen illustrations showing the full wishbone-with-wings shape of the clitoris. "That may be what the G-spot is: the other side of your clit. Mmph!" She gasped.

"Wiggle it around, like back and forth." To demonstrate the movement she wanted, Maddi lifted her hand, made a fist with her thumb on top, and turned it like she was starting a car.

Freya complied, and the resulting stimulation made Maddi shout. "Oh shit, oh shit, oh shit!" Maddi grabbed her thighs and pulled her knees toward her chest. She lifted her head and shoulders from the bed as she let out a low, loud grunt: "Urrrrrrrm!"

"Wow." Freya rubbed Maddi's leg, and then she looked between her wife's thighs. "Ooh, there's a bit of extra wetness here."

Maddi's head dropped back onto her pillow and her legs sunk into the bed. "Hmm, what do you mean?" she said in between pants to catch her breath.

"Well, there's a different wetness on you and the toy. It's not the same as the usual kind of wetness; it's thinner, more like water."

"Let me see." Maddi put her hand between her legs to touch herself and the Crystal Wand. She traced her fingers around her swollen, moist labia and the slick shaft of the toy. "Yeah, it does feel like water. It's not tacky or sticky at all like what usually comes out of me." She brought her hand to her face and sniffed it. "Doesn't smell like anything, thank goodness. At least that means I didn't pee on myself," she chuckled.

"It's definitely not pee," Freya agreed, then her eyes grew wide and her mouth gaped open. "Maddi, I think you just ejaculated!"

The look in Maddi's eyes matched that of her wife. "You mean, I G-spot squirted?"

"Couldn't you feel a difference in your orgasm?"

"Well, it's been so long since I've had a real good, hard come that I probably don't remember how it felt before compared to now," Maddi mused.

"Oh, honey." Freya squeezed Maddi's leg.

"And man, was it good, and hard. Whew!" Maddi took a deep breath. "I don't think I can take another one, so you can go ahead and pull it out."

Freya slowly withdrew the Crystal Wand. "I'd better bring you a towel from the bathroom. There's a wet spot under you."

"Oh." Maddi sat up and placed her palm on the sheet between

her thighs. She saw and felt a damp patch about the size of a drink coaster. She closed her legs and scooted to the edge of the bed away from the patch, while Freya got out of bed and went to the bathroom, taking the Crystal Wand with her to clean it.

When Freya returned from the bathroom, she had a face towel in each hand. She gave one towel to Maddi, who laid it over the wet spot and then carefully stretched out over it. The other towel was wrapped around the Crystal Wand, which Freya placed on top of the tote bag. Freya then got into bed and lay on her side facing Maddi, and the couple embraced each other and kissed.

"I had a G-spot orgasm," Maddi said.

"Yes, you did."

"And I squirted."

"Yes, you did."

"I've never had a G-spot orgasm, not less squirted. Dang! They should call this thing a magic wand. That thing got my poonani back to not only getting me off good, but also it took me to a new level I never got to before I had the surgery and that stupid Lupron shot."

"I think the progesterone cream helped as well." Freya smiled at Maddi.

"Mm-hm, you always gotta credit your natural remedies," Maddi responded with a smirk. "But then you get credit for all this anyway because you suggested getting a G-spot toy."

"But you had the idea of getting the specific kind of toy with the curves," Freya added.

"Yeah, but I would have never bought that toy if it wasn't for you." Maddi caressed her wife's back. "Your eternal optimism got me my groove back—and then some."

"I'm so happy," Freya said, "and I'm also so horny. Are you ready to give me my turn with the magic Crystal Wand?"

"Oh, you want to try it now, huh?" Maddi sat up and reached

for the toy. "Shoot, you already have G-spot orgasms off my fingers, though you haven't squirted as far as I can tell. We use this magic Crystal Wand on you, it might make you flood the whole bed and pass out."

"Actually, that might be a possibility," Freya said. "I'm going to get a big bath towel."

"Good idea, Pollyanna baby." As Freya went to the bathroom to get a towel, Maddi took the lubricant bottle out of the bag and prepared the curvy wand to work its magic on her wife.

HOMECOMING

Jacqueline St-Urbain

Tip of the hat to AZ

Miriam hates the damp. It's not what she's used to. In the prairies, winters are cold and dry. Here in Halifax, it's technically less cold, but fuck is it damp. It's seeping into her bones, making her ache.

Well. Ache more. Fuck. Long-distance relationships are always hard. She misses Anna so constantly the pain is as familiar to her as her own breathing. Regular. Automatic. Essential. But travel is so difficult to manage now with the borders and lockdowns that loving someone long-distance has become its own special kind of awful.

Six months. They have not seen each other in six eternal months. Six months in which they have both been through different separate hells. Six months of depression, loneliness, loss, and uncertainty.

And now. Now, Miriam is waiting. Waiting in this rent-an-apartment for her boi. She refused an airport pickup. She told Anna to present herself at exactly 5:00 p.m. Gave her the code to open the door. "Let yourself in. You know what to do."

She runs a towel over the pristine counter she hasn't made anything on yet. Checks the cupboards for dust. Wipes the faucets clean. They were already clean.

Miriam groans under her breath, remembering the last time they spent together. Anna's heavy silver collar gleaming between her collarbones. The catch in her breath whenever Miriam leaned over to kiss her, and then . . . didn't. Miriam savors the muscle memory of her boi's throat under her hand, Anna pressing her neck harder into Miriam's firm grip. Miriam's fingers deep enough she can feel Anna's pulse submitting to her touch.

"You want a kiss, boi? Come get it." Watching Anna strain against the hand that holds her away, cutting off her breath a bit more with every push. Still not quite close enough just yet. Soon. But not yet.

Push. Pause. Pull. These are the principles Miriam builds her dominance of Anna upon. Push Anna's submission past her resistance. Push Anna's body, opening her up wider, and then wider still. Teasing and using her holes. Pushing both their buttons, and their vulnerability when calling Anna by those names she would never, ever use in public.

Miriam repeats them, the litany of filth rolling through her mind. *Slut. Bitch. Boi. Mine.*

Pausing to make her crave moving forward. Being still to heighten tension, to get Anna ramped up. Waiting can be a powerful aphrodisiac. And a source of elemental frustration, as well. She so enjoys watching Anna suffer.

Then pulling back, making the moment last longer. Longer than that. No. Still. Withdrawing by tiny increments. The intimate, filthy dance has steps she has not used in too long. Miriam is more nervous today than she has ever been with Anna. The filth and tenderness and vulnerability they have shared, so much of it happened too long ago.

The pause was far too long in those six months. The dance came so close to ending entirely.

Miriam is sweating under her cardigan. How is it possible to be cold and hot at the same time? No matter, it's happening regardless. The dance was interrupted by illness, too much distance for too long. She gulps with the thought that she has lost the intimate knowledge she had of its steps, of how to dance it with Anna. Of how to lead.

Miriam shakes herself and tries to focus her mind on being a Dominant. She is trembling with desire mixed with a great deal of fear. She reviews basic top tricks to bypass her nervousness.

She cannot remember a single one.

She holds the edge of the kitchen counter in this strange, sterile little apartment. She closes her eyes and counts to ten slowly. Anna will be here any second now.

At the count of nine, Miriam hears the door click open, and smells winter sashay in on Anna's coat.

Miriam does not turn. Anna has instructions, knows what is expected. Miriam realizes her knuckles are turning white against the dark marble of the counter. She cannot remember the last time she felt this scared and uncertain. Miriam pictures what Anna must look like as she enters.

A slight woman in her early thirties, wearing a black leather motorcycle jacket over her clothes. Anna's blue-black hair is cut very short. While the salons and barbers were closed for months, Miriam's boi shaved her head in desperation, an attempt to feel more like her genuine self. It has not yet fully grown out, and so the sides and back are short, but the top is shorter than usual. Miriam has wondered if it will be long enough to lace her fingers into in order to hold Anna's head just so. There are so many reasons to hope so.

Anna will hang her jacket in the closet and place her well-tended boots by the door. Pull the button-down shirt she is wearing carefully off her shoulders and place it on the back of the nearest chair. Then, her pants. Underthings. Socks.

Miriam still does not turn. She is in full panic mode. This feels so unfamiliar. It's been an eternity since this protocol was set: enter the space. Strip. Kneel. But it's also been an eternity since they shared actual physical space. The phone calls and emails and texts and video have been hollow comfort at best.

She hears Anna's careful steps heading into the living room space. Feels more than hears Anna kneeling.

Still Miriam waits. Does not turn. Does not look.

Perhaps this is pushing the whole pause thing too far. But Miriam keeps pulling blanks. She feels stuck, her mind wading through peanut butter when she wants to be fast and fleet and filled with ideas.

She cannot put it off any longer. She knows Anna is kneeling with her head bowed and her eyes fixed on the bland patterned carpet currently digging into her kneecaps.

Finally, Miriam loosens her death grip on the counter just enough to turn herself. Shifts her body around to look at Anna's bent head, her hands clasped behind her back, facing the squeaky-new leather couch, rather than facing Miriam.

She has done as expected. Anna has remembered.

Miriam is both relieved at the familiarity and made more nervous. She still feels lost, swimming in feelings and utterly undominant. What are her moves in this dance? Will her body and mind remember the steps by the time she needs them?

She takes a deep breath and lets go of the counter.

Swims toward Anna. Toward the couch.

Her body—heavier and older than Anna's—feels once removed. The sensation of plodding through peanut butter is still there. Miriam feels almost dissociated as she navigates the tiny apartment: the kitchen and living room are two sides of one room. She has maybe fifteen feet to travel.

It is over in a blink that lasts an eternity.

Miriam sits down in the center of the couch, directly in front of Anna. Anna remains still, poised, bent, submitting.

Miriam reaches out to Anna. This will be the first touch in six months. Far too long.

And stops, her hand outstretched but not yet touching.

Pauses again. Remembers a fragment of their protocol.

Sends a thanks to whatever gods were watching over her.

"Boi. Do you have it?"

"Yes Ma'am."

Anna's hands are in front of her now, held together with their offering to Miriam. The silver collar, and the ring that locks it. Miriam puts out a hand to accept Anna's offering, and the collar is transferred without their hands touching.

Miriam hopes Anna doesn't see how her hands shake in the exchange.

Anna dips her head lower, in supplication. Her voice is deep, deeper perhaps than might be expected in Anna's small frame. "Please Ma'am, will you collar your boi?"

Miriam's reply is to unspool the heavy links of the chain in her hands, to stretch them out in invitation. Anna moves forward in the ritual motion of asking, indicating her desire to be collared. Miriam slips this symbol of their time together around Anna's neck in silence, and fastens the links together with the locking ring.

This is the first time they have touched, and Miriam is reluctant to end the connection. Her hand rests between Anna's chest and her collar, cradling the locking ring. She can feel Anna's warmth on her fingertips. The sight of Anna on her knees, her collar around her neck once more, brings Miriam into sharper focus. She is starting to remember. *This is how we do this dance. I have not stepped on any toes yet.*

And then her brain informs her of what else she is feeling. Under the backs of her fingers, against her hand, Anna is trembling. She seems so composed, so certain of her moves, but she is shaking like a leaf under Miriam's touch.

They have spent months talking, falling apart, hurting, consciously working to come back together, to find each other again. Anna has been open, honest, present, and kind, but nothing in that talking has prepared Miriam for the rush of emotion that comes when she realizes that Anna is shaking, as nervous and scared about their reunion as Miriam herself is.

Somehow, that helps. A lot.

Still nervous, but encouraged, Miriam counts to five before speaking. She sees a way to move forward. It's not entirely clear, but the next step or two are coming into hazy focus.

"Ma'am?" Miriam has been silent too long. Anna's breathy question brings her back to the present.

Time to push a little.

"Eyes down, boi."

Anna's eyes are already on the floor, but she shifts her body a bit to show she is obedient.

"Turn around. Face the kitchen."

Anna's movement breaks their contact. She spins easily, bracing herself on her arms and moving to face away from Miriam.

Yes. This is better.

Now, Anna can't see into her eyes. Hopefully she won't realize that Miriam is so shaken with uncertainty.

This is Being a Top 101: if you're feeling cautious or unsure, limit your bottom's avenues to connect with you. If they can't see you, they won't see you scared.

Right?

Okay, Miriam tells herself, *you got this. Slowly. Take your time, and play this your way.*

Which is exactly what?

Hush.

Time to find out how her boi's hair is growing out.

"Back up, boi." Miriam puts her hands on Anna's shoulders to guide her. Anna scooches back until she is kneeling between Miriam's legs. Miriam's knees are open, and her dress rucks up along her thighs, allowing the boi to nestle.

Ah. Now the connection feels stronger. Skin-to-skin is warming and comforting.

When Miriam holds her boi by the hair, time stops. She likes to pull it back, to watch Anna's neck lengthen and strain to keep her balance without fighting Miriam's hand.

She does so now as Miriam finds that there is, in fact, enough regrowth to get a good hold. She pulls Anna toward her, and Anna arches back toward Miriam and the couch.

Miriam has Anna in a very vulnerable position, and can feel her trembling still. Good.

Okay. There are two ways this can go. We can do it nice, or we can do it rough.

Miriam and Anna's dance has always been passionate, and underpinned with the complexities of a power-based relationship. The steps are complex, but there is never a moment's doubt who is leading.

Time to lead.

Miriam takes her hand out of Anna's hair only to place it between her shoulder blades. She pushes Anna onto all fours on the carpet. Anna's face is resting on the beige shag. Her ass is high in the air. Miriam can see her cleft, the stark contrast of her black hair on her vulva and ringing her asshole against her pale skin.

Miriam's mouth waters.

Miriam runs her hand down along Anna's spine. Anna's shiver is barely perceptible. Miriam is stroking her ass cheeks now, assessing that paleness. Yes. Too pale.

The first blow is a surprise. Anna jolts forward and catches herself almost immediately, pushing back into position as Miriam angles to give a second. This one is backhand—harder, across the other cheek. Miriam feels a rush and it's matched by the jolt in her clit. Oh, yes, she remembers this feeling.

Remembers how her hand will heat up as Anna's ass gets pinker, then redder. The blows come quickly. There is so much need behind them.

Anna is panting now, her ass high in the air, her face buried in the carpet and her moans muffled.

Miriam is aware that this beating has months of pain, missing, and loneliness fuelling it. Her pent-up frustration and grief of the last half year are driving her hand a bit more than may be technically healthy. But it feels so good, so good to exorcise some of these feelings, to give them an outlet they have not enjoyed for so long. It feels right, damnit.

And so she lets the tightly coiled spring inside her uncoil a little, lets it loose on her boi's upturned ass.

Anna is moaning, almost sobbing. Wait. Not almost. Sobbing. When did that start?

Fuck.

Miriam stops to breathe, to assess. The bit of carpet under Anna's face has turned darker with tears. She's been crying for a while.

Damn.

Well. No safeword has been spoken. What's more, the pouch of Anna's cunt—the black-curled slit of her—is glistening.

Miriam reaches a decision. Topping 101: Know when to change things up.

"Into the bedroom, boi. On your knees on the bed."

Anna takes a shuddering breath, whispers "Yes, Ma'am," as she gets shakily to her feet.

Walks unsteadily into the bedroom, disappearing from Miriam's view.

Miriam pauses. Takes another five slow, deep breaths. Anna can wait. Miriam consciously sets aside her slight concerns about her own motivations. Muscle memory allowed her to give Anna a solid, short but brutal spanking that was definitely powered at least in part by a jumble of pent-up emotions.

She stands up and walks—almost as shaky as Anna—into the bedroom.

Anna is waiting as commanded, on all fours with her feet over the bed and her ass in the air.

Miriam takes in the sight before her, drinking in the view and the arch of Anna's back before stepping into the bedroom. She reaches for the lube and gloves on the bedside table, gives brief thanks that she thought to put them out before Anna arrived.

Miriam watches Anna carefully as she gloves up and pours lube onto her fingers. Positions herself at the edge of the bed, standing between Anna's spread legs. She reaches out with a single finger and slides it along Anna's slit, pressing in just slightly.

Anna moans and moves onto her finger, prompting Miriam to pull away. Anna moans again, this time in frustration.

"Shut the fuck up, boi. I don't want to hear you. Shut the fuck up and be still."

"Yes, M—" Anna catches herself mid-sentence and shuts the fuck up.

Miriam's finger presses once more just a half inch into Anna's labia. Drenched. Nervous she may be, but she is also turned on.

Miriam loves to take her time with Anna. Anna loves and hates it, the stretching-out of the tease, the push-pull of denial and surrender. This isn't the time for those games, though. This feels too urgent. The need to re-establish what they share, what binds them to each other, is too pressing.

Two fingers find Anna's cunt, and slide in easily. Anna moans wordlessly, but she says nothing. Miriam is itching to pull a reaction from her boi, but Anna is determined to obey. Three fingers, then four invade Anna's slick wetness, pushing into her and making her shudder. Still she is silent.

Miriam knows the measure of Anna's cunt, what she can take. She is stretching Anna open, and Anna is eager to swallow Miriam's hand.

"Touch yourself, boi." Miriam's command is spoken through clenched teeth: she is focused on Anna's unfurling cunt. Anna's hand slides under her stomach to circle her clit.

Ah. There it is. She is opening up, and Miriam's hand is pressing in gently as Anna's arousal ramps up and her tunnel becomes slicker.

After that, it gets easier.

Miriam is fully inside Anna now, her hand encased and turning oh so slightly. Anna is gasping, though still unspeaking. Sweat is beading between her shoulder blades as she jerks herself off.

Miriam grips Anna's hip with her other hand, pulling handfuls of flesh between her fingers, squeezing tightly enough that there will be bruising tomorrow. Anna's breathing is speeding up, Miriam is relentless, twisting her hand and pulling it out as far as Anna's muscles will allow.

"Don't forget to ask, boi."

Anna grabs the bed, trembling with built-up tension. Legs spread, Miriam's hand buried deep in her cunt, Anna's voice is tight and thready.

"Please," she begs.

"Please. May I come? Please?" Anna's voice rises almost

comically on the last word. Miriam does not laugh. She can feel Anna's orgasm building around her fist.

"No," says Miriam, almost casually.

"HNNNGG."

Miriam feels the difference in Anna's cunt, a fluttering that tells her Anna is desperately trying not to go over the edge.

"PLEASE," Anna's voice is desperate. She is barely holding on.

"Come for me now," says Miriam, already feeling the ripples in her hand that tell her Anna is losing control.

Anna gasps, groans, and grits her teeth as Miriam feels wave after wave of orgasm tear through her. Her hand feels like it might break—the force of Anna's cunt muscles throbbing over it is both mighty and marvelous. Anna is shaking, her eyes closed and incoherent grunts escaping from her lips. Her body glistens as she spasms, and tightens again around Miriam's fist, holding on as best she can from within. It is hot, it is warm even through the gloves, and it is crushing her. No help for it—Miriam cannot pull out now.

So she pushes just a bit deeper, and is rewarded with a cry torn from Anna's lips as a second orgasm rolls through her body and pushes out from her cunt. Miriam's arm aches, and she loves this, Anna's utter loss of control. She savors it, rolls Anna's surrender over her tongue.

The contractions threatening to break her hand are subsiding. Anna is coming down. She shivers a little as her sweat cools on her skin. Miriam slides out of Anna slowly, strips the gloves off to hold her boi.

Anna rolls over onto her side, curled in on herself on the bed, still shivering.

Miriam climbs onto the bed. Reaches for Anna.

And realizes that she—Miriam—has hot tears rolling down her face. She is crying, suddenly, almost silently.

She hesitates, feeling suddenly terribly vulnerable, heart cracked wide open and exposed.

Anna turns to Miriam, who is sobbing helplessly. Folds Miriam into her arms. Wraps herself around her Ma'am lovingly and holds onto her fiercely as she cries.

And Miriam understands that she has finally come home.

TITUS ANDROGYNOUS is a writer, multi-disciplinary performer, and drag king from Toronto, Canada. Their writing has appeared on stage, in *Xtra* and *Queeries* magazines, and online at DapperQ.com.

STEPHANI MAARI BOOKER, author of *Secret Insurrection: Stories from a Novel of a Future Time*, has erotica published in *Owning It: Embracing Our Bodies, Sexuality, and Power* (Rhiannon Rhys-Jones, Sienna Saint-Cyr & S.B. Roark, editors; SinCyr Publishing, 2018), *Coming Together: Girl on Girl* (Leigh Ellwood, editor; EroticAnthology.org, 2013), and *Longing, Lust and Love: Black Lesbian Stories* (Shonia L. Brown, editor; Nghosi Books, 2007). She also has science fiction, nonfiction, and poetry in many other publications. For more information about her work, go to goodreads.com/athenapm.

SARAH B. BURGHAUSER is a New Mexico-based writer and teacher. She holds an MFA from Calarts, where she has also taught. Sarah has been awarded fellowships with the MacDowell Colony, Lambda Literary Foundation, and Vermont Studio Center. Her first book, *Infringe,* is a lyric coming-of-age tale about being a queer Jew, and the places where sex and spiritual well-being meet.

CASSANDRA CAVENAUGH (cassandracavenaugh.com) is the pseudonym of a trans lesbian, mother of two, and author of sweet, saccharine stories with a dash of levity. Her work has involved everything from twenty-sided dice to the demon spawn of Microsoft Word, but aspires to one day wrap kinky fuckery in one giant pun.

MEG ELISON is a science fiction author and feminist essayist. Her series, *The Road to Nowhere,* won the 2014 Philip K. Dick award. She was a James A. Tiptree Award Honoree in 2018. In 2020, she published her first collection, called *Big Girl* with PM Press and her first young adult novel, *Find Layla* with Skyscape. Meg has been published in *McSweeney's, Fantasy & Science Fiction, Fangoria, Uncanny, Lightspeed, Nightmare,* and many other places. Elison is a high school dropout and a graduate of UC Berkeley. Find her online, where she writes like she's running out of time, at megelison.com & @megelison.

MX. NILLIN LORE is a queer, non-binary, polyamorus, gray-romantic erotica author and transgender sexual wellness speaker out of Saskatoon, Saskatchewan, Canada. For the past few years they have run a successful, multiple award-winning sex blog at mxnillin.com which was named one of Kinkly's Top 10 New Sex Blogs of 2016 and recently placed eighth in Molly's Daily Kiss' Top 100 Sex Blogs of 2019. Their short trans erotica story "Here Comes the Sun" was featured in 2019's *Best Lesbian Erotica of* *the Year Volume 4*, with the spiritual follow-up, "On A Hot and Humid Night," appearing in 2020's *Best Lesbian Erotica of the Year Volume 5*.

KEL HARDY is a white, gender-indifferent lesbian from Toronto. They co-produce Smut Peddlers, a recurring erotica reading with Glad Day Bookshop, the world's oldest LGBTQ+ bookstore. They write erotica in hopes that sex can be reinstated as an essential part of storytelling, as well as to turn people on.

TOBI HILL-MEYER is an indigenous Chicana transwoman with fifteen years experience working in the LGBTQ movement. She is editor of the Lambda Literary Finalist anthology *Nerve Endings: The New Trans Erotic*, author of children's books *A Princess of Great Daring* and *Super Power Baby Shower*, and director of the award-winning erotic documentary series Doing it Online. Currently, she serves as Co-Executive Director for Gender Justice League.

AUGUST IN FLUX lives in a tiny apartment in the San Francisco Bay Area with her proud Filipina wife and their ridiculously silly kid. She enjoys nineties TV, cookies every day of the week, and bougie farm-to-table foods. Her work can be found at augustinflux.wordpress.com, theunderenlightened.com, and in the lesbian BDSM anthology *Say Please*.

KATRINA JACKSON is a professor by day and she writes erotica and erotic romance in her very limited free time. She likes cats, sleep, and coffee.

MEKA JAMES is a writer of adult contemporary and erotic romance. A born and raised Georgia Peach, she still resides in the southern state with her hubby of sixteen years and counting. Mom to four kids of the two-legged variety, she also has four fur-babies of the canine variety. Leo the turtle and Spade the snake round out her wacky household. When not writing or reading, Meka can be found playing The Sims 3, sometimes Sims 4, and making up fun stories to go with the pixelated people whose world she controls.

LUISA MARGO PARK identifies as multiethnic/transnational, of Korean ancestry, a nonbinary femme, and a kink enthusiast who usually publishes in academic journals in another name. This is her first time writing smut. While not related to this genre, Luisa draws inspiration from Kai Cheng Thom, Ocean Vuong, Nikki Giovanni, and Edith Wharton.

BEAR NICKS is a young-ish Black Butch Lesbian, who enjoys writing fiction, short stories, and screenplays. He began writing fanfiction in 2012, which started his love of writing and discovered the true freedom that comes with it. He hopes to share his short stories and movies with the world, sooner than later.

ASH ORLANDO is a playwright, poet, and short story writer from Sydney, Australia. They have performed in The Butch Monologues, the Butch/Stud annual performance night, and various spoken word events. Ash is also a codirector of Gender Creatives, a collaborative group showcasing work by nonbinary artists and writers. They don't know much, but they know they love you, and that may be all you need to know.

QUENBY is a queer performer, activist, and writer based in Leeds. Their eclectic work uses a range of different art forms to explore themes of gender identity, kink, and queer history. You can find them everywhere at quenbycreatives.

THERIN SALEM is a gray-ace writer of mixed European and Lebanese heritage. She always looks for the humor alongside the blunders of life. She lives in Toronto, Ontario, Canada, with her cat.

SONNI DE SOTO is an Asian kinkster of color who knows that while kink isn't therapy, play can often be therapeutic. It can often be the place where we explore our deepest fears within a safe context. De Soto has had the privilege of publishing romantic erotica novels and stories with The Sexy Librarian, Cleis Press, Sexy Little Pages, and many others. Find more from her at patreon.com/sonnidesoto and follow her at facebook.com/sonnidesotostories.

JACQUELINE ST-URBAIN has been a shit-disturber on the Canadian leather scene for almost two decades. The founder of the Unholy Army of the Night and co-founder of Unholy Harvest, Canada's long-running weekend for leatherdykes and other queerdos, Jacqueline writes for a living, but loves writing smut so much more than her day job.

MEGAN STORIES has been writing about the intersections of kink, trauma, asexuality, queerness, and generally being sex-weird since the early 2000s—longer if you count those childhood compositions about Rainbow Brite "nibbling" Strawberry Shortcake. She blogs about these topics at circumstanceandcarefulness.com and lives in Durham, North Carolina, with her crotchety Chihuahua-dachshund. Megan can often be found at queer events wishing more people were talking about kink, or at kink events wishing more people were talking about their feelings.

BD SWAIN (bdswain.com) is a butch dyke who writes queer smut. You'll find BD's stories on her site and in anthologies like *Best Lesbian Erotica of the Year, Volume 4, Best Lesbian Erotica*

2015, *Best Lesbian Erotica 2013*, and *Unspeakably Erotic: Lesbian Kink*. BD lives in Oakland and is currently working on a long-form narrative and a collection of her dirty stories.

LIANYU TAN has always been fascinated by the darker side of love: obsessive yearning and monstrous desires. She usually writes dark romance with a fantastical twist. Her debut novel *Captive in the Underworld* is an F/F dark fantasy retelling of the Hades/ Persephone myth. Lianyu is Malaysian Chinese Australian and lives with her wife in Australia. Subscribe for a free, sexy short story at: go.lianyutan.com/best.

TIARA-JORDANAE is an African American woman, born and raised in Detroit whose dream is to become a kink writer. When not writing, she spends her time exploring narrative worlds in video games, television shows, and other pop culture content. When not at her day job as a project manager, she spends her time editing her first novel for release, a queer erotic thriller about Georgian vampires with Gothic imagery.

SINCLAIR SEXSMITH (they/them) is "the best-known butch erotica writer whose kinky, groundbreaking stories have turned on countless queer women" (AfterEllen), who "is in all the books, wins all the awards, speaks at all the panels and readings, knows all the stuff, and writes for all the places" (Autostraddle). They have written at sugarbutch.net since 2006, recognized by numerous places as one of the top sex blogs.

Sinclair's creative nonfiction and queer erotica writings are widely published online and in more than thirty anthologies, including *Best Lesbian Erotica 2006, 2007, 2009, 2011, 2014, and 2016, Sometimes She Lets Me: Best Butch/Femme Erotica, Take Me There: Trans and Genderqueer Erotica, The Harder She Comes: Butch/Femme Erotica, The Big Book of Orgasms: 69 Sexy Stories, The Sexy Librarian's Dirty 30, Me & My Boi: Queer Erotic Stories, Paradigms of Power: Styles of Master/slave Relationships, Queer: A Reader for Writers, The Remedy: Trans and Queer Healthcare, Queering Sexual Violence: Radical Voices from Within the Anti-Violence Movement, Persistence: All*

Ways Butch and Femme, Nonbinary: Memoirs of Gender and Identity, and others.

Sinclair is the editor of *Best Lesbian Erotica of the Year Volume 4* and *Volume 5, Best Lesbian Erotica 2012, Erotix: Literary Journal of Somatics,* and *Say Please: Lesbian BDSM Erotica.* Their short story collection, *Sweet & Rough: Queer Kink Erotica,* was a 2015 finalist for a Lambda Literary Award, and they were awarded the National Leather Association Cynthia Slater Nonfiction Article Award in 2015 and the National Leather Association John Preston short story award in 2016 and 2019.

They have taught kink, gender, sexuality, relationship, and writing workshops online and throughout the US and Canada. Sinclair is also a facilitator for and co-founder of Body Trust Circle, a sacred somatic collaborative dedicated to the body as a laboratory for transformation. All of their work centers around studies of power and the body—individual, interpersonal, and institutional. They identify as a white non-binary butch dominant, a survivor, and an introvert. Follow all their work at patreon.com/mrsexsmith.